Forgive not Forget

EMILY BANTING

Sapphic Publishing
www.sapphicpublishing.co.uk

Sapphfic
Publishing
www.sapphficpublishing.co.uk

CREDITS:
Editor: Hatch Editorial

1 3 4 5 6 7 8 9 10

ABOUT THE AUTHOR

As an author of LGBTQ+ romance featuring sapphic main characters, I'm passionate about increasing the representation of sapphic women over forty in literature and on-screen.

I write about women in their prime, experiencing everything life throws at them — missed opportunities: regret: lost loves: family problems: aching joints: and menopause.

With a passion for, and a degree in Archaeology and Heritage Management, I never miss an opportunity to sneak historic buildings into my books. The Nunswick Abbey Series features a Georgian country house, a quaint historic village setting and of course, oodles of ruined abbey.

When I'm not hiding behind my MacBook pretending to write whilst secretly consuming tea and biscuits, I bow to the unreasonable demands of my cat overlord and walk my starving velcro Labrador.

Connect with me
www.emilybanting.co.uk

FIND ME HERE

I love to hear from my readers. If you would like to get in touch you can find me here…

www.emilybanting.co.uk

Or follow me here…

 facebook.com/emilybantingauthor

 instagram.com/emilybanting

 twitter.com/emily_banting

 bookbub.com/authors/emily-banting

 goodreads.com/emily_banting

 amazon.com/author/emilybanting

ACKNOWLEDGMENTS

Thanks, as always, to my dear editor, Jess. You are a wonder who works wonders with words!

Also, thank you again to my amazing team of BETA and ARC readers who take time out of their lives for me, especially Andie Trinder-Whittle for her advice and guidance — check her out in chapter 36.

A special thank you to my proofreader, Laure Dherbécourt. You are, as always, spot on with your deliberations!

Lastly, thank you to my readers for supporting a new author. I hope you've enjoyed this third and possibly final instalment of Anna and Katherine's journey. If you desire more from them, get in touch to let me know.

My next book *Broken Beyond Repair* is a standalone, one which I was ready to write after Lost in Love, until Anna and Katherine insisted on more airtime!

CHAPTER 1

A loud whistle rang out, its echo resonating off the nearby ruined walls of Nunswick Abbey. Anna lowered her fingers from her mouth and shot Katherine a satisfied grin. She was only too aware her endless practising had been driving Katherine crazy the last few days. It was a skill she had been determined to learn, and it would prove useful in her new job. Her whistle had drawn the attention of the crowd that had gathered outside Abbey Barn, whose open doors were barred by a red ribbon.

Katherine gave her a wink as she tapped the microphone, clearly as impressed with Anna's whistle as she was.

"Is this thing on?" Katherine's voice bellowed from a speaker beside her feet, causing the crowd to erupt into laughter. She stepped up onto a box to elevate herself above the crowd. "I think that's a yes. Everyone, welcome to Nunswick Abbey, and a special welcome to Abbey

Barn." Katherine gesticulated to the renovated structure behind her. "We hope it will become a cherished addition to the site and prove useful to you as a community. It's available to hire for classes, weddings, birthday parties, Bar-Mitzvah. You name it, it will take anything you throw at it — as long as you don't throw more than eighty people. However, saying that, we can accommodate more in a marquee on our beautiful grounds."

Anna gazed with adoration as her spectacular fiancée worked the huge crowd. They had practised her speech multiple times that week, discussing what needed highlighting and making sure Katherine remembered it by heart.

Though she was normally relaxed amongst a crowd of people, Anna felt nervous. Her confidence had dwindled a little since she'd been promoted. The daily repetition of the abbey's history, followed by immediate thanks, had been replaced by months of behind-the-scenes work, which she wouldn't know had been a success until the event was over. She now relied on a team of people to pull things together rather than just herself, which was bound to leave her a little nervous.

"As you can see behind you," Katherine continued, "work on the visitor centre is running behind schedule. I had hoped to at least present a completed external structure today; unfortunately, work was halted upon the discovery of some human remains."

The crowd drew in a collective breath.

Katherine's hand shot out to calm them. "Historical, not modern, I might add! We hope to resume building work as soon as possible. Once it's completed, you'll find extended food offerings in our new restaurant, with additional seating inside and out; a gift shop full of quality items; and most importantly… our limited-edition print of the abbey by our fabulous artist Michael Warner." Katherine extended her arm to an elderly gentleman at the front of the crowd, and everyone broke into a round of applause. Once the clapping lulled, she resumed her speech. "Interest in the print is already high, so I'm pleased to announce that he has agreed to create a set of four watercolours in total for us and to extend the number of editions available, so thank you, Michael."

The gentleman gave Katherine a nod of acknowledgement in return.

"We have an exclusive offer for you today only, as we are giving you twenty percent off a lifetime membership to the abbey. Now remember, this gives you the benefit of continued free parking, ten percent off purchases in our new restaurant and gift shop, and VIP status for future events, which has been confirmed by our new marketing and events manager, Anna" — Katherine gestured with her hand to the woman standing beside her box — "will include an annual New Year party."

The crowd broke into another round of applause, this time directed at Anna. Her face warmed with either pride or embarrassment — perhaps a little of both. Following the success of the New Year party, Anna had been persuaded by the trustees, though mainly Katherine, that it should be held annually.

"If you would like to sign up, then please see Carrie. Carrie, where are you? Give us a wave."

Carrie shot out from the barn, where she was making

some finishing touches to the room, and gave an enthusiastic wave to the crowd.

"She'll be in the barn to sign you up, which is also where we hope you will join us for a glass of fizz to celebrate, which, after all, is why we are all here today. Before I cut the ribbon, I'd like to take this opportunity to thank Carrie and Anna for all their hard work over the last few months in getting the barn ready for opening. I think you'll all agree, especially those that saw the barn prior to the work commencing, that the team have achieved something truly wondrous."

Carrie gave a little bow before disappearing back into the barn.

Anna blushed at yet another round of applause. It was typical of Katherine not to take any of the credit herself; it had been her project and her vision that had come together to create the space.

"One last thing before I let you all loose at the bar. Please do join us for Easter when we will be holding a bunny trail on Easter Sunday afternoon. There will be plenty of chocolate eggs for everyone."

Anna passed Katherine a pair of scissors as she stepped backwards off the box. A photographer stepped through the crowd and took several shots of Katherine and Anna to a backdrop of yet more cheering and clapping. They posed, each holding one end of the ribbon that was strung across the central, glass double doors of Abbey Barn.

"Without further ado, I declare Abbey Barn officially open." Katherine placed the ribbon between the scissor arms and snipped it.

Anna welcomed this particular round of applause. She had worked tirelessly since the new year to not only ensure everyone knew about Abbey Barn but also to organise the official opening event. Now that the formalities were out of the way, she could finally relax a little.

She and Katherine stood to one side and let the crowd fall into the barn.

Carrie appeared with two glasses of prosecco. "Well done, both of you! I thought you might need these."

They both reached out in desperation. "Thanks, Carrie," they said in unison as she disappeared back into the crowd.

"Shall we sit for ten minutes, let the prosecco to do its work, and then go in with the hard sell?" Anna asked.

Katherine chuckled. "Sounds like a plan."

"Come to my office, we can warm up. I'll show you what I've done with my postage stamp."

"It's not that small!" Katherine protested.

"Can we swap then?"

Katherine nudged into her, conceding the point. "No."

Anna inhaled the scent of the freshly cut grass as they strolled around the outside of the barn. The gardeners had been on-site early that morning to carry out the first trim of the year. Her gaze was drawn to the flower beds where yellow daffodils and multicoloured tulips were in full bloom against a backdrop of low shrubs. The shrubs, once grown, would afford a certain amount of privacy inside the barn.

They reached the end of the barn and turned, following

it around the side until they stopped beside two reclaimed wooden stable doors. Anna unlocked the right-hand one and entered her office. It was a compact yet modern space with built-in shelving and storage. Abutting a wall in the centre of the room was a desk which faced the internal door.

There would have been a time when her office was messy, but living with Katherine had taught her not to leave anything where it shouldn't be. If she dared to do so at Abbey House, Katherine would roll out her usual line of *a place for everything and everything in its place.* Anna refrained from telling Katherine that she knew the saying well because her grandmother used to say it. She didn't think Katherine would appreciate the comparison.

Carrie was the messy one in the office, and Anna was now grateful not to be sharing a workspace with her. She had been due to take the office next door to Anna's in the barn until Katherine suggested it may be more convenient for them to be closer together in the visitor centre. Anna wasn't particularly looking forward to being in the barn alone until someone else filled the other office.

Katherine rearranged a vase of daffodils that stood on the windowsill. "These have lasted well."

"Beautiful, aren't they? My fiancée bought me those," Anna replied, squeezing herself between her chair and Katherine.

"You have a very kind fiancée." Katherine turned and found herself face to face with Anna.

"I do. Sexy too." Anna slipped her arms around Katherine's waist. "I really must get a blind for the window — and the door."

"Why?"

"So I can do this." Anna leaned forward and kissed Katherine lips. "And this." She gently pressed Katherine back against the wall with her body. Her hands worked their way up from her waist and gently caressed her breasts.

"Oh, yes, maybe a blind would look good in here. It would block the low afternoon sun in the winter."

"Mm-hmm, that too," Anna mumbled, her lips brushing Katherine's neck.

Katherine gently eased Anna away from her. "Down, girl. We have an audience awaiting us, and I don't think they want to see me dishevelled."

Anna pulled her best sulky expression as Katherine extracted herself from behind the desk, almost knocking a box from it.

"Okay, this office is too small, but you're a very resourceful woman; I'm sure you'll make it work. What's in the box?" she asked, opening it before Anna could answer. "Chocolate eggs. Have you got enough?" Katherine smirked.

"Attendance at a new event is always difficult to judge," Anna remarked as she took a seat. "Do you want to be the one to explain to the youngsters that we have run out of eggs?"

Katherine pulled her lips to one side. "Good point. They won't miss one, though, will they?" Katherine's hand dove into the box to extract one. She tapped it on the desk and then tore off the foil wrapper, stuffing it into her mouth. "Mmm, these are good."

Anna shut the lid and placed the box under her desk.

"That is exactly why they are in here; I can't trust the staff not to eat them all before the event."

"Miss Walker, are you expecting me to believe you haven't tasted the goods?"

"I may have taste-tested them, as part of my job."

Katherine's eyebrows shot up. "Them?"

"One," Anna quickly corrected herself.

Katherine smirked and, reclaiming her glass, perched on the space the box had left on the desk. "Cheers." She held her glass out to Anna.

"Cheers." Anna took a sip and tilted her head. "I think we may have the hard work ahead of us. At least you do."

"We'll get there. I just hope we get the all-clear on Monday so we can get building again."

Anna's eye caught Harry's in the photo that sat in pride of place on her desk. "It's a shame Dad's not here to see this."

Katherine squeezed her arm. "I know, he would have been so proud to see you today."

"Us," Anna corrected her.

Katherine nodded. "Us."

"Maybe next time. He's best left in his armchair until his cold improves."

"Come on. We better get out there and help Carrie." Katherine yawned as she rose from the desk.

"I'll join you in a minute."

"Oh yes, and what might you be doing in the meantime? Stuffing your face with chocolate eggs?"

"No, I'm nipping to the ladies' actually."

"Like I believe that," Katherine called back as she left the room.

Anna's stomach grumbled. She covered it with her hand, regretting skipping breakfast; there had been far too much to do that morning. She pulled the box closer to her with her feet and removed an egg, unwrapping it as quickly as she could before stuffing it into her mouth. They really were incredibly good.

CHAPTER 2

Katherine was already working her magic with a small group of people as Anna emerged from her office. Their focus was fixed on her — it was clear they found her as hypnotic as Anna did. As she passed Katherine, she allowed the palm of her hand to lightly brush the back of her pencil skirt. A brief glance over her shoulder told her it had the desired effect: one side of Katherine's mouth creased slightly, and her eye subtly pulled away from the man she was speaking with to gaze at her.

"Ah, Anna, there you are," Carrie said, approaching her. "Would you mind grabbing some prosecco and refilling glasses as you do your walkabout? The girls are struggling with everyone at the bar."

"Yes, of course."

Anna joined two young ladies at the bar who had been hired for the day. The abbey couldn't take on any more full-time staff at present, and relied on temporary and seasonal staff for more menial tasks. Casual staff were great on the abbey's bank balance, yet left a lot to be desired when it came to skill.

"Anna, what an excellent job you ladies have done with this place."

Anna looked up from the bottle of prosecco she was uncorking and greeted the purveyor of Nunswick's tearoom. "Gloria, how are you?"

"Good, love. The little abbey is going up in the world."

"It is, bless it."

"Who would have thought it a year ago, eh? Now you and Katherine are at the helm." Gloria turned to the point in the room where Katherine was holding court.

Anna smiled. They had come a long way, possibly the hard way. They had everything ahead of them now, though, and nothing to stop them.

"Anyway, I'll leave you to get on. I only came for a nose around and a glass of prosecco." Gloria helped herself to two half-filled glasses on the bar, poured one into the other, and winked at Anna before wandering off.

Anna stuffed a handful of freshly updated leaflets complete with interior shots into her back pocket, uncorked the bottle in her hand, and immersed herself in the crowd.

She took every opportunity to discuss the highlights of the barn and the abbey as a unique setting for any event. The majority of the guests were locals, come to have a look like Gloria. She hoped they would be drawn in by the barn and that, if they wouldn't book it for a family event, they might become regulars at one of Katherine's exercise classes.

As she manoeuvred her way back to the bar to get the

crowd a third bottle of prosecco, a hand caught her arm. She turned to see a woman with shoulder-length, chestnut brown hair and a friendly smile. There was a familiarity about her that Anna couldn't quite place.

"Anna? Anna Walker?"

Anna eyebrows rocketed up her forehead. She recognised the voice. "Laura?"

"Yes."

"Golly, I haven't seen you since…" Anna thought for a moment.

"School," Laura put in.

Anna shook her head. Had it really been that long? "How are you?" she asked. "What have you been doing all these years?" Anna looked at the two children standing beside Laura. "Been busy, I see."

Laura let out a nervous laugh. "Yes, this is Tom. He's thirteen."

Tom partially nodded in Anna's direction and then picked at his fingers.

"And this is Abigail. She's —"

"Abi, and I'm eight," Abigail answered before Laura could finish her sentence. "Are you a tour guide?"

"No, I'm the marketing and events manager."

"So why do you look like a tour guide?"

Anna pulled herself upright. Luckily, she could see the funny side of the comment.

"I was a tour guide, and I suppose I've continued to dress the same." She leaned closer to Abigail. "Adults are creatures of habit! Perhaps it's time for a change. What would you suggest?"

Abigail eyed her, then looked around the room. She

pointed at Katherine. "Like that lady." Abigail looked back at Anna and examined her. "But I'm not sure you can carry that skirt like she can."

Anna smirked at her harsh, yet quite accurate observation. This was one terrifying girl that stood before her, yet Anna liked her manner. She was straight-up, a trait Anna generally liked in people — though such naked honesty from a child may become increasingly hard to take.

Laura shifted uncomfortably. "Sorry. She's one for saying what she thinks. She wasn't born with a filter."

"It's fine, honestly. I kind of like it."

Abigail folded her arms and looked at her mother indignantly.

"So what have you been up to these past" — Laura paused as she did a quick calculation in her head — "twenty-odd years?"

"Not a lot until I moved back here last year to be closer to Dad."

"How is he?"

"He moved into a home last year. He has Parkinson's."

Laura scrunched her face. "I'm sorry to hear that."

"Thanks."

"I've just moved back myself with these two. I lost my husband last year. We needed a fresh start, didn't we?"

Tom and Abigail lowered their gaze to their feet.

Laura continued. "I thought, why not return home to Nunswick?"

"I'm sorry." Anna scrunched her face. "It's as good a place as any for fresh starts, that's for sure."

"Have you got a husband?" Abigail asked suddenly.

"Erm, no, I don't." Anna wasn't sure if she should say anymore, then realised how ridiculous it was. She shouldn't have to hide her relationship. Children weren't homophobic unless they had been taught to be by their parents or peer group. Abigail didn't seem like the sort of child who would be influenced by anyone. "You know that lady that carries off that skirt in a way I couldn't?"

Abigail nodded.

"I'm going to marry her."

Abigail's eyes twinkled. "Really? That's epic. Can I be a bridesmaid?"

Anna and Laura both laughed.

"Can I come back to you on that? We may well have a vacancy."

"Sure," Abigail replied with a shrug.

Anna caught Laura's eye. She was relieved to see her smiling.

"Congratulations."

"Thanks."

"Look, you're clearly supposed to be working, I don't want to keep you any longer. Why don't you pop over to ours at the weekend so we can catch up properly? I'll try to keep the child interrogations to a minimum."

"I'd like that. To catch up, I mean." Anna looked down at Abigail and winked. "I'm always up for interrogations."

Abigail gave her a cheeky grin in return.

Laura fished her phone from her bag and passed it to Anna. "Pop your number in and we can sort something out."

Anna tapped at the phone and passed it back. "Great, it will be good to catch up."

"Can we go now, Mum?" Tom mumbled. "I'm so bored."

"See you soon then. Sorry about the grumpy teenager." Laura rolled her eyes.

Anna smiled and shook her head to rebuff the apology. She'd had enough experience of pre-teens and teens during tours to know most held no interest in history. They resented being dragged around historical properties in the name of valuable family time when they would prefer to be shouting down a microphone in their bedroom at an equivalently grumpy teen whilst playing a computer game.

Laura led the children away, and Anna headed back to the bar with the realisation of how far she was from her own schooldays. They had been part of the same group at school, then headed to university with promises to keep in touch, which had amounted to the odd text message or email in the first few months. As they found new friends their priorities changed, as did phone numbers and email addresses.

As the number of guests dwindled to zero over the course of the afternoon, Anna commenced the task of clearing up. Katherine had gone to the meeting room with some of the trustees for a chat about the staffing issues the abbey had faced since Margaret had left. By the time she and Carrie had packed everything up, Katherine still hadn't appeared, so Anna headed back to Abbey House alone. The least she could do was get dinner started. Katherine would be wiped out by the time she got home.

CHAPTER 3

atherine took the seat at the head of the meeting room and relaxed into it. It was only mid-morning, and she was already tired. It had been a busy weekend with the grand opening of the barn to deal with. She removed a shoe and rubbed at her ankle; she was sure it was swollen. She'd have to ask Anna for a rub when they got home and face a telling off about overdoing it.

She was already aware that she had been working harder than she should have. What should have been a smooth operation of fitting out the interiors of Abbey Barn whilst patiently awaiting the construction of the extension of the visitor centre had turned into a nightmare with the discovery of human remains in the foundations. The discovery had come as a complete surprise to the staff. The abbey records showed no burials in that area of the site, and the excavation of the original visitor centre foundations had thrown up no evidence of burials or human activity.

When the trustees had submitted their request for planning permission, the planning office had stipulated that an archaeologist must be in attendance during the excavation of the foundations — much to the annoyance of Mark, the construction company's project manager. Sophie, the archaeologist who had been assigned to oversee it all, was now the most unpopular person on-site, having called an immediate halt to all work until it could be fully assessed. Katherine found herself caught in the middle, under pressure from Mark to get the archaeologist off-site as soon as possible and from Sophie to be allowed to carry out her work unhindered.

A specialist osteoarchaeologist had been called in to excavate the remains, which had caused further delay. On top of all that, Anna had been trying to organise the official opening of Abbey Barn, which had already been announced to the press. Though they had hoped to show off the exterior of the completed, new extension to the visitor centre during the event, visitors had been greeted by ugly steel hoarding, which obscured their view of the visitor centre altogether. The ticket hall and offices were on the opposite side of the construction, so they had remained open during all the upheaval. That was one thing to be thankful for, though their budget was feeling the effects of the closure of the café.

Carrie and Anna arrived and took seats on either side of her. Katherine was so deep in thought she hadn't realised she was still rubbing her ankle as Carrie tucked her chair in beside her.

"Are your feet as overworked as you are?"

Katherine slipped her foot back into her shoe and sat upright. "I think so, yes."

Carrie poured herself a glass of water from the jug on the table. "How did the meeting go with the trustees?"

"We agreed that I would continue with my role and the added elements I had taken on of Margaret's responsibility since her absence. So I'm now officially in charge of the abbey. You're to take over the day-to-day operation of the site and staff management, reporting to me with any problems."

"It won't make much of a difference to me. I'm not sure what Margaret brought to the table anyway."

There was a resounding groan of agreement around the table.

"As you know, the other trustees all have jobs outside of the abbey, and having just taken on a restaurant manager we can't afford to take anyone else on. These delays really are having an effect everywhere. I did stipulate that we would have to reassess roles as we go, so if you're feeling the strain, do let me know. It's going to be a difficult few months with this continued reduced income. It will be worth it, and we'll get through it by working together and keeping all lines of communication open."

Carrie and Anna nodded their agreement.

Katherine had increased her hours since the new year, much to Anna's concern. Katherine had assured her she would reduce them again once the site was finished. With this date ever-changing and with an increased workload due to Margaret's departure, she wondered if she would ever be able to return to her part-time hours.

"Has there been any word from Margaret?" Carrie asked.

"The trustees finally received a response — she was in Spain." Katherine was pleased Anna had persuaded her to let Carrie in on what had really happened with Margaret. It made life easier, being able to talk freely, and Carrie deserved to know the truth.

Anna rolled her eyes. "No doubt trying to ruin someone else's relationship."

"The good news is she was happy to leave her investment in the abbey, so financially we are more secure now than we thought we would be. The bad news is — "

"She's still tied to the abbey," Anna finished.

Katherine tapped her notebook with her pen. "Indeed."

"Well, as long as she keeps out of our way in Spain, then we have nothing to complain about. Right, ladies?" Carrie said in an upbeat tone.

"Right," Anna and Katherine repeated dully.

They both knew Carrie well enough to know her optimism alone could have carried the *Titanic* safely to New York, had she only been on board at the time.

"The new restaurant manager, Daniel, starts in two weeks. Carrie, I know I suggested that you stay in your current office, but he's requested one and he'd like it to be in the same building as the restaurant rather than out in the barn, which is understandable."

Carrie shrugged. "Oh, of course, I don't mind moving into the barn."

The relief that crossed Anna's face didn't escape Katherine. Despite reassurances that she would be fine alone in the barn, Katherine hadn't been totally convinced, and so had suggested to the restaurant manager that he might like to have his own office and then offered Carrie's. She felt a little sneaky arranging it that way, but decided it was for the best.

"There was no delaying the start of his contract, then?" Carrie continued.

Katherine sank a little into her chair. "No, it was signed before the building work was stopped, so we didn't have a leg to stand on legally. He'd already handed his notice in too. He kindly agreed to take some annual leave initially, which is why he won't start for two weeks, not today when he should have been managing the fitting out of the restaurant." She looked at her watch. "Sophie and Mark should be along any minute with the results of the survey."

"How many wedding enquiries did we get at the opening, Carrie?" Anna asked, opening her laptop.

Carrie checked some papers in front of her. "Fifteen. I think seven were quite serious."

"I can't possibly organise that many. I've never organised a wedding."

"You're organising ours?" Katherine pointed out.

"You know I mean from the other side."

"It's an event, Anna. Treat it like any other. We're only supplying the venue and staff this year, so it's only a matter of coordinating, and you are a coordinating genius."

Anna lifted one side of her mouth.

"How about we see how things go this year and what bookings we get for next year, and we'll think about hiring a dedicated wedding coordinator," Katherine said.

"That's all I ask. With all the other events the abbey will be holding throughout the year, it's going to be stressful enough without being held responsible for multiple bridezillas' big days."

"Did the people come from the registry office this morning, Katherine?" Carrie asked.

"Yes, they seem happy with the barn as a venue; they were perhaps a little concerned about the building work, despite me showing them endless folders with all the health and safety measurements in place."

"How long until we get approval?"

"They will put the notifications out immediately, which gives anyone twenty-one days to object. They said there may be a stipulation that we don't take confirmed bookings until the building work is complete."

"I'm not sure anyone would want to get married with a building site for a view anyway," Carrie replied, examining her notes. "The more serious enquiries we got on Saturday were all for next year anyway."

"If we're unlikely to have any weddings this year, then we'll need to work hard to increase the number of other bookings on the barn," Katherine remarked.

Anna let out a groan as she exhaled. "No pressure then."

"On that note, I know you have the Easter bunny trail coming up, but the trustees have requested you submit your plans for the rest of the year with full costs and predicted revenue."

A knock at the door interrupted them before Anna could voice an objection to the trustees' request. Sophie popped her head around the door.

"Come in, take a seat." Katherine gestured to the table.

Sophie took the seat next to Anna, and Mark placed himself opposite her, beside Carrie.

Katherine wasn't keen on this seating arrangement and hoped the project manager and the archaeologist wouldn't butt heads, literally across the table.

"What's the verdict?" she asked.

"I have good news and bad news for you," Sophie said. "The good news is we are happy that the burial was one-off in that area, so you can recommence building work."

Mark sat back in his seat and let out an audible sigh of relief. "The bad news?"

"You'll be pleased to know it won't affect you," Sophie replied, meeting Mark's glare.

Katherine raised her eyebrows and braced herself. "Go on then, hit *me* with it."

"The team would like to extend the survey to the rest of the site. No survey has been carried out before. We only have the historical records and very basic information gathered from when the Government took over the site during World War II. It's a good opportunity for the abbey, a chance to see beneath the soil. We'd like to extend it to your garden if we may, Katherine."

Anna grinned. "You'll have to ask Virginia's permission, not Katherine's."

"She won't say no to me. We've become firm friends."

They all let out a light laugh, dispersing the tension in the room. Katherine's cat had been a common sight at the abbey in the last weeks, more so than usual. She'd been found nosing inside the cabins of the diggers, Mark's temporary site office that had been placed in the car park, and even the trench itself, much to the annoyance of the archaeologists.

"How long will it take?" Anna asked.

Sophie scrunched her face. "A week to survey, another few to analyse the data and decide on a plan of action."

Carrie fidgeted in her seat. "What then? You find something and shut us down?"

"We would initially put in test pits to look at any anomalies we find, but there is nothing that would cause the site to be shut down. It's unlikely we'd do any excavation unless we found something particularly interesting. At most, we'll just need to cordon off areas. I know you will have concerns, but this is a good chance to add to what we know about the abbey's history."

Mark leaned forward and stared at Sophie. "You're sure it won't interfere with the construction work. We really cannot accept any more delays."

"The area you are working in holds no further interest for us."

Katherine looked to Anna, who shrugged.

"Can you supply a written report on your intentions, timings, number of staff on-site?" she asked Sophie. "I'll need to feed it back to the rest of the trustees for their approval."

"You'll have it first thing tomorrow," Sophie replied, standing up. "It might be that we find nothing, and we'll be on our way. Anything we do find will only add to the history of the site."

Sophie's last comment made Katherine feel like it was her duty to agree whether she liked it or not, which was likely the intention. She would be standing in the way of increasing knowledge about the abbey, and that would be working against their aim.

"I look forward to receiving it. I'll try and have an answer from the trustees by the end of the week." Katherine gave her a weak smile; it was all she could manage. One problem resolved, yes, but another one potentially created.

"If you could. We have some test pits going in up at Halsey Castle this week and next, so it will be a few weeks before we can get back on-site anyway. We'll have the results from the carbon testing on the remains in a few weeks, so we'll reconvene then."

Katherine nodded her agreement as Sophie and Mark made their exit, ten paces apart.

"Well, at least Mark's happy," Carrie said when they were out of earshot.

"For a change," Anna added with a smirk.

"He's under a lot of pressure from all sides, as am I." Katherine rubbed at her furrowed forehead. "Who knows what this additional survey will throw up? I think we'd be mad to disregard it. I wonder if they would do it anyway, even if we refused."

Anna's forehead creased as her gaze turned to Katherine. "You think they could?"

"I wouldn't like to bet against it. I'm sure they could get any permits they wanted and wave them at us."

"Best put it to the trustees then," Carrie added, rising from her chair. "I'd best get back to the rabble."

"And I have an exercise class to prepare for. Then Anna and I are leaving early," Katherine said, a little smirk dancing on her lip.

"We are?"

"Yes, we're going clothes shopping. You said yourself you need to smarten up for your new role. Apparently, a little girl pointed out she looked like a tour guide, Carrie."

Carrie snorted. "Get her out of the abbey jumper before her skin fuses with it permanently."

Katherine stroked at her chin. "I'm thinking a nice sharp suit, white shirt, maybe a pair of braces."

"Oh yeah, is that some fantasy of yours?" Anna raised one eyebrow at her.

"I'll leave you ladies to discuss that one in private."

"Sorry, Carrie, too much information?" Anna called after her.

Carrie stuck her head back around the door. "Just a bit. Good luck with the hunt."

Katherine stood. "Right, I'm going to squeeze this body into some Lycra and get to Pilates."

"Oh, can I watch?" Anna pleaded as they left the meeting room.

"I'm not sure the group would want you watching them during Pilates."

"No, I meant watch you squeeze into Lycra."

Katherine twitched her lip at the accuracy of the word *squeeze*.

CHAPTER 4

*A*nna left Abbey House with a promise to Katherine she would be back in good time for dinner. She felt like a kid going out to play with her friends. She'd always had to be back before the lampposts came on; it was the best way for an eighties child to tell the time. Technically she was going to visit a friend; she'd had a text from Laura inviting her and Katherine over for a cup of tea on Saturday afternoon. Katherine had suggested she go alone so they could catch up properly and said that she would meet her another time.

A little flutter of excitement had been with her all day at the prospect of hearing what Laura had been up to over the years and sharing her own news in return. Anna had very few friends, if any, outside of work, and she relished the thought of having someone close by who shared her experiences from long ago. It was grounding in a way. She might even have someone other than her dad, Gloria, and Carrie to invite to the wedding. She and Katherine had agreed to draw up a list of names each so they could finalise invitation numbers. So far Katherine hadn't been forthcoming with hers, and Anna was embarrassed to show her list to Katherine, who no doubt had endless friends, colleagues, acquaintances from the past to invite.

A rustle in the bush at the end of the driveway alerted her to Virginia's presence. The cat leapt out, running ahead of Anna by a few paces, and stopped in her path so she would have to be greeted. Anna stooped over to stroke Virginia's head. Before she could reach it, though, Virginia dived back into the bush as a figure in a black coat flew past on a bike on the road beside her. It took Anna by surprise as much as it had Virginia.

She watched as the bike left the road and mounted the elevated pavement in front of the shops where Gloria was clearing tables outside the tearoom. As the bike reached Gloria, it jumped off the raised pavement and into a puddle on the road below, before popping a wheelie down to the other end of the village. Anna was sure there was something familiar about the figure in black.

Gloria had almost fallen over backwards in shock. She steadied herself on the nearby table.

Anna ran over to her. "Are you okay?"

"Little thug!" Gloria shouted after him. "It's the second time he's done that this week. I'm sure he's aiming for me. He's a menace."

"I'm sure he's just trying to have a bit of fun. He could perhaps do it somewhere more appropriate, though."

"He'll have my elderly customers over and drive away business if he keeps it up." Gloria moaned, then collapsed into a nearby chair.

Anna stepped forward to help, though this prompted Gloria to bat her away.

"I'll be all right, love, just give me a second. Did you want anything?"

"No, thanks, I'm heading to a friend's for a cuppa. Do you remember Laura, whom I used to go to school with?"

Gloria thought for a moment. "Jean's daughter?"

"Yes, she's recently moved back to the village."

"Jean was a good 'un, like your mum. We all used to hang about together back in the day. It was a different village then. Everyone was younger."

Anna braced herself for a long speech about the old days.

"We'd all look after each other's kids. Then you all grew up and left, and we all stayed and grew old. It's nice that some of you have come back, though I'm not sure this village is built for youngsters like that." Gloria nodded down the road. "It's a shame my Mandy hasn't come back. I've lost track of how old my grandkids are now. Haven't seen them since they were bubs. All I get is an email with some photos every few months."

"Australia is a long way away."

Gloria thought for a moment and then stood up. "Anyway, I can't sit around here gassing all day. I've got work to do."

Anna did her best to contain a grin. "Bye, Gloria."

It saddened her that Gloria had little contact with her only child, Mandy. Mandy was two years older than Anna, and she could remember playing with her when she was little. They had sat together on the bus to school until Mandy became more interested in boys and joined them at the back. Anna was grateful to never have had that debilitating problem.

She continued down the road, sneaking a look at their old house across the road as she passed it. It looked quite fine kitted out with a new front door and windows. The small area to the front had been tidied up and gravel put down for the bins to stand on. It was quite transformed. Her thoughts drifted to the inside and how it had been ripped apart during its renovation. It irked her that the council hadn't taken the bother to do it whilst her dad was living there. She stopped her thoughts from going any further. The house may have been run-down, but it was home, and she preferred to think of it as it had been.

Because she spent most of her time at the top of the village, she rarely needed to go to the bottom end anymore. The main road through the village exited at the top end, beside Abbey House, as well as the bottom. She hadn't been down this end for months; it was like a trip down memory lane. She passed the surgery where she had met Katherine and the library where she used to walk with her dad until Katherine took over that responsibility. The church lay beyond, set far back from the road, and then there was the patch of land where the village hall once stood. A playground sat to one side of a large, grassy area that had once been the hall's car park. It was nothing more than a wasteland now. The playground was very much neglected, with one broken swing, a roundabout, a small metal slide, and a lone spring rider in the shape of a horse, poised to throw any loose-handed passenger from its back.

Anna stopped outside what had been Laura's mum's house and unlatched the gate. It was one of the oldest properties in the village and one of the last before the main road swept you out and along the valley. The house was set back from the main road, and as soon as she proceeded up the path to the front door, she heard a voice shouting from inside.

"Mum, Anna's here!"

Abigail's face appeared at one of the upstairs windows. She waved enthusiastically at Anna.

Anna waved back. She was starting to think she had the beginnings of a fan club.

Laura opened the door as Abigail thundered down the stairs behind her.

"Come on in."

"Anna!" Abigail cheered. "Can I show you my room?"

"Later, love. Let Anna have a cup of tea first."

Anna winked at her. "Can't wait."

Abigail beamed and raced back up the stairs.

"Come through to the kitchen."

Laura led Anna through the hallway to the back of the house. It was much changed from how she remembered it. What had once been drab, brown and orange seventies interiors were now bright and modern blues and greens. As they arrived in the kitchen, it was obvious the house had been fully renovated. The small kitchen at the back was now an open-plan kitchen diner with sliding doors onto a patio. It was a similar style to that at Abbey House, on a much less grand scale.

"Take a seat. Tea?"

"Please. Milk, no sugar." Anna pulled out a chair at what looked like an IKEA dining table. "Have you renovated? I don't recall it being like this."

"Yes, before we moved in. Can you imagine living in it how it was?" Laura chuckled as she moved around the kitchen.

"No, not really."

"It was like something out of a horror movie."

Anna didn't think it had been quite that bad but understood where she was coming from. "You were renting it out, weren't you?"

"Yes, we didn't see the point in selling it when Mum died. It made more sense to have the rental income; we always planned to move back here when we were older." Her tone softened as she continued. "Steve always dreamt of having an acre of land in the countryside. I don't know what he planned to do with it; I don't think he did either."

Anna waited patiently as Laura stirred the tea, drifting off into her thoughts. A bang from upstairs roused her.

"Sorry. What was I saying? Yes, so I ended up moving back a little earlier than planned and without him."

"How did he die, if you don't mind me asking?"

Laura brought two mugs over from the counter and sat opposite Anna. "He was stabbed during a terrorist attack whilst on duty. He was in the Metropolitan Police. They say he died a hero. Like that's supposed to make it okay."

Anna let out a long breath. "I'm sorry to hear that. I can't imagine how difficult it must have been for you. How have the kids handled it?"

"Abi misses her dad obviously; they were very close." Laura passed a mug to Anna, then opened a biscuit tin and offered her one.

"No, thanks."

Laura placed the tin on the table and extracted a

digestive biscuit. "I think she's handled it better than Tom. Abi's at that age where they spring back; Tom, on the other hand, he's angry. About everything. I don't know if it's his age or his dad — or the move. He had to leave his friends back in the city. To be honest, I was glad to get him away from them. He was less impressed."

The front door slammed.

"Speak of the devil."

Tom slunk into the kitchen. His black coat instantly gave him away as the phantom bike rider that had terrified Gloria.

"Have you put your bike in the shed?" Laura asked him.

He turned with a harrumph and left the room.

Anna and Laura caught each other's eyes, both poised for the slam of a door that followed a second later.

"Sorry. Kids, eh?"

"I think he may have had a run-in with Gloria earlier."

"Gloria? Used to run the tearoom?"

"Still does."

Laura's jaw slackened. "I thought she would have retired by now if she wasn't already six feet under. What did he do?"

"He caught her unawares, that's all."

"I'll have to pop in and say hello. I'll take Tom to apologise. He's mad keen on bikes, got that from Steve. At least it's a bit safer around here than in the city, angry shopkeeper aside."

A set of thundering feet coming down the stairs echoed around the open-plan kitchen just as the front door opened and slammed again.

"Ow." Abigail's voice came from in the hall.

Tom entered the kitchen followed by Abigail holding her arm.

"He bashed me."

"Did not," Tom grunted back.

"Did."

"You were in my way."

"Enough!" Laura snapped. "Tom, grab a snack and go to your room, please. I don't appreciate you taking out our neighbours with your bike."

Tom exhaled loudly and scowled at Anna.

Abigail took a seat next to Anna.

"Are you coming to the Easter bunny trail on Sunday afternoon?" Anna asked Abigail, feeling a change of focus was needed.

"Can I help?" Abigail asked.

"Well, you wouldn't be able to take part then."

Abigail shrugged. "I don't mind."

"I will need help putting some signs up and then handing out trail sheets. Can you help with that?"

Abigail beamed and nodded. "Easy."

"I'm not going," Tom interjected. "It's for babies."

"I'm not sure they'd want you there anyway with that attitude," Laura replied, to which Tom stormed off out of the kitchen.

Anna tried once again to steer the conversation back to more pleasant ground. "I can take Abigail to the bunny trail and drop her back in the afternoon," she told Laura.

"I'm eight," Abigail said. "I don't need dropping back."

Laura laughed at her daughter. "You send her straight

home if she's any trouble. Now upstairs with you, Abi. I'll bring Anna up before she leaves, don't you worry."

Abigail's hand dove into the biscuit tin before she skipped out of the room.

"Are you sure you don't mind?" Laura asked.

"Not at all. An enthusiastic and willing helper is always welcome at the abbey."

CHAPTER 5

*A*fter they had been over their schooldays and every teacher and fellow student they could remember, Anna moved the conversation on to more current times.

"So, do you work?"

"Not now, no. Not since the kids were born," Laura replied wistfully. "I was in catering. It's how Steve and I met actually; I was working an event he was at. I was in the process of starting up a catering business when I fell pregnant with Tom. With Steve's hours being irregular, it was too difficult for us both to have jobs and be there for the kids." Laura extracted another biscuit and munched on it thoughtfully.

Anna refrained from commenting on how many women had given up their careers for their husbands and children; Laura was fully aware of what she had lost.

"Have you never thought about getting back into it now the kids are older?"

"I can't now. I'm hoping to have an operation soon — if I can convince the stupid doctors to give me one."

Anna laughed internally; relieved Katherine had stayed at home. She wasn't sure if she should ask what was wrong or wait and see if Laura was forthcoming.

"Nothing serious, I hope?" she ventured.

"Not serious enough for them to take it seriously, yet enough to cause me day-to-day misery. I have fibroids," Laura finally disclosed, as if she had sensed Anna's awkwardness. "They've cursed me most of my adult life, and now with Steve gone, I just want a hysterectomy. My previous doctor thought that at forty I may want to have more kids. When I pointed out that my husband was dead, he suggested that my next husband may want them. As if my choice not to have any more was irrelevant."

Anna spat out a laugh and then held her hand to her mouth. "I'm sorry, I don't think I've heard anything so ridiculous."

Laura grinned, much to Anna's relief; she did have a habit of smiling or laughing at inappropriate moments, something she blamed her dad for.

"It's fine. I'm hoping that, now that I've changed location, a new consultant may agree with me, I'm waiting for an appointment."

"Fingers crossed. It must be awful if you feel the need to have a hysterectomy."

"It is. Imagine the worse period pains, and then imagine you have them most of the time. Stress makes it worse, so Steve dying... let's just say I've had to learn to manage myself a little better now. If it wasn't for the kids, I think I would have fallen apart."

Anna nodded; she knew all too well about managing herself.

"Have you considered going private? Assuming you could afford it?"

Laura fell silent for a moment. "I hadn't, no. I suppose I could afford it."

"There's nothing more important to spend your money on than your health. It's just a shame some have to; you'll also be freeing up treatment for someone less able to afford it."

"I'll look into it. The condition is really holding me back."

"And no doubt making you a bit depressed, which then impacts the kids."

Laura nodded; her gaze fell to the cup in her hand. "A lot depressed, and yes, I do get a little grouchy sometimes."

Anna squeezed her arm.

She smiled. "It would be great to get it sorted soon. I could finally draw a line under it and move on. Anyway, enough about me and my sad life. You've fallen on your feet, it seems — shacked up with a gorgeous woman in the most sought-after house in the village."

"I rather have, haven't I?" Anna replied, unable to contain the huge grin forming on her lips. "Kat is…" She was lost for words. How did one sum up a woman like Katherine? "Exceptional. I adore her."

"Good, I'm glad you found someone. She seems like she means business."

Anna's grin tightened again. She knew exactly what Laura was implying.

"She has a vulnerable side too. She lost her first wife and unborn child a few years ago. I don't think she's over it or if she's even come to terms with it. She acts like she has, but then something happens and hell shines through to take her down."

Laura nodded as if she understood. "So will you two be having kids?"

When she was younger, she had thought children would be in her future. Whether that was simply part of growing up, to daydream about being a mum, she wasn't sure. At that age, you want to experience everything — or at least feel you should. Not only had her ex, Jess, not wanted children, Anna herself had never been in a stable enough environment in the past to contemplate them. Her dreams had fallen by the wayside.

"I don't know. I always wanted them when I was little, but then life takes over and pulls you in other directions. It's hardly a straightforward process when you're gay."

"It's hardly impossible, though. How does Katherine feel?"

Anna rested her cheek on her fist. "We haven't really discussed it. She wanted them once, so maybe she would want them again. She hasn't said anything. I think we're a little too old now to be thinking about that anyway."

"Too old? Rubbish. At the least, it sounds like a conversation you might want to have. You've certainly got the house for it." A smile formed on her lips. "Do you remember us trying to find a way into Abbey House because you wanted to see inside, but it meant breaking a window and you couldn't bring yourself to do it?"

Anna laughed. "Neither could you."

"It wasn't me that wanted to go in." Laura took a sip of tea and then another biscuit. "So, when did you come back to the village?"

"Last year. Dad wasn't coping on his own and I wasn't in a great place with Jess, so I came home to Nunswick."

"No regrets?" Laura questioned.

Anna took it as a sign that Laura was still in those early days of regret. It was something she had experienced early on until she realised how much her dad had needed her. The only regret she had was not doing it sooner.

"None. Give it time. The kids will settle. Who wouldn't choose the country over the city? You'll find your feet."

Laura nodded. "So you and Katherine must have hooked up pretty quickly then if you're already engaged."

"It's certainly been a rollercoaster, I can tell you. She lost her job because of me. She was a doctor — is a doctor, technically," Anna quickly corrected herself, as Katherine would have, had she been there.

Laura shot a bewildered look at her.

"Our relationship was a little inappropriate, considering she was my dad's doctor."

"Ah. I see."

"Margaret, my boss at the time, had a crush on Katherine and reported us to the General Medical Council to try and break us up."

"What a bitch."

Anna laughed. "Obviously, it didn't work. She did cause a lot of problems between us over Christmas, though. Kat just couldn't see what she was like. They were quite good friends, and Kat really felt betrayed by it."

"I can see why. How's your dad doing now? You said he was in a home?"

"Yes, and he's doing okay, as well as you can expect for a Parkinson's patient. He had a fall last year, and I was working full-time. It was the only option."

"That must have been hard. Mum died in her sleep, so we never had to make that decision."

"It would have been if it had been my decision. Dad decided it was right." Anna laughed to think back at her behaviour. "I fought it, much to Kat's annoyance. She said from the start he needed to be in a home, as if it was the easiest decision to make."

"Send him my best next time you see him."

"I will; we're visiting tomorrow. We haven't seen him in a while as he had a cold; otherwise you could have said hello at the opening. He insists we don't visit when he's ill as he doesn't want to pass it on. He knows how busy we are."

"I can't get over how much the abbey has changed. The visitor centre is quite something."

"It will be if we ever finish the extension."

"Didn't it only open last year? Why are you extending already? Is it that popular?"

"It had its first full season last year, and yes, it's that popular. We're extending the café to a restaurant and adding a proper gift shop. It's a shame you weren't here for the new year. I held an epic party." Anna drained her mug.

"Well, we'll be here this year and can't wait. Shall I take you to see Miss Impatient?"

"Yes," Anna replied eagerly. She liked Abigail; the girl was refreshing.

Laura led the way upstairs, passing Tom's room first. The door was ajar and revealed carnage comprising of open video game boxes, clothes, and empty bowls and glasses.

Abigail's room was as Anna had expected to find it. Typical pink walls held shelves of books, and more importantly, a bean bag sat in a corner, ready for the girl to collapse onto to read them all. A desk in one corner was heavy with colouring pens and pencils, and the walls around it were plastered with drawings.

"When are you getting married?" Abigail asked once she'd given Anna the tour of her room.

"We were going to do it in the summer, but with all the delays at the abbey, we haven't set on a date."

"You're getting married at the abbey?"

"Yes, in Abbey barn, but it has to be given permission to hold weddings, and we're waiting to receive that before we can choose a date." Katherine had said it would be tempting fate to choose a date and then wait for permission.

"Will you both wear dresses?"

"I'm not sure." They hadn't thought as far as what they would wear.

"I can't wait to get married so I can wear a beautiful, long, white dress."

"You can wear one of them anytime you like, you know."

"Who did the body you find belong to? Was it gooey?"

Anna was caught off guard by the sudden change of

direction. She looked to Laura, wondering if it was okay to say. Laura put her hand over her mouth to conceal what Anna could only assume was a smirk. She was going to receive no help from her.

"It's the remains of someone from long ago. When the abbey was in use, we believe. We're still waiting for the carbon dating. That's something that tells us how old it was. And no, it wasn't gooey." Anna looked at her watch. "Sorry, I better be going. I promised Kat I'd be back in good time for dinner."

She followed Laura downstairs, Abigail close at her heel.

"Thanks for coming," Laura said as she held the front door.

"It's been great catching up. If you need anything, just ask."

"Thanks. I look forward to meeting Katherine."

Anna turned on the doorstep. "You'll have to come for dinner. Kat loves cooking."

"I'd like that, especially if it includes a full tour of Abbey House."

"Without a doubt," Anna smirked. "I'll message you once I've spoken to Kat about a date. Perhaps after Easter."

"Can I come too?" Abigail asked, her eyes wide and bright.

"Of course, and Tom."

The glow in Abigail's eyes dulled.

"I'll see you on Sunday, Abi."

The shine returned as her mouth curled into a smile.

Anna walked down the path to the gate, pleased to

have potentially added three people to her wedding invite list; she was now up to six. Something niggled in the pit of her stomach and deflated her mood. Laura was right: She was going to need to have a difficult conversation with Katherine about children. Regardless of her own feelings, Anna needed to understand where she stood on the subject. It would be terrible if they each assumed the other didn't want children only to find out ten years down the road that they both had and neither had bothered to mention it.

CHAPTER 6

*A*nna stepped out of the car outside Baycroft, instantly regretting putting away her scarf after a single week of milder weather. Katherine, getting out the passenger side, looked perfectly cosy in hers, with matching gloves. Although Anna loved spring and autumn, she cursed the changeability of the weather during those seasons. You knew where you were with the winter; you were in a coat. In the summer you weren't. In spring and autumn you could be in a coat or a jumper, even a coat and a jumper. The only thing you could rely on in spring and autumn was that whatever you were wearing wasn't right.

There was no one at reception when they arrived, so they went straight to Harry's room. Anna tapped lightly on the door and leaned her head around it. "You here, Dad?" It didn't feel right to walk in. She didn't want him to answer the door or shout, so it seemed the sensible answer. It wasn't like he would be in a state of undress at the times they visited.

"Anna," Harry called back. "That you?"

They entered to find Harry in his usual laid-back position in his recliner. He hurriedly tried to return the chair to its upright position as they approached.

"Here, let me help you, Dad."

Anna pushed up the back of the chair, and Harry slowly returned to a vertical position.

"Thanks, love."

"How are you feeling, Harry?" Katherine asked, taking her usual seat. "Any better?"

"Right as rain, doc," Harry replied unconvincingly.

The door opened and a lady entered. Anna wondered if she was a member of staff or a resident. Though her face was certainly older, her dyed blonde hair was perfectly styled into a bouncy, layered bob, and her make-up was flawless.

"All right, my love," she said as she closed the door. She tried to mask her surprise when she saw Anna and Katherine.

Harry's face brightened. "Mabel!"

Mabel approached them. "Sorry, I didn't realise you had company. Shall I pop back later?"

"Come," Harry said. "I want you to meet my daughter."

"Oh, is this Anna?" Mabel turned to Katherine. "Nice to meet you, love. I've heard so much about you. Harry never stops talking about you."

Katherine's mouth opened to answer.

"No, that's Katherine, her fiancée. This is Anna." Harry pointed at Anna in the chair opposite him.

"Oh, sorry, love," Mabel said, approaching Anna before

stopping suddenly to take her in. "Oh, yes, I can see the resemblance now. You've got his nose."

Mabel turned to Harry and squeezed his nose, making him laugh like an infatuated teenager. Anna's forehead puckered as her eyes met Katherine's.

"You warm enough?" Mabel asked, tucking in the sides of Harry's lap blanket. "I can fetch you another throw."

"I'm all right, though I've got a bit of a sore throat coming on."

Mabel nodded. "I'll refill your cup with some fresh water." She scooped up his lidded cup and disappeared into the bathroom.

They sat in silence whilst Mabel hummed to herself over the sound of the tap. Anna frowned at Katherine and twitched the side of her face. Katherine gave a slight shrug in response.

Mabel returned from the bathroom, squeezed the lid of Harry's cup back on, and placed it in front of him. "That okay there? Can you reach it okay?"

"Perfect. Thanks, love."

"Well, I'll leave you to your visitors. I'll see you at lunch, my love, and then perhaps we can finish that book this afternoon." Mabel rechecked Harry's blanket and then made for the door. "It was nice to meet you both."

"And you," Anna and Katherine replied together as Mabel left the room.

"A sore throat. I thought you were feeling better, Harry?" Katherine asked, covering a wry smile as she spoke.

"She likes to look after me, doc. We're sort of going about together now, you know."

46

Anna wasn't entirely sure she did know. Katherine nodded as if she knew. *Going about together.* Was that older-person speak for going out with someone?

"Do you mean she's your girlfriend?" Anna asked pointedly.

"Yeah, if you like, love."

Anna sat back in her chair and tried to comprehend the concept of her dad having a girlfriend at his age. She opened her mouth to make a further enquiry until the glare she received from Katherine made her close it instantly.

"That's nice, Harry," Katherine interjected. "We're pleased for you. Aren't we, Anna?"

"Err, yes, of course," was all the reply Anna could muster.

"Must be nice to have a bit of female company."

"It is, and you want to know the best bit, doc?"

Anna blinked, unsure where the conversation was about to go.

"What?"

"She loves war films. Can you believe it?"

"Really?" Katherine laughed. "She sounds like the perfect woman."

Anna could believe it a little less than Katherine could.

Harry coughed and Anna shot out of her chair.

He put his hand out to stop her. "I'm all right, love."

"How are you getting on with your physio?" Katherine asked once he'd settled himself.

"I'm getting a full workout, doc, believe me. She's a hard taskmaster."

Katherine knew precisely how Harry was getting on.

She had kept in touch with his physiotherapist, Holly, since he left the hospital at the new year, and had shared their conversations with Anna. During their last conversation, she'd said he wasn't being particularly cooperative of late.

"You're doing everything she said?" Katherine gave him one of her stern looks with a raised eyebrow.

"Well, it's hard work, doc. She tires me out, and then I've got no energy for Mabel."

Anna's jaw dropped. "Dad!"

"Oh, not like that. I'm too old and decrepit for any of that business. She gets grumpy with me if I fall asleep during a movie."

"For pity's sake, Dad, sod — bloody Mabel," Anna stuttered. "You need to do your exercises."

"Anna!" Katherine snapped in a firm voice. She sat forward in her chair and looked at Harry. "It's important for your health that you do as Holly says, Harry, not just for your Parkinson's. For your lungs too. The breathing exercises are essential for your recovery from pneumonia."

"All right, Lucy. I'll try and do better."

Katherine looked at Harry and placed a hand on his. "I'm Katherine, Harry, not Lucy. She's your carer."

Harry nodded. His eyes flickered, confused.

"Dad, are you okay?"

"You look tired, Harry. Shall we leave you to it?" Katherine flashed Anna a stare.

Anna followed Katherine's firm instruction and rose from her chair. She kissed Harry on the forehead as she always did.

"What the hell just happened?" Anna whispered the second she closed the door to his room.

"I'm sure he's fine. I think he's tired and became confused under pressure."

"You don't think he could have dementia or something? I've read it's more common in Parkinson's patients."

"He just forgot my name," Katherine said. She waved goodbye to the receptionist, and they exited into the car park. "Actually, we don't even know if he forgot my name; Lucy's just came out instead. Lucy is his primary carer; her name is on the tip of his tongue. I don't think we can assume he has dementia because of that."

Anna nodded with relief.

"Saying that… I don't think we should rule it out either."

Anna stopped in front of the car. "I've watched my dad being robbed of the use of his body. I…I don't think I can watch him being robbed of his mind as well. What if he forgets who I am?"

"It's unlikely to progress that far."

"You mean he'll die from Parkinson's before he dies from dementia?" She pinched her warm, wet eyelids together.

"Hey." Katherine reached out to her and pulled her into a hug. "Let's not worry about anything until we have something to worry about, okay?"

Anna gave a nod to placate Katherine. She couldn't simply turn her worry off. It wasn't a tap.

"I'll call Holly and Lucy tomorrow, just to mention it, see if they've noticed anything. I'll drive."

Anna sat in the passenger side without complaint. Katherine always insisted on driving when she knew Anna's mind was preoccupied.

"I bet she doesn't really," Anna said, tapping the heated-seat button on the centre console.

"What?"

"Mabel. Like war films," Anna clarified. "I bet she's humouring him. What do you think she's after? What has he got to offer that could be of value to her?"

"A sense of humour? Kindness? Friendship? I'm amazed you asked the question."

"You know what I mean."

"No, I really don't, Anna. If Harry has found a bit of companionship, then who are you to object? Depression is a common long-term effect following pneumonia in the elderly. It's more important than ever that he keeps good company… whilst also doing his physio."

If Mabel thought she could replace her mother, she'd have to think again. When she'd squeezed her dad's nose, as her mum often did, anger had caught Anna in her throat rendering her speechless. It had been difficult enough passing the responsibility of care for him onto someone else, but to see him lovestruck with a new woman had been a shock, one she'd had to contain out of politeness. What if Mabel tried to come between them or interfere in his care? Even Anna knew these were irrational thoughts, but it didn't make it any easier to accept.

CHAPTER 7

$\mathcal{K}$atherine pulled the car up outside Abbey House to see Virginia stretched out on the doorstep. She and Anna pulled on the walking boots that were now housed in the back of the car. There was a time when she washed her boots after use and returned them to their designated position in the understairs cupboard, but Anna had been quick to point out that they would be best left in a box in the back of the car. With less time on her hands nowadays, she didn't argue.

As they walked down the high street to the pub, Katherine slipped her hand into Anna's and gave it a squeeze, receiving a squeeze in return. Their Sunday had become a routine of a morning visit to Harry, followed by a walk and lunch at the pub. It had been a ritual started over Christmas. The pub had been an inviting haven on a Sunday, with its log fire and tasty roasts.

Once the weather improved, they decided they didn't want to give up their pub lunch. It saved Katherine cooking once a week, and although she enjoyed cooking, it was nice to have a break considering the amount of work that went into making a roast dinner for two. Throw in her ever-increasing workload at the abbey, and it became a no-brainer. It also freed her up for a phone call to her best friend Rebecca in the afternoon, a time for them to catch up on the week. She was looking forward to telling her that the building work had resumed.

Anna had been quiet on the journey home; her mind must have been racing with thoughts of Harry and his future, what was left of it. Experience taught Katherine that, though she didn't want her fiancée to worry, she had to share any concerns about Harry immediately. Hopefully a conversation with Lucy and Holly would reassure them that all was well. Harry's carer and physiotherapist knew him now better than anyone and would be the best judges of his cognitive abilities.

They arrived at the pub in short order. Katherine waited outside whilst Anna went in to retrieve Moose. Walking Moose, the pub's chocolate Labrador, had also become part of their Sunday ritual. Knowing how busy the landlord, Chris, was on a Sunday, they had suggested they take Moose on their walk before they came in for their lunch. Chris had jumped at the idea, as had Moose, several times.

If anyone could take Anna's mind off Harry, it was Moose. The enthusiastic, chunky Labrador always lifted her spirits. Anna stepped out the pub door with Moose, who sat to be greeted by Katherine. He'd learnt early on that he would get no attention from Katherine unless he sat nicely. She wasn't used to being around dogs, and their wild jumping was the one thing she disliked about them. Luckily, Moose had soon got the idea.

They proceeded back up the high street to Abbey House, Anna being pulled along by Moose who knew exactly where they were going and couldn't wait to get there. They joined the footpath beside Abbey House and followed it around the back of the property, where they were scowled at by Virginia from her perch on a fence post. Moose was too busy sticking his nose into everything to spot her. Katherine had noticed on their walk the previous Sunday that Virginia had followed them the whole way around — a good twenty paces behind, of course. She wouldn't be seen dead walking with them.

The River Wick flowed smoothly beside them. It was more a stream than a river in the spring and summer. Its deep-cut sides were very appreciated during the autumn and winter months, when they contained the heavy rain from the surrounding hills. Without them, the lower parts of the Nunswick Valley would likely flood.

Anna let Moose off the lead, and he ran to the nearest inlet to the river and splashed into the water.

Katherine scooped up Anna's free hand as they continued along the bank. "I was thinking we should make a walking map," she said. "Document all the routes we've marked out around the village. We could get Michael, the artist, to do an illustration. I'm sure the designers of the barn leaflet could pull something together. What do you think?"

"What does the abbey, whom I presume is paying for it, get out of it?" Anna said.

"Take your marketing hat off for a moment; it's more a

chance to give back. Anyhow, it might draw more people to the abbey, like walkers, nature enthusiasts. We have the facilities to accommodate them. It would also draw people to the local amenities; we could even ask them to advertise. If we marked out how the walks linked up to the routes in the surrounding areas, it would encourage people down from the hills."

"Or up into them."

Katherine ignored her comment. "Do you think you could come up with a few hundred words to add to it, maybe work out some costings?"

"Yes, boss," Anna mumbled.

Katherine regretted bringing up the subject. She had intended to draw out Anna's enthusiasm, but it appeared to have only added to her worries.

Luckily, Moose was there to lift her spirits. Anna stood by the bank and threw in a stick for Moose to retrieve. It was his favourite game, and he never tired of it. Occasionally, he would climb the bank and shake himself off, causing Anna to leap back beside Katherine, who always kept a safe distance from the splash zone. They finally managed to persuade him away from the water, and all three followed the path down to the other end of the village and back to the pub.

Whilst Anna returned Moose to Chris at the bar, Katherine placed herself at their usual table, which now permanently reserved for them on a Sunday. She was glad to see a roaring fire in the hearth. Even though it was a spring day, the chill in the air had numbed her nose. Anna returned a few minutes later and sat down with two glasses of wine and the local Sunday paper under her arm.

Moose followed her as far as the hearth, where he proceeded to circle in his basket a few times before finally curling up into a ball. He was fluffier than before; Chris must have towelled him down.

Moose stared up at Katherine with his big, brown eyes before closing them and reopening them several times, fighting the urge to sleep. She watched him with envy; she, too, felt the urge to curl up in a ball and go to sleep. Although she wouldn't like to admit it openly, she was becoming a fan of the docile Labrador. She knew Anna wanted one, and although she was warming to dogs, there was a significant difference between borrowing one for an hour on a Sunday and owning one.

Anna opened the paper and flicked through it.

Katherine disliked free newspapers. She thought they were a waste of good paper and primarily focussed on advertising double-glazed windows and used cars. As the paperboy was too lazy to walk down the drive of Abbey House, she never had to deal with them. Anna, on the other hand, liked to know what was going on locally and would spend the first half of a glass of wine each Sunday thumbing through the pub's copy. Katherine watched as she blew at the side of the paper, catching the page with her thumb and turning it over.

"Oh, look. It's us at the opening." Anna smiled and folded the newspaper back on itself. Katherine watched as her eyes darted through the article, but then, slowly, the smile and colour drained from her face. Anna silently passed the newspaper over to Katherine.

Katherine examined the picture of her standing next to Anna outside Abbey Barn, cutting the ribbon. It wasn't a bad photograph of them. The headline read *Body Unearthed*, and a subtitle followed: *What other treasures lay undiscovered?* She read through the brief article, which focussed on the remains rather than the barn opening. Katherine had made a point of trying to keep the find away from the local press. It had been Anna who insisted on inviting them to the opening based on the idea that it would be good for business. Now their discovery was plastered all over page four.

Katherine passed the paper back to Anna. "Sensationalist bullshit. It wasn't a body; it was historical skeletal remains, for pity's sake. They are hardly the same thing. Why do you read this rubbish?"

"Dad doesn't get this paper, so I keep an eye on the obituaries for him." Anna closed the paper and returned it to the bar.

She let out a loud sigh as she sat back down. Her eyes drifted down to Moose in his basket beside the fire. His lips and jaw twitched as he chewed in his sleep. She felt a little envious of the dog, lying so blissfully without a care in the world except for where his next biscuit was coming from.

CHAPTER 8

*A*nna slipped quietly from the bedroom the next morning to dress for work, leaving a lightly snoring Katherine to sleep in. Lying in was something Anna encouraged. When Katherine was awake, she worked to her full capacity, despite knowing she shouldn't. If she wasn't physically active, you could guarantee she was mentally active; one of those types that never turned off.

With Katherine's dressing room already full of her clothes, Anna had suggested she make use one of the many spare bedrooms to store her few possessions. Although Katherine had assured her that she could clear space in the wardrobes of the master dressing room, Anna had insisted it was fine. She liked the idea of a space she could call her own. Much to her surprise, Katherine had left her to her own devices with the design and allowed her to make her mark on it. As such, she proudly entered the room, with its duck-egg blue, Chinoiserie-papered walls which matched the practical, contemporary, Georgian-style fitted wardrobes.

Katherine had inadvertently had a hand in the interior decorations. While perusing an antique centre shortly after Christmas, she had spotted a particularly elegant George IV mahogany dressing table, complete with figured top, a central drawer flanked by two deeper drawers, and a shaped kneehole. The drawer fronts were fitted with brass lion-head handles, and the whole thing was raised on ring-turned, tapered legs. Anna wasn't one for dressing tables and thought a desk would be more useful, but Katherine's find worked for both purposes. It contrasted elegantly with the room and sat in front of the sash window. She'd paired it with a mahogany, tanned-leather Chesterfield office chair.

In one corner, beside her bookcase, Anna had placed a modern Queen Anne winged chair in matching tanned leather, a replica of which Katherine disapproved. Anna pointed out that not only did her back require support, so did their bank balance, and a replica was perfectly suited to both requirements.

She adored the room so much she would often find herself wandering into it to admire her work. It couldn't have contrasted more with the dark, cramped, slightly damp room of her childhood.

She opened the wardrobe, which was a little fuller since their shopping trip, and extracted her new tweed jacket, chinos, and blue shirt. As much as she liked her new look and Katherine's reaction to it, the more formal attire was taking a bit of getting used to. Having only worn the abbey jumper and her baggy, beige trousers until now, this was a fresh look entirely. Katherine had tried to persuade her towards a more corporate suit with a white shirt, but Anna felt it didn't suit her or her position and decided on the more relaxed country look. The outfit required certain footwear, which was unsuitable for wandering around a ruined abbey, so she left a pair of wellies by her office door in case she was caught out and needed to go into the abbey ruins.

Once dressed, she headed downstairs to the kitchen to feed Virginia and fill up a stainless-steel thermal mug with peppermint tea, something that had become a morning essential. Five minutes later she was out the door of Abbey House and through her office door in Abbey Barn, the easiest and most beautiful of commutes. Her office location came with the added benefit that she could come and go as she pleased, without having to open the visitor centre.

Resisting the lure of a chocolate egg breakfast, Anna fired up her laptop. Having chased quotes for printing at the end of last week, she was relieved to find several in her inbox. They would allow her to finalise her ideas for the rest of the year and finish the report for Katherine to pass to the trustees. She had hoped to have a couple of weeks to finalise everything as she was still waiting for quotes; Katherine had given her a week, despite her pleading. Sometimes she felt Katherine was a little harder on her at work because of their relationship; it was understandable, though, that she couldn't be seen to be lenient with her.

Anna's plans for the abbey were quite ambitious, considering it was their first year with a more formalised structure of events. The Easter bunny trail would be in one week's time, followed by a summer gala, then Halloween with a guided, nocturnal ghost walk, and then the trialling of a Christmas market, inspired by their trip to Bath back in December. The market was the event she was most looking forward to, and it would no doubt prove to be the most difficult to organise. That would need to be dealt with alongside the New Year's Eve party plans but having already organised one successfully, she hoped it would require less attention this year.

With the work being carried out at the abbey, there had been a need to extend the hardstanding car park. It would prove to be an invaluable additional space for Christmas market stalls. However, with the ever-increasing popularity of the abbey, she feared by the holidays, they would require all the hardstanding for car parking.

Once the work on the visitor centre extension was complete and all the machinery and equipment removed from the site, Katherine had agreed to Anna's idea to install car parking machines to help towards maintenance costs. Katherine had insisted it be more of a token gesture rather than an extortionate fee. It was important that they keep peace with their neighbours and encourage people to park in the abbey car park rather than finding free parking around the village. Anna had eased her concerns with the suggestion to have a refund voucher printed on the rear which could be redeemed against any purchase made in the restaurant or gift shop. She'd also agreed to put signs up in the parking hot spots in the village, stating 'No Nunswick Abbey Parking'.

A knock on the external barn door startled Anna from her thoughts. Carrie entered with a parcel.

"This just arrived," Carrie said, placing the box on Anna's desk.

"Great, that will be the print for the egg hunt," Anna said, running a pen through the tape of the box to open it.

"We have a rather pressing matter, I'm afraid." Carrie contorted her face. "I know Katherine isn't due in for a few hours, but it might be best if you fetch her anyway."

Anna stood instinctively, reading the tone of Carrie's voice and the look on her face.

"What is it?"

"Come and see. Boot up."

Fully booted, Anna followed Carrie across the site to the chapel wall at the far end of the site.

"There." Carrie pointed at the exterior chapel wall, which was covered in purple spray paint.

"Graffiti! Where did that come from?"

"I think we'd all like to know that, and that's not all."

Carrie turned and pointed to several disturbed areas on the ground. "Someone's been digging?"

Anna approached the nearest hole and examined it. "Night hawks."

"Night what?"

"Night hawks. Illegal metal detectorists," Anna replied with a sigh. Katherine was going to be fuming. She'd been right to be wary of newspaper reports. "I'd best get Kat."

"I rang Sophie immediately to check that it wasn't anything to do with her surveying the area."

Anna gave her a hopeful look, and Carrie responded with the shake of the head.

"Back in a bit," Anna said, turning and heading for

Abbey House. She checked her watch; it was ten thirty. Katherine should be up and dressed by now.

As she entered the house, she could hear Katherine talking to someone, she assumed on the phone as they hadn't been expecting visitors. Katherine was pacing the kitchen, mobile to one ear. It was never a good sign when Katherine paced.

Anna listened in, trying to gauge who she was talking to with that deflated tone of voice. She allowed her eyes to soothe a wave of anxiety as they wandered to Katherine's long stockinged legs and high heels. The navy blouse she was wearing drew Anna's eyes as it revealed flashes of vanilla cleavage as the buttons strained to contain her breasts.

Katherine came to the end of the conversation, and Anna's heart sank as she signed off.

"Okay, thanks, Lucy, let's do that. Let me know the results as soon as you have them."

Katherine hung up the phone and met Anna's gaze. "I didn't expect to see you here. That was Lucy."

Anna pre-emptively pulled out a stool at the island and sat. "Give it to me."

"It's nothing to overly worry about. Holly was with Lucy, so we all had a chat. Holly hasn't noticed anything except what she'd already alerted me to."

"His stubbornness to participate in physio."

Katherine nodded. "She's only been working with him for a few months and doesn't know his cognitive ability as well as Lucy."

"So what did Lucy say?" Anna asked, wishing Katherine would get to the point.

"She feels there is a marked difference in his cognitive state since his pneumonia that warrants some initial investigations."

Anna fidgeted in her seat. This was all she needed. *Poor dad.*

Katherine walked to her side and placed a hand on her shoulder, sensing Anna's irritability as she always seemed to do.

"Lucy couldn't put her finger on anything specific, which is a good sign. He'd certainly not called her by the wrong name; she simply felt following his confusion yesterday and a niggling in the back of her mind as to his recent cognitive abilities it's worth doing some tests, that's all."

Anna nodded, but her brain trying to process everything rendered her temporarily speechless.

Katherine placed her hands on either side of Anna's face and leaned in for a kiss. "Let's not worry until we have the results, yes?"

The touch of Katherine's soft lips against her own was usually enough to wash away any worries. Not in this instance.

"Why are you home anyway?" Katherine asked.

Anna let out a sigh.

"Oh, what? Should I sit down too?" She lowered herself onto the stool beside Anna.

Anna turned to face her and slotted her knees between Katherine's. "There's been some vandalism at the abbey. Graffiti, and what looks like night hawks."

"Night what?"

"Hawks. Metal detectorists," Anna replied,

exasperated by yet another person unfamiliar with vocabulary she really felt they should know. Anna watched Katherine for a moment as she silently processed her news.

"It's not something to do with Sophie?"

"No, Carrie already checked."

"I suppose we should report it to the police then. Can you get back to the site and make sure no one touches anything? Just in case they want to see."

"You think they would investigate it?"

"I don't know. Until they say otherwise, we should treat it as a crime scene."

Anna stood and was about to leave when Katherine's hands slid around her waist and pulled her back. She was about to point out that it was no time for funny business when she realised Katherine had rested her head against her stomach. She wrapped her arms around Katherine's shoulders and held her tight.

Katherine finally let her go. "Have I told you how hot you look in that jacket?"

"Only a million times." Anna laughed, relieved that Katherine was in good spirits.

"What a day, eh? And it's not even eleven o'clock."

Anna hummed in agreement. "Our two loves not in great places."

"Let's deal with the one in our control," Katherine said, lifting her phone from the marble work surface. "Have you sent over the event schedule and budget yet?"

"On it. You'll have it by lunchtime." Anna kissed her head. "See you in a bit."

CHAPTER 9

Katherine placed the phone down on the work surface and stretched her arms across it. The police were interested enough in the vandalism that they were sending someone out to look at it as soon as they had the available resources. This was all she needed, more bad publicity for the abbey and more things to worry about. She was already physically exhausted and mentally drained; she wished everything would stop for a few days so she could get her breath back.

She inhaled and exhaled slowly to calm herself.

There was much on her plate; the last thing she needed was this vandalism mess. Bigger things were already on her mind, things like Harry's well-being. She needed to listen to her own advice to Anna regarding Harry and stop fretting. His memory slip could simply be some impairment following his pneumonia or even some low-level depression clouding his mind. As much as she didn't wish either on Harry, she certainly didn't wish dementia or Alzheimer's on him either.

Withdrawing her lunchbox from the fridge, she popped it into her handbag and fetched her coat from the understairs cupboard. With a quick check of her belongings, she called out, "Bye, Virginia," as she always did whenever she left the house. She had no idea if Virginia was even home. When she had lived alone, there was only her to let the cat in and out, so she had a fairly good idea of her whereabouts. Now that Anna let her in and out as well, Katherine had completely lost track of the cat's movements.

She scrunched her way across the drive, cursing her heels as they sank into the gravel. It reminded her that she had been meaning to ask her gardeners to lay a path between the borders and the gravel so she could leave the house without nearly breaking her ankles. Now that it was spring, it was the ideal time for them to do it. She removed her phone from her bag and set a reminder for the morning of their next visit.

As she entered the abbey's staff room to put her lunchbox in the fridge, she realised she hadn't asked Anna the location of the graffiti. She'd have to find her. After making two cups of peppermint tea, she took them over to Anna's office. It was a crisp day, and a frost still lay on the ground in parts where the morning sun couldn't reach. Katherine entered Anna's office to find her tapping away at her keyboard.

She placed a cup on Anna's coaster and smiled. It was a gift she'd given to Anna on the first day in her new office and was printed with a Jane Austen quote: "Perhaps it is our imperfections that make us so perfect for one another."

"Thanks, I need that," Anna said, immediately lifting it to her lips for a sip.

"You're welcome. Can you show me where the graffiti is?"

"Yes, two seconds, I'm just sending you the report. It's all done."

"Great," Katherine replied, adding some false enthusiasm; it meant one more thing she had to deal with that day. It would need to be checked before sending it on to the trustees — not that she didn't trust Anna to do her job properly, but there was no room for errors. Once the trustees had Anna's report and her own projections on the abbey's running costs for the remainder of the year, financial decisions would be made as to further investments needed.

Katherine nosed in a box on Anna's desk, hopeful it might contain the chocolate eggs. She'd skipped breakfast, and the few sips of tea she'd had were doing nothing to quell the rumbling in her stomach.

Anna reached under her desk and presented her with a chocolate egg and a snigger.

Katherine contemplated rejecting it, but she needed the sugar hit, so she took it from Anna and devoured it.

Anna returned to her laptop with a grin plastered across her face.

"Don't judge me. I skipped breakfast," Katherine mumbled through a mouthful of chocolate.

"I'm not," Anna replied, her grin widening further as she shut her laptop lid. "All sent."

Katherine ignored her and extracted some paper from the box on the desk.

"Is this for the Easter bunny trail?"

"Yes, and the printer sent some samples for our wedding invitations."

Anna passed Katherine a swatch book from her desk.

Katherine took a cursory look through it and handed it back to Anna. There was no time to be dealing with invitations. She had no one to send them to anyway.

"Let's look another time. Do you want to show me the graffiti?"

"Okay," Anna replied softly, placing the swatch back on her desk. "It's up at the far end."

Katherine waited for Anna to put on her wellies, inwardly wishing that she'd thought of keeping a pair of wellies on-site, and then followed her out. They passed several visitors on the way to the far end of the site. Katherine hoped they wouldn't wander as far today. It would be best to keep this bit of vandalism as quiet as possible.

"Why did they have to do this to the chapel of all places?" Katherine groaned as they approached the chapel where the extent of the damage became clear. "It's our best feature."

"And our special place," Anna said, eyeing Katherine.

Katherine smiled at her and then looked around. "Whoever did this must have chosen it because it's in a quiet corner. The other side, with our window, is overlooked by Abbey House." Katherine thought back a few months to when they had sat in the chapel window to watch the New

Year's fireworks and surprised one another with marriage proposals. She looked at Anna, who immediately caught her eye; they must have been sharing the same thought, as affectionate smiles radiated from their lips.

Carrie appeared with some cones and tape and began cordoning off the area in front of the wall.

"I guess this must be a result of the newspaper article yesterday," she said. "It advertised to every treasure hunter in the local area that there might be something to be found here. They certainly didn't hang about."

"Sorry, I thought it would be good publicity," Anna said.

"I'm sure it was," Katherine reassured her. She must have been feeling an unfair weight of responsibility for the spin the newspaper had put on their opening.

"Did you call the police, Katherine?" Carrie asked.

"They said they would send someone over."

Carrie lifted her eyebrows. "When exactly?"

"When resources would allow, whatever that means. They said they needed to see it to make sure it wasn't someone's tag."

"It doesn't look like a tag; it's very amateur. Though who am I to know what constitutes art?" Carrie said with a chuckle.

Katherine crossed her arms. "We need this gone before Sunday's event; the site needs to be presentable."

"Shall we have a backup plan in case they don't come anytime soon? I can see if I can find something to put in front of it or cover it?"

"Great idea, Carrie."

"What about the holes?" Carrie asked, poking at one with her foot.

"We can fill them in. The police weren't really interested," Katherine replied. "They said it was likely the two were connected, which was unusual."

"Unusual how?" Anna asked.

"Metal detectors — "

"Detectorists," Anna corrected her.

"Detectorists... aren't usually graffiti artists and vice versa. They said it was more likely they would find the culprit through the graffiti, and then they could look to prosecute for the detecting if they found the graffiti artist owned a detector or if they could place them with someone who had one at the time of the vandalism. Without catching them in the act, it's difficult to place them here, and the police don't have the resources to sit on-site waiting to catch someone."

"We have to hope they didn't find anything before Sophie's team had a chance."

"Agreed. They also suggested we hire some site security. I pointed out that we can't afford that. They suggested some form of deterrent instead."

"Shall I get some signs made up to say there is twenty-four-hour on-site security?" Anna shrugged. "It might deter people."

"That's a great idea," Carrie replied. "Did you two not hear anything last night? Like a car? Or beeping?"

Katherine and Anna's eye's locked as they both shook their heads. Katherine hoped Anna was also thinking back to what had kept them distracted until late the previous evening.

"I suppose with the car park locked, they would have parked in the village and entered the site on foot," Carrie continued to surmise.

Katherine reread the sentence she'd already read twice. It was no use; she needed a break and a cup of tea. As she passed the meeting room on the way to the staff room, she spotted Anna through the glass window.

"What are you doing in here?" she asked.

"Sorting the signs for Sunday's event. There's no room in my office to do it, and the barn is in use." Anna checked her watch. "Aren't you supposed to be in there for Pilates?"

"I hardly think this is the time for Pilates, do you?"

"Yes, I think it is exactly the time that you should take an hour out to relax."

Katherine rolled her eyes. "Well I don't have time anyway; I need to send the report off to the trustees by the end of the day. Do you want some tea?"

"No, thanks, I'm nearly done here. Then I have to do some prep on-site."

"I'll probably see you at home later then. Lasagne tonight?"

"Okay, I'll make it; you look done in already. Don't worry, I'll create it to your exacting standards."

"Thank you." Katherine checked to make sure they were alone and placed a kiss on Anna's cheek. "Love you."

"Love you too," Anna replied, taking a handful of Katherine's bottom and giving it a light squeeze.

Katherine continued to the staff room. Her spirits were lifted by Anna as usual, though she now carried a slight sense of guilt for not having gone to Pilates. She was glad she had decided to hire a teacher for the exercise sessions, a retired woman from the village who had contacted Katherine when she'd first put the form up in Gloria's tearoom. Katherine was relieved to pass it all over to her experienced hands. She had once thought of taking a course and teaching it herself until she became a trustee and realised it would be too much. As it turned out, she got far more out of the classes by attending them than she would have by teaching them, even if it was from the mutual amusement at the noises the human body made when put into various positions.

CHAPTER 10

*T*he morning of the Easter bunny trail was, to Anna's relief, a clear one. Blue skies greeted her as she pulled back the curtains of her dressing room. It was everything an Easter Sunday should be.

She would leave Katherine to sleep as long as possible. It had been a long week dealing with further enquiries from other local newspapers, who were all interested in the human remains. Katherine had given them a polite "thanks but no thanks", which Anna felt was very reserved.

The previous day, which was supposed to be a day off for them both, had been disturbed by a call from Carrie in the afternoon to inform them that the police had arrived. Their visit had taken up several hours, though it had at least brought with it the relief that they could finally clear off the graffiti and have a presentable site for the Easter event. Once the police were off-site, Anna and Carrie removed the old banner that Carrie had used to cover the graffiti and scrubbed the spray paint from the wall. Carrie had the foresight to order some special heritage graffiti remover, designed to remove the paint from porous surfaces without damaging the underlying stone. It worked like a dream. Anna hoped they wouldn't need to use it again.

Anna and Katherine had only just arrived home from their weekly visit to Harry before the police had arrived. Because they had been unable to see him on Sunday as usual, they had switched the day of their visit. Harry didn't mind; he was always pleased to see them whenever they had time to drop by. Anna felt guilty, as though she didn't make enough time, but working full time made it so difficult. She was at least lightened by his chipper mood and clear mind during their visit.

They had hoped to have Harry's test results by now, so they would know what they were dealing with, but Lucy hadn't received them from his general practitioner. As much as Anna had tried to keep her mind off her dad for the rest of the week, she hadn't managed to. She'd almost lost him twice in the last year, and now the thought that she was set to lose him whilst he was alive was too much.

Anna inhaled the fresh air as she closed the door behind her, listening as always for the chink of the lady knocker and hoping it wouldn't wake Katherine. This was only her third event at the abbey, and although lower-key than the New Year's Eve party and Abbey Barn's grand opening, she still felt the butterflies. She crossed over the road and headed down the high street to collect Abigail. She was looking forward to spending the day with Laura's youngest and getting to know her better.

Unexpectedly on-site the previous day, Anna had taken the opportunity to give herself a head start on the setup of the bunny trail. All she needed to do this morning was stake out the trail signs and put out a table in the barn for the start and finish points, which Abigail would help her with. They would also need to put out a supply of pens and pencils so visitors could complete the trail form if they didn't have their own.

Her mind slipped back to the swatch of wedding invitations the printers had sent with the forms. She regretted showing them to Katherine when she was unable to give them her full attention. Recently, though, it felt like Katherine was always unable to give the wedding her full attention. The invitations were more for Katherine's benefit anyway; it wasn't as if Anna had many to send. Then there were decisions to be made over flowers, cake, and the wedding breakfast. She'd need to find a suitable time to raise each of them again.

Abigail opened her front door before Anna was halfway up the path.

"Happy Easter, Abi."

Laura appeared in the doorway in her dressing gown and handed Abigail her rucksack. "She has a bottle of juice in her bag. I wasn't sure if she'd need a packed lunch, but I could bring one over later?"

"No need, it's all taken care of. Katherine will be bringing us a picnic over at lunchtime."

"Great, thank you, and thank you for taking her. She's spoken of nothing else all week, have you, Abi?"

Anna watched as Abigail narrowed her eyes at her mum.

"Me neither." Anna scrunched her face at the girl. "Let's leave your mum in peace."

"Thanks again. It's back to bed for me, I'm really suffering this morning," Laura said as she rubbed her lower abdomen.

Anna crumpled her face in sympathy.

They walked in silence a little way back up the high street. Anna wasn't entirely sure where to start a conversation with an eight-year-old. Her experience with children was all from the tours, where they would ask the questions and she would answer them. Once she was in the flow of conversation with them, she was fine. Luckily Abigail spoke, breaking the silence.

"Mum says you used to live in that house." Abigail pointed at Anna's old house as they approached it. "Is that true?"

"Yes, it is. We moved to Nunswick when I was a baby, so nearly forty years ago." Anna gulped down the word forty.

"It's a very small house," Abigail observed.

Anna laughed at her frankness. "Yes, it is; only two bedrooms."

"Did you have to share a room with your brother or sister then?"

"No, I'm an only child."

Abigail's eyes lit up and her lips widened. "You're so lucky. I wish I was."

Anna did her best to demur from her comment. "Tom's not that bad, surely."

"He didn't use to be. Now he plays his music too loud,

he hogs the PlayStation, and his room smells." Abigail wrinkled her nose.

"Well, becoming a teenager generally makes people less likeable. All the changes they go through to develop into adults takes a lot of work, and sometimes it makes them a bit selfish and grumpy."

"You mean puberty," Abigail replied frankly.

Anna focussed on the road ahead of them. "Err. Yes."

"Don't worry, I know all about that."

"Good. It's important to know."

"I won't be like him, though."

Anna withheld a chuckle. "The future's unpredictable. Although you might not want to be a typical teenager, you may still end up being one. I hope you don't, though."

Abigail found a small rock and began kicking it along the pavement. "Mum says that too. She doesn't want two of us playing loud music. She said she'd have to cut her ears off."

Unable to withhold her amusement any longer, Anna let out a small giggle. The girl beamed at her; she appeared to enjoy making people laugh.

They reached Anna's office, and she unlocked the door. Abigail followed Anna inside.

"Is this your office?"

"Yes, all mine."

"Well it's too small to share with anyone; it's the same size as the stationery cupboard at school."

Anna again stifled her amusement. "Are you allowed in there?"

"Sometimes my teacher asks me to collect supplies from there. It smells nice. I like it in there."

"Katherine would love a stationery cupboard here and at home. You can meet her properly at lunchtime. Right, we'd better get set up; we'll be opening soon. Firstly, we need to put the signs out. They are for our avid hunters to find. If you look on the back, you can see the clues for the next sign, and they all lead back to the barn where they'll collect their eggs. They also need to complete this." Anna took a sheet from the box on her desk. "On the back of each sign is a jumble of letters that they need to rearrange and write down."

Abigail examined the back of a sign. "A Giddy Roof, Good Friday."

"Hmm. It's probably a good thing you aren't doing the trail; it might be a bit easy."

"Do I still get an egg?" Abigail raised her eyebrows in hope.

"Of course, all helpers get an egg. Some get two." Anna winked.

Abigail's eyes sparkled at the thought.

"Can you take the mallet? I need someone to hammer these in for me. I'll bring the signs."

They made their way across the abbey's lawn, stopping at all the places Anna had scoped out the previous week. Some were obvious and should be easy for their youngest visitors to solve; some were not so obvious and hidden within the flower beds.

They placed the last sign near the car park to direct all those who had come for the bunny trail to the barn.

"Was history your favourite subject at school?" Abigail asked, suggesting an interest in Anna's place of work.

"Yes, I've always loved learning about how people used to live. That knowledge connects us to our past, don't you think?"

Abigail nodded. "My dad used to take us to museums all the time." She looked down and scuffed at the ground with her tan suede boots.

Something tugged in Anna's chest. "I love museums," she said. "Anytime you want to go, you let me know."

Abigail looked up. "Really?"

"As long as your mum agrees."

"She will! She can't take us far anymore. She's not very well, and it's so boring sitting at home."

"Hopefully she'll get better soon, and I will let you know anytime I need a helper. Perhaps we could tag along on a tour of the abbey one day or I could give you a private tour."

"That would be so cool."

With the registration table set up and a box of pens available beside the bunny trail sheets, they were ready for their audience. Anna placed two chairs behind the table for them both, and they waited. Carrie would be opening the site in five minutes, and a queue was already forming in the car park.

"Do you miss being a tour guide?" Abigail asked.

Anna thought for a moment. "I'll always be one at heart," she decided. "I love sharing stories of the past."

Abigail's lips twitched with excitement. "Can you tell me some about the abbey?"

Anna hesitated, unsure whether to tell Abigail the story about the two nuns who fell in love at the abbey. She decided it wouldn't be appropriate; it had a terrible ending that involved a bricked-up wall.

"Maybe a ghost story?" she suggested.

Abigail nodded eagerly.

When Anna had been a tour guide, she was constantly asked about ghosts, so much so she ended up including them in the tour at relevant spots around the site. She racked her memory for the least scary one in her repertoire.

"There is supposed to be the ghost of a nun who appears to people in the chapel and beckons them with her hand to follow her, only to then disappear into the wall."

Abigail crinkled her nose. "Is that true?"

"I've never seen anything myself, but what is truth anyway? It's only someone's version of what happened. Someone else could have been there at the same time and told a completely different version of it. That's the fascinating thing about history; it's often written and told by the winners, whether that's about war or how people lived. The rich wrote the books, so they would record the poor as lazy people who stole from them. The poor, if given a voice, would say they were hungry and were taking what was kept from them by the wealthy landowner."

"A bit like Robin Hood."

"A bit, yes. Robin Hood is documented in history as a fictional character, but it is possible he may have been real. Often these stories that pass down are based on a real character. Unfortunately by the time they reach us and our books, they are so distorted from the truth that they seem fanciful." This sparked a thought in Anna's mind, and she turned fully to Abigail. "It's not just history this happens with; it happens with you and Tom. He has one version, and you have another of a falling-out you have. It doesn't mean either is lying; you've just interpreted the situation differently. You both have your version of the truth."

"Is that why Mum never takes sides?"

Anna laughed. "Quite possibly."

A large group of mums with a brood of enthusiastic youngsters and countless pushchairs piled into the barn, much to Anna's relief. The worst part of any event was waiting for the first attendees to arrive. She armed them with trail sheets and pens and sent them off in the right direction.

A woman with four children was next in the queue. All of them looked to be under the age of ten, and their mother's forlorn face and puffed eyes said that even though the bunny trail hadn't even started, she was already at her wit's end. Anna had always been baffled as to how one woman could look after so many children. One or two would be a good number. Surely it was just crowd control after two.

She watched as Abigail drew on the back of the trail sheet. It always amazed her how creative children could be; they had the least experience of anyone in the world, yet they could conjure the most wonderful things from their imaginations. A naivety towards the world was likely the cause; their view hadn't yet been distorted by the reality of life and all its struggles.

"What do you want to be when you're older?" Anna asked, genuinely intrigued to hear Abigail's answer.

"I want to be a journalist… I think. I want to tell

people's stories. I'd like to hear people's stories of the past before they all die." Abigail rested the end of her pencil in her mouth and pouted. "I don't think that's a job."

"You should meet my dad," Anna said. "He always has a story, and I think he'd like you."

"Can I? I love old people."

"Of course, again as long as your mum agrees. One piece of advice: If you do become a journalist or anyone with any influence in the world, always tell the truth."

"Why wouldn't I?"

"Some journalists don't. Their job is to share information, and sometimes information is a bit boring, so some people embellish their stories."

Abigail looked at her blankly.

"Make them more interesting than they are," Anna explained. "You could be a researcher, that's similar. I used to do that before I moved back to Nunswick. I worked at The National Archives, and my job was to help people find information in all the old records."

"What were they looking for?"

"Family history, mainly."

"Why don't they know who their family are?"

"As each generation lives, they don't always think to record who their family members are, their birth dates, things like that, because they know it. Then fifty or a hundred years pass, and people forget things or forget to tell the younger members of the family."

"That's sad."

"It is. It's not done intentionally; we don't appreciate that our family in the future will forget things or not even know them in the first place. In the past, they had family

Bibles that were passed down the generations. In the front, they would record all the members of the family and their dates of birth. Nowadays people want more information than that; they want to know where their family came from, where they lived, what they did for a job."

"And you could find all these things out for them?"

"Not always, but I gave it a good try. If the records survived history, then we can find out the basics about people. Things like their jobs can be more difficult. We use something called a census to find out."

Abigail frowned. "Could we see who lived in Granny's house before her? It's very old."

"Yes, of course."

Abigail fell into silence and returned her attention to her drawing until the next family arrived.

Katherine arrived bang on one o'clock as promised, carrying with her a promising picnic basket. Anna's stomach rumbled at the sight of it.

"You must be Abigail?" Katherine said as she approached their table.

"Abi," Abigail replied pointedly.

"Sorry, Abi," Katherine corrected herself, pulling the sides of her mouth down and eyeballing Anna.

Anna smirked.

"Do you work here too?"

"I do. I'm a trustee. My key role is to make sure the abbey is safe."

"So you're like a guardian of the abbey?"

"Something like that."

Abigail looked down and played with her fingers. "My dad was a guardian, too, of people. Everyone says he's a hero. I still miss him, even though he's a hero."

"I expect you do," Katherine said. "The world may have gained a hero, but you lost a dad. I'm also a guardian of people; I make sure that everyone at the abbey is safe, be that staff or visitors. I'm also responsible for ensuring they have an enjoyable time whilst they're here, so they return. Anna helps with that bit, and you are today, I see."

Abigail's lips curled with pride.

Katherine took over the slow stream of visitors to give Anna and Abigail a break whilst they ate their lunch. The picnic basket revealed ham rolls, crisps, fruit, and small bottles of fruit juice.

"Do you want me to stay and help?" Katherine asked as they finished up.

"No, I don't think you need to." Anna grinned at Abigail. "I have my helper."

Katherine nodded. "I'll pop back later and help you clear up. I've got a few bits to do in my office anyway. I'll leave the basket with you in case you get peckish. Bye, Abi."

Abigail looked up from her drawing and smiled at Katherine. "Bye. Thank you for the lovely picnic."

After lunch, there was a constant stream of people coming into the barn, either to start the trail or collect their eggs at the end. Anna had expected the afternoon to be busier than the morning, with people likely to be having a family get-together and a big lunch. The demographics certainly indicated this, as more grandparents arrived with the younger families.

Anna admired Abigail's tenacity; it was tiring dealing with so many people, yet she soldiered on, not complaining once. They split the duties equally, with Anna welcoming those starting the trail, explaining what they needed to do and handing out the trail sheets, whilst Abigail handed out the eggs on their return.

As the afternoon drew to an end, Anna realised how much she had enjoyed Abigail's company. She'd asked lots of interesting questions and had an eagerness to learn more about the world. She loved that about children; they had a raw passion to learn. Her enjoyment today had purely come from passing on knowledge as a teacher would to a student, rather than a mother to a child. Though the more she thought about it, the more she could see herself steering a young person through the world, being able to teach them about it every day, helping them take their first steps, giving them their first solid food, watching their faces as they tasted things for the first time. Her stomach tingled at the thought.

Would Katherine feel the same? If Anna could be a good mother, Katherine could be an even greater one. Although they both had a caring nature, Anna had always felt Katherine was more mothering than she was. She had an instinct for things, was nurturing, full of empathy and compassion. They were traits that had made her a great doctor.

A ping from her phone pulled her from her thoughts. It was a text from Katherine.

Give me 5 mins and I'll be there. Shall we walk Abi home together and see if we can get something to eat at the pub? X

Anna tapped out a reply.

Sounds like a plan. I'm starving! X

CHAPTER 11

atherine was surprised to see everything cleared away as she entered the barn. Anna and Abigail were waiting in their coats. "You've cleared up already! I was coming to help."

"There wasn't much to do. Abi collected all the signs from around the site."

"It took me three trips!"

"Only three?" Katherine replied. "You must be very strong."

Abigail's eyes sparkled at the compliment.

"I've done everything in here," Anna said. "Oh, hang on one moment, though."

She disappeared into her office, returning moments later with an abbey guidebook.

"This is for you. It'll tell you all about the history of the abbey," Anna said, holding the book out to Abigail.

"Thank you." She opened it and shoved her nose into it. "I love the smell of new books."

Anna and Katherine chuckled at her.

"We do, too, don't we, Kat?"

"Yes, you're in good company here. Sniff away," Katherine replied, picking up the picnic basket. "I'll run this back into the house as we pass."

"One last thing." Anna extracted two chocolate eggs from her pocket. "For my helper. Don't eat them all at once."

"Thank you, I won't. I'm not Tom. I'll have to hide them, though, or he'll eat them."

Katherine locked up Abbey Barn, and they made their way across the site.

"You live in that house?" Abigail asked as they stopped at the end of the driveway of Abbey House. "It's beautiful, like something from a fairy tale. The flowers are lovely," she added, admiring the crocuses, daffodils, and tulips that covered the beds around the drive.

"I can't claim any credit for them," Katherine said, as much as she'd have liked to. "I have gardeners that do it all for me. I'll be back in a moment."

Katherine crossed the drive and placed the basket inside the front door. As she pulled the front door shut, Virginia shot out.

Katherine startled at the sudden movement. "I nearly squashed you. Silly cat!"

Her voice caught the attention of Anna and Abigail at the end of the drive.

Abigail noticed the cat and approached her slowly. "Hello, kitty. What's her name?"

"Virginia," Katherine replied proudly as she reached the group.

Abigail crouched to pet Virginia. "Strange name for a cat."

Katherine's mouth opened a little as Anna choked back a laugh, covering it as a cough.

"But I like it," Abigail said, giving a nod of approval.

Katherine turned to Anna and flicked her eyebrows up. "Come on. Let's get you home, Abi."

"Bye, Virginia," Abigail called back as the three of them joined the high street.

To Katherine's relief, Virginia didn't follow them. Although it was a safe village, on occasion, someone would speed through. She was much happier when Virginia hunted in the fields at the back of the house and the abbey, as long as she didn't make a nuisance of herself. Anna had mentioned twice that Virginia had appeared in her office when she'd left the door open. She had made a point to shoo her out. The last thing they needed was her thinking she was welcome there and turning up in the middle of a wedding ceremony.

"Do you not have any pets, Abi?" Katherine asked.

"No," Abigail replied, pulling her lips to one side.

Katherine looked down at the girl. "I'm sure Virginia would like to be your friend."

Abigail looked behind her; Virginia was licking her paw at the end of the drive. It drew the smile from the girl that Katherine had hoped for.

"So, do you enjoy school?" Katherine asked.

"I love school."

"Any particular subjects?"

"I love English the most, then history, then art."

Katherine racked her brain for another question. She

had hoped that school would have been a great conversation starter; she'd forgotten children generally answered the question asked of them, especially around those they didn't know so well.

Anna stepped in to help her out. "Katherine used to be a doctor, you know."

"Really? What's the worst thing you've seen?"

Katherine was relieved that the girl was opening the conversation, though less impressed by her morbid fascination. It was a question she had often been asked when she was practising, and it was one she hadn't missed. Any answer would have to be tailored to Abigail's age.

She thought for a moment, then said, "I once had to drain a cyst on a man's back."

"What's a cyst?"

"Imagine a small bag full of yucky, white-yellow goo under your skin."

Abigail scrunched her face.

"I had to cut into it a little and squeeze out all the pus. Strangely it was quite satisfying, for him and me."

"What's pus made of?"

"White blood cells. Our body releases them to help fight bad things. Sometimes it goes a little wrong and they build up."

Abigail opened her mouth to speak until a squeak behind them turned their attention to Tom braking his bike behind them. He swerved around them and hopped his bike off the curb before hightailing it down the road.

"He's such an idiot," Abigail tutted.

As they reached the gate of the cottage, Abigail ran up the path and knocked on the door.

Laura answered.

"I hope she's been good," she said, playing with her daughter's ponytail as she hugged her.

"Of course," Anna replied. "She's been an immense help. I couldn't have managed without her."

A smile formed on Abigail's lips. "Thank you for having me. I really enjoyed myself."

"Anytime," Anna said, giving her a wink.

Abigail disappeared into the house.

Anna turned to her fiancée. "Laura, this is Katherine. Katherine, Laura."

Katherine stepped forward a little and held out her hand across the threshold. Laura shook it.

"It's nice to finally meet you," Laura said, leaning against the doorframe.

"Likewise."

"I was sorry to hear about the graffiti at the abbey; it must have been awful for you."

"Thanks. Yes, the abbey means a great deal to both of us, so in a way, it feels like a personal attack," Katherine replied.

A bang of the garden gate drew their attention to Tom at the bottom of the path. He lowered his bike onto the grass and slunk towards the cottage. Anna and Katherine separated to allow him through.

Laura caught him as he passed and placed her hands on his shoulders. "This is Tom, Katherine, my eldest."

"Nice to meet you, Tom."

"Yeah," Tom replied, giving a slight lift of the head in her direction.

Anna had warned her about the grumpy teenager, so Katherine wasn't surprised by his curt remark.

He shrugged his mum off and entered the house.

"Err, shoes off," Laura said.

"I'm just getting my phone from upstairs."

"Tom, shoes," Laura added firmly. "Look at them! They're filthy."

Tom let out a long groan and sat on the bottom step of the stairs to remove his shoes.

"So what can you do about the graffiti, then?" Laura asked, returning her attention to Katherine.

"We've put some signs up insinuating we have security when we don't. Hopefully, we can deter whoever it is. It's about all we can do; we don't have the funds for anything else."

"Fingers crossed they do the job."

"Mum?" Abigail's voice echoed through from the kitchen.

"I better…" Laura nodded back. "Thanks again for letting Abi help today."

"Anytime," Anna said. "She's a delight."

"Do you mean that? It's just that…" Laura fidgeted.

"Of course, what do you need?" Anna reached forward and placed an encouraging hand on her arm.

"I finally have an appointment with the consultant. A private one, as you suggested, but it's this week and at a time when the kids are due home from school."

"Do you want me to meet them at the bus stop?"

"Would you mind? Tom has a key. He doesn't need watching. I'm more concerned for Abi."

"It's fine."

Katherine had a better idea. "Why don't they come back to ours? I'll make dinner, and then you can join us when you return."

Laura's face dropped. "Are you sure? I don't want to take advantage."

"What are friends for?" Anna flashed Laura a smile.

Her hand slipped into Katherine's and gave it a squeeze. Her plan obviously met Anna's approval.

"Thank you both," Laura said. "I can't express how much I appreciate it."

"Text me the details," Anna called as they edged their way back down the path.

They followed the path up to the pub for a much-needed meal. Katherine had only nibbled a ham roll when she'd prepared the picnic, expecting to return to Abbey House for her lunch. Instead, she'd been unable to resist the urge of popping to her office to get some work done.

"What do you think of Abi then?" Anna asked, interrupting Katherine's thoughts of a roast.

"She's sweet. I think you might have been much the same at that age, full of questions."

Anna spat out a laugh. "You'd have to ask Dad. I'm sure he'll delight in telling you…" The creases of laughter fell from her face. "If he can remember, I suppose."

Tom shot past them on his bike, heading back up the high street.

"Must be tough on them all," Katherine observed, "losing a father and husband."

"Hmm. Have you…" Anna hesitated.

"Have I what?"

Anna shook her head and looked down. "Never mind."

"Come on, it must be something?" Katherine squeezed her hand to encourage her.

"Have you ever… thought about kids? Since Helena I mean. You know… us having kids?"

Katherine stopped in her tracks, lightheaded at the unexpected question.

"Have you ever thought about filling the house with little voices?" Anna took her hand. "Kat, say something?"

All thoughts of children had been pushed deep into the back of her mind; Helena's accident had suggested it just wasn't something that was supposed to happen for her. And Anna had given no indication before now that she wanted a family.

Katherine managed to shake her head. She felt blindsided. "I don't know," was the only response she could find.

"That's okay. Have a think, that's all."

Anna walked on, still holding Katherine's hand. She let herself be guided as they entered the pub.

"You settle in," Anna said. "I'll see if Chris can rustle us up a roast."

Katherine almost fell into her chair, her legs weak beneath her. So many thoughts raced around her head she could barely focus on any of them.

Anna arrived with two glasses of wine and placed one in front of Katherine. "Two roasts coming up. Are you okay? You look as white as a sheet."

She felt as white as a sheet. If it wasn't for the pounding of her heart, she'd have thought she'd been drained of blood. Anna had pulled the ground out from underneath her feet with her question. Lifting the very welcome glass of wine to her mouth, she downed half of it.

"Steady on," Anna said with a nervous laugh.

Katherine wiped her top lip with the tip of her tongue and set the glass down.

Anna reached across the table and placed her hand on Katherine's. "Sorry, I shouldn't have said anything. Have I upset you?"

"No, I'm just a little… shocked, that's all."

She'd spent the last few years thinking about what she'd lost, not about replacing it. Was that even possible? Would she even want to if she could? Her head spun and a pulsing sensation gripped at her neck.

Moose appeared beside the table and sniffed at Anna's leg, making her jump.

"Hi, Moose." Anna stroked the bear-like dog behind his ear, just where he liked it. He groaned and pushed back against her with some force.

"Okay, enough Moose. Go to your basket." The Labrador trundled off to the next table, in search of more attention. Anna rolled her eyes after him.

When Anna's gaze returned to meet Katherine's, it made her feel as if Anna was waiting for her to say more. There were no words, though. She tried to compose herself and find some. The least Anna deserved was a response.

"I didn't think you wanted children. I don't know why I thought that. I assumed," Katherine said softly.

"I did when I was younger, but then I sort of gave up

on the idea." Anna's eyes brightened. "I think we could be great parents, though, don't you?"

"I've not really thought about it. I've not thought beyond us to be honest."

Katherine grappled with herself to find a new subject to discuss. Her thoughts were failing her when she needed them most. Her mind filled instead with the images that ran through it whenever she thought of Helena and the baby: the police turning up at her hospital bed the following morning; the thought of Helena being somewhere in the basement of the same building, stone-cold in a mortuary drawer with their baby inside her; returning to the empty house after; seeing their bed as Helena had left it after leaping out of it for the final time to rush off to the hospital. Then having to deal with the funeral, a quiet empty house, and all the things they had already bought for the baby. Thankfully Rebecca had dealt with most of the logistics; Katherine had been left to deal with her emotions — or not, as the case had been.

She could feel her eyes beginning to moisten. "I'm going to pop to the ladies."

Within moments she was facing herself in the ladies' room mirror. She unravelled some toilet roll from the nearest cubicle and wiped her eyes and blew her nose, thankful she was alone. Starting a family with Anna should have been the easiest and fastest question to answer, and under normal circumstances, it would have been. As she was increasingly aware, her life didn't operate under normal circumstances. Despite her attempts to move on, just when she thought she had, something would pull her back, and the feelings of guilt would start all over again. Each time she would wonder if she would ever be able to move past it properly. Any answer that she gave Anna would need to be based on how she felt about it now. She couldn't let feelings from the past get in the way. It wouldn't be fair to Anna.

The only problem was, she didn't know how she felt.

CHAPTER 12

*A*nna scrubbed at the last remnants of purple spray paint.

"There, nearly done. I'll soon have you back to normal." Anna placed a hand on the stone wall. It broke her heart that someone had once again sprayed the chapel, particularly as it was such a special place to her and Katherine.

A check of her watch told her that Tom and Abigail's school bus would shortly be arriving. With a final scrub and a rinse with a clean bucket of water, she stood back and admired her work. Although the wall stood free of spray paint, it showed the scars from the two vigorous brushes it had undergone in one week. The natural wear and colour of the stone had gone, and with it the lichen and moss that naturally formed in the cracks. Something had to be done to catch these vandals, and if the police weren't going to help, then it was up to them.

She returned the buckets and brushes to the cleaning cupboard in the visitor centre and scrubbed her hands in the large sink until the water flowed as clearly as it was going to. Cupboards like this one always reminded her of the janitor's cupboard at school. They all came with a large butler sink, a big metal bucket on wheels — or a yellow plastic one in more modern times — and that strange, not necessarily unpleasant odour of scented cleaning products mixed with bleach.

All cleaned up and with buckets washed out, she entered what was a busy visitor centre for midweek and exited through the main doors. The extension beside the entrance was progressing well. The foundations had been laid as soon as the builders had been allowed back on-site, and now a fully formed, hollow structure sat upon them. When finished, it would mould itself seamlessly with the current, glass-fronted structure as if it had always been part of it.

Anna left the site and passed Abbey House, where Katherine had spent the morning dealing with Sophie's crew as they finished up their survey of both the abbey site and their garden. Their van was no longer in the car park, so Anna assumed Katherine would now be preparing for the children's imminent arrival.

Following Katherine's unenthusiastic reaction to her mention of children at the weekend, Anna had added the topic to her list of things she and Katherine needed to have a serious discussion about. This one was slightly more important than that of invitations and wedding dates, but it wasn't something Anna was in a hurry to bring up again. It was going to be a sore point for Katherine, and she didn't want to push it too much. There was a case that needed answering, but only when Katherine was ready.

A bus passed Anna as she made her way down the high street, splashing into the rain-filled potholes that were a permanent feature of the road. It stopped a little way down from the row of shops. She jogged to meet it, concerned that Tom and Abigail would forget she was collecting them and head home. They were old enough to walk up to Abbey House by themselves, though Anna didn't trust Tom not to wander off and do as he pleased.

The bus pulled away, revealing an eagerly waiting Abigail and less-than-impressed Tom.

"Hi, kids. Good day at school?" Anna asked as she approached them.

Tom shrugged.

"Hi, Anna. It was great! I had cookery today," Abigail answered, opening the Tupperware she was holding. "Would you like a biscuit?"

"I don't mind if I do. Thanks, Abi." Anna reached in and extracted a perfectly shaped shortbread biscuit. She took a bite, surprised by how good it was. "Mm, that's tasty! And with a hint of lemon, my favourite."

They walked along the path back up the high street to Abbey House. Anna noticed that Tom turned his head away as they passed Gloria's tearoom.

"Do you think Katherine would like one of my biscuits?" Abigail asked as they approached the driveway.

"I'm sure she would. If she doesn't, can I have hers?"

"Of course. You can have another if you want. I need to save one for Mum. When will she be here? Do you know where she's gone?"

Anna wasn't about to elaborate on Laura's whereabouts

if she hadn't told the children herself. "I'm sure she'll be here in an hour or two. Then we can all have dinner together," she said, placing her key in the front door.

"What is for dinner?" Abigail asked as they stepped into the hallway.

"Shepherd's pie," Katherine answered as she crossed the hall to welcome them. "I hope you all like it."

"It's Tom's favourite," Abigail replied, earning her a shove in the shoulder from Tom.

"No, it isn't. Pizza's my favourite."

"Well, we'll remember that for next time, won't we, Anna?" Katherine replied, widening her eyes at her fiancée before leaving the room.

"Indeed we will. Just pop your shoes, bags, and coats by the door so you don't forget them." Anna knew full well this went against the rules of putting all outdoor wear and accessories away in the enormous cupboard under the stairs. Anna had been quite surprised the first time she had seen it. It wasn't far off the size of her bedroom in the old house. "Let's get the kettle on and make some tea to go with those biscuits, shall we? Come through to the kitchen."

Awestruck at her surrounding and not looking where she was going, Abigail nearly tripped over herself.

Anna looked down at her. "Don't feel like you have to take it all in now. I'll give you the full tour shortly."

The smile that washed over Abigail's face told her she was as excited to see the house as Anna had been when she'd first arrived. It wasn't every day you were allowed to see inside such a house.

"Can I watch television?" Tom asked as Anna led them through the sitting room to the kitchen.

"Do you not have any homework to do?"

"No," Tom replied flatly.

"The remote is on the table. Would you like tea or something else to drink?"

"No, thanks," Tom replied, collapsing onto one of the enormous sofas.

Anna led Abigail through to the kitchen where Katherine was already filling the kettle at the sink.

Abigail spotted Virginia outside on the patio and ran to the glass door. Her appearance attracted Virginia to the door, and she opened her mouth in a silent meow to those on the inside.

"Can I let her in?" Abigail asked in a high-pitched squeal of excitement.

"Of course," Katherine replied. "She doth command it."

Taking a stool at the island, Anna watched as Virginia entered and brushed herself against her new friend. To Virginia, Abigail was just another person that she could boss about. Whilst Abigail was entertained, Anna took the opportunity to discuss the latest graffiti.

"Did you speak to the police?" she asked Katherine.

"Yes, and I emailed the photographs you took," Katherine confirmed, as she placed her best Denby teapot on the island.

"Did they have anything to say?"

"Not that they hadn't said already," she said, filling the teapot with water from the kettle.

"Security?"

"Mm-hm."

"Well, I've come up with a plan. If the police can't do anything, then we need a better deterrent than some signs. We need a tent."

"A tent?" Katherine laughed. "How on earth is a tent going to help us?"

"We're going to camp out, catch the culprits in the act."

"Us, camp out? In a tent, on the abbey grounds?"

"Yep," Anna replied, peering over at Abigail to make sure she was still occupied. Confirming she was, Anna leaned closer to Katherine and whispered, "Have you ever done it in a tent?"

Katherine bit her lips together and then checking for herself that Abigail was preoccupied, mouthed, "No," at Anna.

"I have," Anna whispered back.

Abigail got up from the floor where she had been stroking Virginia and climbed up on a stool beside Anna.

"Anyway, I'm not sure I'm the kind of woman who sleeps in a tent," Katherine added.

"Are you going camping?" Abigail asked. "We have a tent you can borrow. Dad used to take Tom camping." She paused for a moment, then added, "And me, sometimes."

Tom appeared in the doorway. "I'm bored. Can I go home and get my bike?"

"I'd rather you didn't, Tom. Your mum has placed you in my care, and whilst you're in my care, I'd rather know where you are," Anna replied firmly. Tom had to be the only child to ever get bored when they had every channel available to them under the sun.

"I'll only be outside in the street, where I always go. It's not like there is anywhere else to go around here."

It was a reasonable request, and one Laura wouldn't have a problem with; however, Anna strongly felt that for the few hours she was responsible for her friend's son, she wanted eyes on him at all times.

"No, Tom, sorry. Perhaps when your mum arrives you can ask her."

"When will that be?"

Anna checked her watch. Laura's appointment was happening now, and as it was a private consultation, likely it would be running to time. "Soon," she replied, not wanting to make any promises.

Tom turned with a grunt and returned to the sitting room.

"He's cheery today." Katherine poured the tea into the mugs.

Abigail rested her head on her hands. "He's always like that since Dad died."

Katherine passed the mugs around and then sat on the stool opposite Abigail. "We all react differently when someone dies. When you lose someone very close to you, or not even close to you, it can change you and change your behaviour. It can take a long time to get over it. Sometimes you never do."

Katherine fell silent, as she often did when she spoke about loss. Anna watched her as she stirred her tea. She often wondered if Katherine was truly over the loss of Helena and the baby, if it was something someone could ever move on from or get over, as Katherine had said.

"Now, pass me one of those biscuits before Anna eats

them all," Katherine said, snapping her attention back to their afternoon snack.

After tea and biscuits, Katherine prepared dinner whilst Anna gave Abigail the full tour of their home. Anna thought it was amusing to see the girl's jaw drop as hers once had at the beautiful feature wall in the bedroom. It was a wonderful opportunity to explain how houses used to be built, and Abigail drank it all in.

"When I grow up, I want to live in a house like this. I don't suppose I will."

"When I was growing up in Nunswick, your mum and I used to play around the abbey. It was just a ruin in those days, not a tourist attraction like it is today, so we could do what we wanted — within reason, of course. It was in the garden of this house, and there was no fence then to divide them. I'd look at this house and think, 'Firstly, why is no one looking after that poor house?' It was in a bit of a state in those days. And secondly, I'd think, 'I'd love to live there.' And hey, presto — I do."

Abigail's face lit up.

"You see, dreams can come true. We never know what is just around the corner." Anna couldn't help grinning back at her. She extended a hand to the girl. "Come on, let's see if Katherine needs any help with the dinner."

CHAPTER 13

*A*s Anna and Abigail crossed the hallway, someone knocked on the door. Anna opened it to find Laura on the doorstep.

"Mummy!" Abigail shouted, wrapping her arms around her.

"Hey, darling. Have you been good for Anna?"

"Of course."

Laura flashed a questioning look to Anna, and she nodded to back up Abigail's statement.

Abigail stepped back to allow her mum to enter.

"Hi, Tom! How was school?" Laura called to her son, receiving a half-hearted grunt from the sitting room for her efforts. She rolled her eyes, took off her coat, and looked around the hall with her mouth open. "Finally, I get to see what this place looks like inside."

Anna laughed as she closed the front door. "It only took us about thirty years to get in."

"I think it was worth the wait."

"I'm assuming Madam would like a full tour?"

"Madam insists."

"Abi, will you tell Katherine I'm going to show your mum around? Then why don't you go and watch television for a little while?"

"Okay." Abigail skipped off across the hall into the sitting room.

"I love your knocker. Very apt."

Anna smirked. "She's delightful, isn't she? A friend of Katherine's bought it for her. Shall we start upstairs? I'll show you my dressing room."

"Dressing room! Are you about to make me very jealous?"

"I can't promise I won't," Anna replied as she led Laura up the ornate, wooden staircase and into her dressing room.

"Oh my God, Anna! Is this even real?" Laura gasped.

Anna burned with pride over the room she had designed.

Laura examined the walls. "Look at this wallpaper."

"I took the slightly darker blue of the birds and had the wardrobes painted in it."

"It all matches beautifully," Laura said as she wandered around the room. "Love the chair."

"That's a replica."

"Feels genuine enough to me," Laura said with a groan as she relaxed into the Queen Anne chair.

Anna took a seat in the Chesterfield office chair and spun around.

"How did your appointment go?" she asked, bringing the chair to a stop.

"Brilliant. The consultant — female, I might add —

completely agrees with me. She said I've been suffering long enough and that it's my body, my choice."

"Great. When can you book the surgery?"

"Already booked: a week from Friday." Laura beamed.

Anna shook her head in bewilderment. "What? So soon?"

"I'm going private; she had a space, and I took it. It won't be cheap, but I'm so done with this, Anna. It's consumed me for most of my adult life. I can afford it, so I'm doing it, and I can't wait."

Anna's eyes warmed with moisture to see her friend taking back control over her life.

Laura pulled her smiling face straight. "Obviously, I'm also bricking it that something might go wrong, and... I have a massive favour to ask."

"Anything."

"Can you take me to the hospital on Friday morning?"

"Of course. How is that massive?"

"And look after the kids for the weekend," Laura continued with a grimace.

"Oh, I see." Anna thought for a moment, slightly overwhelmed by the request. It wasn't anything she couldn't handle, though; they were easy-going, one more so than the other.

Laura's face crumpled into an apology. "Sorry, is it too much to ask?"

"No, no, it's fine. I'm sure we'll have a great time."

"Honestly? I don't want to put you out."

"Honestly, it's fine," Anna reassured Laura — and herself.

"Thank you so much. Tom doesn't need much

attention, as you know. It's more a matter of feeding and making sure he's home when he's supposed to be, and it might be better if you stay at ours, if that's okay? They'll feel more settled there. It's going to be worrying enough for them as it is."

"That's fine, I don't mind a sleepover. I'm sure Katherine will enjoy having the bed to herself."

"She's welcome, too, of course. I did mean both of you if she's up for it. If she's not, that's totally fine, too, of course. Whatever works for both of you. Speaking of which, have you had the conversation with her?"

Anna wrinkled her face.

"Oh! That bad?"

"I think I took her by surprise more than anything. She'd assumed I hadn't wanted kids, which was a fair enough assumption. She didn't say no. She was quite shocked. Very shocked, actually. I'm going to let her sit with it for a bit, you know, give her time to think it over and see how she feels."

"Sounds like a plan," Laura agreed, stroking the fabric on the arms of the chair.

"I don't want to push her into anything." A smile edged onto her face. "I'm quite excited by the idea. I think we'd make great parents."

"So do I." Laura sat up. "Come on. Show me the rest of your fine pad before I curl up in your fancy chair and fall asleep."

Anna leapt to her feet. "Okay, the bedroom next. Prepare yourself!"

After Anna had finished showing Laura upstairs, they made their way back downstairs to finish the tour, hopeful that the aroma that had been filling the house was an indication that dinner was almost ready. The sitting room and kitchen were their last stops, where they found Tom and Abigail entranced by the television.

"Have you done your English homework, Tom?"

"I'll do it when I get home," Tom replied, glancing sheepishly at Anna before returning his attention back to the television.

Anna let out a quiet sigh at how gullible she'd been.

"Hi, Laura." Katherine wiped her hands on a tea towel as she entered the room.

"Katherine, you have the most beautiful house."

"Thank you. I can't take all the credit. The developers did most of the work, and then I added my personal touch. Would you like a glass of champagne?"

"Please. What are we celebrating?"

Anna laughed. "Nothing, Katherine's a fan. Look." She opened the fridge to reveal a stack of champagne bottles.

"Golly, how the other half lives."

"I don't hear you making any complaints when I pour you endless glasses, Anna," Katherine said with a wink as she passed her a glass.

"Admittedly I've become quite accustomed to it. I wouldn't want Katherine to drink alone. Anyway, she buys it in bulk, Laura, so it's no more expensive than a decent bottle of wine. We restrict ourselves to a couple of bottles a week; we don't live off it."

"Unfortunately," Katherine added with a sly grin.

Laura took a sip from her glass. "Who could blame you if you did?"

"Dinner won't be long; shall we eat in here or the dining room?" Katherine asked.

Katherine had previously suggested to Anna that they make more use of their opulent dining room. This wasn't exactly the best time to do that, though, as children could be messy. As if reading her thoughts and having just had a tour of the dining room, Laura answered correctly.

"In here is fine, isn't it? I don't want the kids making a mess."

"Fine," Anna answered before Katherine could object. "I'll lay the table."

The table was a new addition to the kitchen. When Anna had moved in, they had taken their meals in the dining room, and although it was a nice space, with sage-green wallpaper and a pedestaled mahogany dining table from the late Regency period that sat twelve, it didn't feel particularly cosy for just two people. On their search for furniture for Anna's dressing room, they had come across a table that suited the more modern style of the kitchen. It seated six in a much less formal manner. Placed in front of the long, sliding patio doors, it made a welcome addition to the kitchen.

With Abigail's assistance, the table was soon laid, and Katherine presented them with a steaming dish of shepherd's pie, served with peas and carrots, and gravy. All the eyes around the table widened with delight.

"This looks delicious, Katherine," Laura said. "Thank you. It's so nice to have a night off from cooking. Sometimes it can be so difficult to just stand for long periods of time in the kitchen."

The centre of Katherine's brow furrowed at her confession. "You're welcome. Dig in."

Anna allowed them to get halfway through their dinner before she announced that she wanted to pick their brains about something. She and Carrie had a meeting at the end of the week in which they were expected to present their ideas to Katherine for the new gift shop. She and Carrie had split the list of merchandise they would need to source to fill the shop. Now was a perfect time to extract some information from potential customers.

Luckily her audience was ready and willing to help.

"Abi, what would you like to see in the abbey shop for kids?"

"Stationery, so maybe notebooks, pencils, erasers."

Katherine gave Abigail a wink. "Great idea."

Abigail returned her wink and raised it with a cheeky grin.

"Tom?"

Tom shrugged as if out of habit. A moment later he spoke. "Chocolate bars, pen knives?"

"We saw some nice den kits and outdoor things when we went to Halsey Castle, didn't we, Tom?" Laura added.

Tom nodded and then looked down at the plate. Anna felt she'd extracted all she would from him.

"When the kids were little, I used to meet up regularly with a group of friends at a historic house," Laura said. "They had a wonderful shop. Tom used to love the wooden swords and slingshots, that sort of thing when he was little, didn't you?"

Tom nodded his agreement and smiled momentarily

before his eyes fell back to his plate, the smile slipping from his face along with it.

"What about you, Laura?" Anna asked, quick to move the focus away from Tom and whatever memory had come to him.

"Well, I can't resist a mug, an apron, or an oven glove."

Having taken copious notes on her phone, Anna let them finish their dinner, which was followed by a Katherine-made chocolate cake.

"How on earth do you find the time, Katherine?" Laura asked, eyeing up the cake.

"Easily. Cooking is my essential relaxation time. I wouldn't be sane without it."

"Lucky for me," Anna piped in.

"Relaxing! It's not a word I would use to describe cooking — not for these two."

"Don't look at it as a daily chore," Katherine advised. "Look at it more as a gesture of love, and you'll probably begin to enjoy it more. I receive a great deal of enjoyment from seeing others enjoy my food."

"Well I certainly enjoyed that," Laura replied. "I think it's the best shepherd's pie I've ever tasted."

Tom laughed. "It's definitely the best one I've had."

"Oi, cheeky," Laura said, sticking her tongue out at her son.

It was the first time Anna had seen Tom laugh; it suited him.

After dinner, Laura insisted she had taken up enough of their day and would leave them to their evening. As Anna showed her out, she suddenly remembered to ask about the tent.

"Abi mentioned you might have a tent we could borrow."

"Yes, it's in the shed somewhere. Are you going camping?"

"Not exactly. We've had more graffiti at the abbey. We're going to see if we can catch them at it."

"Golly, that's dedication. I'll get one of the kids to drop it round tomorrow."

"Thanks."

As Anna closed the door on them and returned to the kitchen, she felt the atmosphere that had accompanied the children and filled the house that afternoon had been suddenly drained from it. She'd enjoyed their company more than she thought she would; they brought an energy to the house that suited it. The acoustics were different with them there as their voices reached parts of the house the soft tones of adults would never fill. It was an atmosphere she immediately missed.

CHAPTER 14

*K*atherine's lips parted as she regained her breath. "That's certainly one way to be woken up."

Anna's bare body emerged from under the duvet. Katherine writhed as Anna placed kisses on her soft belly, working her way up as far as her neck. Goose bumps washed over her body, and she shivered. She made to embrace Anna, but her body was still weak and trembling from her touch.

"I hate to interrupt this. Aren't you going to be late for work?" Katherine added, as Anna's lips pushed against her cheek and then nibbled her earlobe.

Anna looked at the clock on Katherine's bedside. "Shit. I'm opening up for Carrie this morning too. She has a dentist appointment."

"And don't forget Becks is coming tonight."

Anna's warmth pressed into her belly as she sat back and straddled her.

"Oh, I had forgotten. Now that we have the tent, I thought we could camp out tonight."

"Sorry. Rain check?" Katherine replied. Though she didn't want to camp out at all, she didn't want Anna going out there alone.

"I'll hold you to it," Anna said, leaning over and teasing one of Katherine's nipples with her tongue. "What time are you coming in today?"

"Our meeting isn't until two, so I thought I'd just come in for that. I've worked my hours and then some this week. I'd like to prepare for Becks's arrival."

"Takes all morning to put a crate of champagne in the fridge, does it?"

Katherine dug her fingers into Anna's side, making her squeal and jump out of the bed.

"I'll see you later," Anna said as she ran from the room. Her head suddenly reappeared around the door, and she blew Katherine a kiss.

Katherine sank back into the bed with a satisfied smile and closed her eyes. She had no intention of falling asleep, she was simply going to rest her eyes. Virginia woke her an hour later when she meowed in her face with fish breath.

"Oh, Virginia," Katherine said as she flung a hand over her nose. "Haven't you brushed your teeth this morning?"

Virginia leaned her head down and rubbed it against Katherine's face, then curled up in a ball on her chest. Another five minutes in bed wouldn't do any harm, and it was nice to have Virginia all to herself for once.

Katherine basked in the silence. The noise from the abbey construction work had a habit of penetrating the walls of Abbey House over the past few weeks. She was pleased that the major work was now finished, and silence had been restored to her home. Though it had been nice to have Laura and the children over earlier in the week. It had suited Abbey House to being filled with the chatter and laughter of children. Was it something she would want full time?

If she thought logically about the question of children, Katherine had to admit she'd never had the intention of falling in love again and dealing with everything that brought with it. After Helena, she swore she wouldn't put herself on the line again, but then she'd met Anna, with all her wit and charm. It was inevitable that they would end up here, talking of children, yet she hadn't seen it coming. In fact, it had completely floored her.

What had made her think Anna wouldn't want children? She'd certainly never raised the subject of having children before now. Had she hoped that Anna would assume she didn't want children because of her past? Surely Anna was a little too old for pregnancy, and it would bring added complications, as she and Helena had found. Was she too sold for child-rearing herself? She'd started a new chapter of her life, one that was past children. She'd had her chance, and it hadn't worked out. Could she go through all those hopes and heartaches again, especially when it would be like history repeating itself, a history she was trying to escape from? With that thought, she sat up, today wasn't the day for it. Virginia took the hint and walked to Anna's side of the bed before curling back up into a ball.

She dressed quickly, not realising an extra five minutes

had led to an extra thirty minutes, and she had so much to do before she left for work. With Rebecca's room cleaned and the bed made, the bathroom spotless and public areas of the house cleaned, she moved on to the kitchen, ensuring she had all the ingredients for dinner that night. A quick check of the fridge told her she already had enough bottles of champagne chilling. She made herself a sandwich to take to the office, only to find Anna had already packed her one. She felt awash with love, and not just for the delicious sandwich that would be inside the lunchbox.

She shouted goodbye to Virginia as she closed the front door, only to turn a shade of pink when she spotted the postman halfway down the drive. With rational thought, she realised the postman wouldn't know Virginia was a cat even if he had heard her. She left him to pop the letters through the letterbox and made her way to the abbey. A quick bite to eat and a check of her emails would take her until the meeting started with Carrie and Anna, then back home.

Katherine leaned around the meeting room door to find Anna and Carrie working away behind a laptop. "Ready for me?"

"Yep," Carrie replied.

"Always," Anna added with a wink.

Katherine took a seat on the opposite side of the table and opened her notebook. "Blow me away."

Carrie tapped a key on the laptop, which projected an

image onto the wall of the meeting room. "I've visited some local and national heritage sites in the last few months whilst Anna has focussed her attention on online offerings from the better-known charities. From this, we created a list of categories for the shop. We have home and garden, books, gifts, stationery, and accessories. We've kept the items on the lower price end whilst retaining quality. We don't want to be investing too much money in high-end items we aren't sure will sell."

Carrie led them through a few slides showing practical, well-made offerings for the garden, ranging from bird boxes to metal animal sculptures and outdoor planters.

"Where we can, we have chosen items that fit more with an abbey environment. For example, this range of outdoor metal mirrors is in the shape of a Gothic window. These are at the higher end yet more fitting. In the meantime, we'll focus on mugs, aprons, tea towels, and coasters, all with the same branding." An image of the items appeared on the next slide, complete with a logo of the outline of the six windows of the renowned east chapel wall and "Nunswick Abbey" written underneath in a monastic font.

Carrie sat down and Anna took over the laptop.

"Books. We have our extremely popular and beautifully written abbey guidebook."

Katherine lowered her glasses and looked at Anna over the top of them. "Now on its third print run, I believe."

"Indeed," Anna replied with a pinking to her cheeks.

Katherine wasn't sure if Anna was blushing with embarrassment or from her having lowered her glasses; she knew the effect that had on Anna.

Anna showed several slides of popular books that had an abbey theme. "There are fiction ones, mainly crime and historical, but also nonfiction ones about abbey architecture and history. Also a few ghost stories."

"Wouldn't the ghost books be more fitting in the fiction section?" Katherine smirked. She and Anna had different views on ghosts. Katherine felt there was no scientific evidence for the existence of ghosts whilst Anna preferred to keep an open mind.

Anna folded her arms and glared at Katherine. "See me after class, Dr Atkinson." She returned her attention to the laptop. "We also have children's books, including colouring, sticker, and fiction. All the books would be sale or return, so no risk to us on these."

"Excellent," Katherine responded, impressed by Anna's efforts to reduce risk to their small retail budget.

"Other items for children will include the stationery, which we have decided will be uniform for adults and children. Pencils will have a natural wood finish, notebooks will have kraft covers, rulers will be wooden, and we even have eco pens made from recycled cardboard. All in one colour print to keep the costs down. Then we have the den kits, slingshots, crossbows, key rings, and water bottles."

Anna flicked through several slides showing proofs from the merchandise company they were working with. "Then we have cotton and jute bags, and of course, travel mugs. Something else I've been working on is a toy bear in embroidered, hooded robes." A bear in brown robes with a rope tie around his waist flashed on to the screen. On the back of the robes was the abbey logo. "This is a rough visual of what I'm thinking. I may even turn him into a key ring."

Katherine nodded. "Fantastic, he's cute."

"We also have our range of art, which you're dealing with, Katherine, and I understand we'll be having them made into greeting cards too?"

"Yes, Michael has been so supportive. I'm hoping to persuade him to allow us to use one of his watercolours on some of the homewares. Let's see how they go down first as prints and cards." She sat back and closed her notebook. "Well, I must say I wasn't quite expecting this range of quality items from you both. I think they'll all fit very well."

"We think going with a slightly broader offering to start with, but purchasing lower quantities, will allow us to hone it, see what sells and what doesn't," Carrie said. "As you may have noticed, we've avoided all clothing and food. We suggest adding these later, a second phase."

"Perhaps once we have a retail manager, you mean," Katherine said.

"Yes!" Carrie and Anna replied in unison.

"Well, fingers crossed for one of those. I think you've done a fantastic job between you, considering this is well outside the remit of your job roles. It just shows what we can achieve when we pull together. I assume you can email that presentation over to me and that you have a budget for me to show the trustees? They want final sign-off due to the costs involved."

Anna tapped furiously at the laptop. "In your inbox now."

"Fantastic," Katherine replied, standing up. "Thank you, ladies."

Katherine made her escape to her office, desperate to get the files off to the trustees so she could clear her desk for the week. She was looking forward to a relaxing weekend with Rebecca. She'd earned some quality downtime, and it had been too long since they had seen each other.

Her return to her desk revealed several emails, one of which was from Sophie. She read it and exhaled noisily just as Anna entered.

"Everything okay?"

"Sophie's just emailed. They've analysed the results from earlier in the week and now request permission to dig some test pits," Katherine read from her laptop. "They want to verify the position of the foundations of the monastic buildings that used to accompany the abbey and also look at some of the larger anomalies that have come up."

"That's good, isn't it?" Anna tried to find the bright side. "It would be useful to us to have the positions verified. All we have now is information from hundreds of years ago."

"I guess. It's just… what if they unearth something that will cause problems for us? I really can't take any more delay and upsets."

"It's not near the building work, so how would it affect us if they found something?"

Katherine pulled a moue. "I know, my head just goes to the worst-case scenario at the moment. It's better to plan for the worst and at least be prepared."

"Oh you're not one of those 'fail to prepare, prepare to fail' lot, are you? You must have been a barrel of laughs at school," Anna teased.

A smile tore into Katherine's lips, despite her utmost effort to prevent it.

"Leave it all until Monday," Anna suggested. "It's nothing that can't wait until then. You'll be refreshed and better able to focus."

Anna was right. It wasn't anything that couldn't wait until Monday; she had to get out of the habit of trying to clear things. By Monday there would be a new list of things to do and challenges to overcome, as seemed to be her daily routine.

She shut her laptop.

"Okay, I'll see you at home." Katherine placed a kiss on Anna's cheek.

"I'll try not to be too late, but I've got a lot to finish up."

"Maybe you should take some of your own advice and leave it until Monday," Katherine replied as she headed for the door.

Anna narrowed her eyes. "Go on, off you go. Smart-arse."

Katherine felt a pat on her bottom as she left the office.

Virginia was behind the front door as Katherine arrived home a few minutes later, likely drawn to the pile of post on the doormat, which always needed to be sat on. Katherine's suspicion was confirmed when she picked up the letters, warmed from the cat's body. Virginia placed herself on the threshold of the door before Katherine could close it and looked out.

"Well, are you in or out?"

Virginia mewed at her and then turned around and headed back inside, only to turn around again and shoot out the door just before Katherine shut it. She rolled her eyes at the fickle cat.

She popped Anna's post on the Regency hall table that she and Rebecca had bought at auction shortly after she moved in, and took a closer look at the rest of the post. One envelope was stamped with *Her Majesty's Prison*. She drew in a sharp gasp of air as a rush of heat and panic swept over her body. Shoving the unexpected letter back into the pile, she used it to fan herself, panting out slow breaths to control her emotions.

Regaining her composure, she headed to the kitchen at a pace, throwing the letters onto the kitchen island. She extracted a bottle of champagne from the fridge and opened it at lightning speed with the help of a nearby tea towel. She filled a glass, then waited only seconds for the bubbles to settle before downing it and refilling it.

Her mind raced with thoughts about what the letter could mean, yet she found herself unable to open it and find out. Once opened, there was no going back. The bubbles fizzed in the glass beside her. She needed something more. Extracting the whisky from the drinks cupboard, she half filled a glass and downed that. She could feel the liquor's warmth loosening her body and refilled the glass with her shaky hand.

CHAPTER 15

A loud knocking stirred Katherine from the sofa where she lay. It took a moment for her to come around fully. She hadn't been sleeping so much as dozing amongst her thoughts. Lightheaded from the whisky, she toddled to the front door and opened it.

"Bloody hell, Kat. What happened to you?" Rebecca remarked, concern filling her face as she fully took in the state of her friend.

Katherine examined herself in the hall mirror whilst Rebecca entered and set her suitcase down.

Her reflection was somewhat of a shock. Her mascara had smudged, her usually perfect hair was flat on one side from where she'd lain on the sofa, and her puffy eyes stared back at her in bewilderment. She ran her fingers through her hair, but there was little she could do to fix her face without a wash or a make-up wipe, and the only thing she wanted now was another drink.

"Kat, what the hell is going on? Why do you look like you've just been dragged through a hedge backwards?"

"I need a whisky. Want one?" Katherine picked up her glass from the sitting room table as she made her way through to the kitchen with Rebecca close at her heel.

"I knew today was going to be difficult for you. I wasn't expecting you to look like this, though. Talk to me."

Katherine reached for the letter marked HMP and pushed it across the island at Rebecca. She turned her attention to refilling her whisky glass and gulped it down, grateful for the burn in the back of her throat as it gave her a moment of distraction. She watched as Rebecca examined the envelope.

"You haven't opened it," Rebecca said, her tone softer than before.

Katherine shook her head and took another sip of whisky, her hand shaking as she raised it to her mouth. There would be no avoiding the envelope with Rebecca involved; it would have to be opened.

Rebecca took the glass from Katherine and placed it down before wrapping her arms around her. "Shall we at least see what it says before we go into full meltdown?"

Katherine nodded as her body relaxed against her oldest friend. "You open it."

"Where's Anna?"

"At work."

Rebecca pulled back from the hug. "Why isn't she here? You shouldn't be alone. I would have come earlier if she wasn't going to look after you." Rebecca paused and glared at Katherine. "You have told her it's the anniversary today? Kat?"

"I assume she forgot, and that worked for me. I just

wanted it to pass like any other day. Then I'd know it was getting easier, that I was getting over it."

"Words fail me, Kat."

"Every year at this time, I feel myself slipping, and then I spend the following weeks, months even, trying to claw my way back to normal again. I just wanted this year to be different, to be easier."

"You could at least pause and remember. Share a moment of quiet reflection with the woman you love for a woman you once loved."

"I need to move on, and Anna would have only made a fuss. I was sailing through, you know, until that bloody letter arrived."

Rebecca's eyes bored into her as her hands tore into the letter. Katherine felt a reprieve as Rebecca finally turned to the contents of the letter. She braced herself as she sat, her hand clutching at her glass.

Rebecca took the seat beside her and closed the letter. A nod told Katherine everything she needed to know.

"I'm not going," she said.

Rebecca's eyebrows shot up. "Seriously? You're not even going to ruminate on it?"

"Why should I go and listen to them tell me how hard their life has been since they killed my wife and baby? Why should I go to help make them feel better?" Katherine snapped back as she grabbed a handful of tissues from the box beside her to quell the flow of tears.

"I asked you to consider restorative justice at the time, if you remember." Rebecca replied firmly. "I understood it was too difficult for you then, but you promised me you would think about it in the future. It's supposed to help both parties heal. It's not just about making them feel better, but yourself too."

"I only told you that to shut you up. I never had any intention of doing it," Katherine scoffed.

She hadn't wished to lie to Rebecca at the time, but it had been the only way to get her off her back about it. Right now, she needed her best friend's support, not an argument. She needed her to understand why she was refusing to meet with the person who had killed Helena and the baby.

"Anna wants children." Katherine's voice felt like gravel in her throat.

"What the f…" Rebecca stopped herself and huffed.

Katherine realised how naive she'd been for believing she could make a fair decision about children based on her current situation, when her past was her present and her future. It was all-consuming; there was no escaping it. She couldn't go through it all again.

"I can't do it. I can't give her what she wants because of what he did to me in the past. Every step with Anna would be a reminder of the same steps I took with Helena. This time I wouldn't feel the same excitement I'd felt the first time. I'd be dreading every moment, knowing they should have been moments I shared with Helena, and that's not fair to Anna. I have to hope she can accept a future with just me in it."

"Anna should have realised you wouldn't want children. It's a little heartless of her to have brought it up."

"No, it's not." Katherine shook her head. "It's reasonable for her to ask what her future looks like, and it's ridiculous she has to ask. Why have we not discussed it before? Has she been afraid all this time to raise the subject? She said she wanted them when she was younger, but then let go of the idea. At least she was brave enough to raise it before we got married."

"You don't think the restorative justice scheme would help you with this — or help you in any other way?"

Although Rebecca's voice remained calm and firm, Katherine could sense the disappointment within it. She tried not to care. She wasn't going to allow herself to be bullied into this so-called solution.

"I'm trying to move forward with my life. I have been moving forward. I can't and won't go back."

"This is an opportunity to help you move forward, Kat," Rebecca pleaded.

"No, it's a way to drag it all back up. I don't care what they have to say, and I have nothing to say to them. I owe it to Anna to properly put the past behind me. It's already affected her life too much."

"I think you owe it to Helena to go and hear out the person that killed her." The calmness in Rebecca's voice was beginning to edge away; the firmness very much remained.

It took a moment for Katherine to respond.

"I don't want to fight with you, especially not when you've only just arrived. I'm not feeling myself at the moment, and this hasn't helped. First the building hold-up, then Harry, now this. I feel like my head will explode." Her heart pounded even harder in her chest from saying it out loud.

"Why don't you see a doctor?"

"I am a doctor. I'm fine. It's just… why did it have to arrive today?"

"I guess they are thinking about it too."

"I don't want to share my memories with them. They're mine. That just makes it worse." Noticing her glass was empty again, Katherine refilled it, only to empty it again.

"You're clearly stretched thin, Kat. This is exactly why you were supposed to be keeping low hours: to give yourself enough downtime to process things when it gets too much."

"Well, this can go in the bin for starters… one less thing to deal with." Katherine placed her hand over the letter on the work surface and scrunched it into her palm.

Rebecca stared in disbelief as Katherine dropped it into the bin. "Seriously? That's it."

"Yes," Katherine replied. She felt lighter already.

Rebecca reached into the bin. "I'm showing it to Anna, even if you're not."

Katherine intercepted Rebecca as she withdrew the letter. "No, you're not. She doesn't need to deal with any more of my baggage. Leave it."

Rebecca managed to keep a grip on the letter.

Katherine danced around her, determined to get it back.

"What on earth is going on?" Anna's voice filled the kitchen, rooting Katherine and Rebecca to their spots.

CHAPTER 16

*S*ilence fell as Anna entered the kitchen and read the room. It was unnerving. She'd never heard so much as a cross word between the two of them before.

"Why are you arguing over a piece of paper?" She approached them as they hovered over the bin. Her heart quickened in her chest at their continued silence. "Will one of you tell me what's going on?"

Katherine avoided her eye. On closer inspection, she could see why.

"Katherine, look at me." Anna placed her hand on Katherine's face and tilted it towards her. Her gaze was met with a set of puffy, red eyes. "Why have you been crying?"

Katherine reached out. Instead of coming to Anna for a hug as she was expecting, Katherine snatched the letter from Rebecca's hand and shoved it back into the bin.

"It's nothing."

The smell of whisky on Katherine's breath caught Anna by surprise.

"Hardly," Rebecca chimed in, reaching back into the bin to extract the letter. She took a couple of steps back, out of Katherine's reach, and then passed the letter to Anna. "Read it."

Taking the nearest stool, Anna sat and devoured the letter. She barely understood it but knew it was from the prison. She reread it more carefully, noticing out the corner of her eye that Katherine had sat beside her and was reaching for a glass of whisky.

She put the letter down, unable to fully take it in, and looked to Rebecca. "Can you just explain it to me please, in layman's terms?"

Rebecca sat opposite her and topped up the glass of champagne left abandoned earlier by Katherine. She gestured the bottle towards Anna.

Anna declined. One of them needed to keep a clear head.

Rebecca took a couple of large swigs before answering.

"It's called restorative justice. It's a programme that brings together the offender of a crime and the victim in the hope that opening the lines of communication can assist in the rehabilitation of the offender. The idea is to bring closure for the victim, or at the least... some answers."

"Kat doesn't have to do it, though, if she doesn't want to?" Anna asked, sensing this was what had drawn the tension into the room. She reached out and placed a hand over Katherine's, pleased that it earned her a faint smile in return. She'd never pushed Katherine for details before regarding Helena's death. She'd always been led by her willingness to talk about it, which was rare, and all Anna could do was respect those wishes.

Rebecca shook her head. "It can be requested at any time by either party, and it seems that it has been requested… and it arrives today of all days."

Katherine's head snapped in the direction of Rebecca.

"What's today?" Anna asked, her eyes darting between the two of them as they glared at one another.

"It's the anniversary," Rebecca answered softly.

Anna closed her eyes and exhaled. *Idiot!* How could she have forgotten such an important date? "Why didn't you remind me this morning? Oh, Kat, I'm sorry. I shouldn't have needed reminding, should I?"

"I didn't want you to remember; I didn't want to remember. I just wanted to get through the day, no fuss," Katherine replied, wiping tears that sat in her eyes. "I'm sorry I'm such a mess. I just want it to go away, and I'm really trying —"

Anna stood and pulled Katherine's trembling body into hers, rubbing her hand soothingly up and down her arm.

"I don't want to go, Anna. Please don't ask me to."

"You don't have to do anything you don't want to."

Her reply earned her a glare from Rebecca before she turned her attention to Katherine. "The fact that it is still too hard to talk about tells me you aren't over it, Kat. Take this opportunity!"

"How many times… I'm not going."

Anna pondered interjecting. Arguing wasn't going to get them anywhere, and she feared for Katherine's emotional state.

"It could help!" Rebecca slammed her hands on the work surface.

"Or it could make things worse!"

"How? How can it make things worse than this? It's already preventing you from having children."

Silence cut through the air like an executioner's blade.

Anna blinked and pulled back from Katherine. "What?"

Rebecca hung her head. "Sorry, Kat. I shouldn't have said that."

Katherine sighed. "I'm sorry, Anna, I… don't want children. It was hard enough for me to open my heart to you. I just can't go through it all again."

Without time to properly process Katherine's explanation, Anna went with the response required of anyone in this situation. "It's okay. I understand that you want to protect yourself." This wasn't the time to allow her disappointment to overwhelm her, as much as it was trying. Katherine was all that mattered at this moment.

Katherine stepped off the stool. "I'm going for a lie-down. Sorry, I hadn't got around to making dinner. There is plenty of food in the fridge. I'm sure you can fix yourselves something."

"Do you want me to come with you?" Anna asked, unsure if Katherine should really be alone at this time.

"No, I just need to shut my eyes," Katherine replied, squeezing Anna's hand as she passed.

Once Katherine was out of sight, Anna found herself under Rebecca's scorn.

"Well, thanks for the support there," she said. "Really helpful."

"What?" Anna was taken aback by her tone.

Rebecca got up and examined the contents of the fridge. "This is a really good opportunity for her; you should have been encouraging her, not holding her back."

"She doesn't want to go; I'm not going to force her."

"We can't just let her do what she wants; we have to push her towards what's best for her. Do you think if I'd sat back the past few years and let her do what she wanted, she'd be here? She'd be fucking dead."

Anna throat tightened at Rebecca's words.

"She would have been able to deal with this better if she'd been following the rules and looking after herself, but no, she exhausts herself at that bloody abbey instead." Rebecca threw out a dramatic arm in the opposite direction to where the abbey stood in relation to the house.

Anna thought it best not to correct her and sat back as a packet of tomatoes skidded past her on the work surface, followed by a cucumber. She quickly lifted the glass it was heading towards, allowing it to pass freely underneath.

"She is quite clearly your problem now; she's stopped listening to me."

Problem. The word cut through Anna. Katherine wasn't and never would be a problem to her. She watched in silence as Rebecca made herself a cheese-and-salad sandwich. Was this a little glimpse of barrister Rebecca, bullish and scary? If it was, she certainly wouldn't wish to oppose her in a courtroom.

"I'll eat this in my room," Rebecca said, cutting her sandwich in half with a bread knife and letting it carelessly fall onto the work surface with a thud.

So much for a fun and relaxing weekend.

CHAPTER 17

*K*atherine woke with a start the next morning. Fragments of the previous evening's conversations flashed in her head, and she desperately tried to piece them back together into something coherent. As she lifted her head from the pillow to check the time on her bedside clock, she was surprised to find her head didn't react badly. No doubt thanks to Anna's insistence that she eat a sandwich, drink a pint of water, and take a couple of painkillers, all before she'd shoved her into the shower, helped her into her pyjamas, and put her to bed. She hadn't even said anything about children or the restorative justice programme when she'd held her and kissed her head as she fell asleep.

They had both cleared the weekend for Rebecca's visit, and with no plans for the day, Katherine decided not to wake Anna just yet. She slipped gently from the bed, donned her warm, fluffy dressing gown, and headed downstairs.

"You're leaving?" Katherine said with false surprise as

she noticed Rebecca with her suitcase in the hallway. She hadn't expected her to stay; it would have been too awkward following the previous evening's exchanges.

"Yes, I must get back to London. Something has come up at work. Sorry."

Katherine knew Rebecca well enough to know when she was lying. She also knew that Rebecca would be aware that she knew she was lying. They went through the motions anyway for the sake of politeness.

"I'll call you sometime."

Katherine nodded, not wanting to feed into the false niceties for fear they would never end. She had nothing to say, no words of regret or apology to issue, all she wanted now was to move past last night and the letter. Her only regret was having fallen out about it, when really, Rebecca should have been more supportive of her decision as Anna had been.

Rebecca opened the front door and slipped away without even so much as a look back.

Now she had another problem to add to the knot in her stomach: her broken relationship with her best friend. How she would resolve that one was a problem for another day. After Rebecca had some time to cool down, she hoped she would be back on the phone, checking in on her.

As she entered the kitchen, she noticed the letter was still on the work surface. She filed it where it belonged, in the bin. Its arrival had knocked her for six. Until that point, she really felt that she had a grasp on the day, rather than it having a grasp on her. Would she ever truly be able to escape her past?

Virginia caught her attention at the window as she filled the kettle. The outside window sill was another one of the cat's favourite spots in which to sit and mew for the door to be opened. Katherine let the cat in and returned to her tea-making; it was definitely a peppermint morning. When she returned to the bedroom, she found Virginia curled up in a ball on her side of the bed. She shooed her to one side so she could get back in. Once she was settled, Virginia curled up on top of her stomach.

Anna lay so peacefully beside her that Katherine decided she wouldn't wake her. She reached for a book instead. She had just finished one, and she hovered momentarily between rereading one of her favourites, *The Price of Salt*, and a new one that Anna had told her she should read. She opted for familiarity; she needed that now.

Half an hour later a soft voice came from beside her.

"Morning."

Katherine popped her book down, forgetting Virginia was still on her lap. She was mewed at with disgust. "Sorry, Virginia." She looked down at a bleary-eyed Anna. "Morning, beautiful. Becks has left."

"Without saying goodbye?" Anna questioned, sitting up.

"I caught her sneaking out earlier. We've never fought like this before, ever. What did you two talk about when I came up?"

"Nothing, really. She just made a sandwich and took it to her room. I don't think she was impressed by either of us."

"Sounds like Becks. As much as I love her, she does tend to only see things her way."

"Comes from being a barrister, I expect."

"No, she's always been that way. Compromise is for other people. I couldn't have done without her these past years, though."

"I'm glad she was there for you. But perhaps it's time that she had a little less say in things," Anna said, reaching for her phone.

Anna was right. Katherine had relied heavily on Rebecca for emotional support and guidance to navigate her way through the world following the loss of Helena. If she was going to move forward, then perhaps it was time to cut her tie to Rebecca's support. She had Anna now, after all.

"Since Becks has gone, shall we camp out tonight? The weather looks mild according to the Met Office," Anna said.

"Do you really think our graffiti artists will return?"

"Yes, I do. The first time it happened it was on a weekend."

"I'm not keen, but I don't want you out there by yourself."

A hand slid across her stomach, under the duvet, as Anna turned towards her and snuggled into her. Virginia eyed the duvet, her paw striking at the ruffled fabric as it buckled and bowed.

"We can call it glamping if you prefer," Anna said. "I've borrowed a blow-up bed from Gloria, and we'll fill the tent with duvets and pillows. We'll make a little love nest."

Katherine had to admit a love nest sounded appealing, somewhere they could hide away from the world and all the problems it brought with it.

Anna continued with her plan. "We could have an early dinner and head over at seven o'clock and take some snacks for a midnight feast."

"Midnight feast," Katherine chuckled. "How old are you?"

Anna's hand slid up to Katherine's breast. "I'm as old as the woman I feel," Anna replied, caressing it. "So, in this case, nearly fifty."

"Thank you for the reminder."

The last time Katherine had participated in a midnight feast was in the Girl Guides; it was the first and last time she went camping too. Five-star hotels had been built for a reason — for people like her — and it was rude not to use them.

They lay in silence for a while, listening to the light purrs from Virginia.

"Do you want to talk about last night?" Anna finally asked.

"Not particularly, do you?"

Anna's phone rang before she could answer. A stifled ring came from somewhere in the duvet. A few moments of searching revealed it.

"It's Lucy," she said as she read the caller display. "I wonder if they have Dad's results."

"Only one way to find out."

Katherine listened to Anna speaking with Lucy. She could gauge from her tone that it was the news they were dreading to hear. She held her breath as Anna finished the call.

"Okay, we'll see you tomorrow then as arranged, and we'll talk to him. Thanks for ringing." Anna hung up. "They've had the results sent through and emailed them on to both of us. She wanted to let us know they would be coming rather than them just appearing without warning."

"And?"

Anna nodded and looked down to where Katherine had just placed a hand on her arm. "It's Parkinson's dementia."

Katherine pulled Anna into her. "I'm sorry."

"Is it different to regular dementia?" Anna asked with a sniff, her voice shaky.

"It's the name given when a Parkinson's patient develops dementia after a year or so of motor problems. It's dementia, no matter how you wrap it." She reached for her phone. "I'll read the report now and translate for you."

"Thank you." Anna wiped her face and gave a weary sigh. "I think I'll take a shower."

CHAPTER 18

"*J*'m not sure about this," Katherine called out to Anna. Anna was a good two metres in front of her and making good headway despite carrying two duvets and two pillows. Left to carry the tent, which had shrunken considerably since she'd last seen one, Katherine found herself sent straight back to her Girl-Guiding days. Trampling across a field led by a domineering brown owl that, now that she thought about it, had probably been the same age as she was now. How on earth had she reached the age of a brown owl?

"Come on, it will be fine," Anna reassured her.

"I can't even remember how to put a tent up."

Anna stopped by a crop of trees where she had already placed a picnic basket, the blow-up bed, a rucksack, and two fold-out chairs.

"Luckily for us, I do, and luckily for you, it only takes one pair of hands," Anna bragged.

"In that case, I shall sit and observe," Katherine said, relaxing back into the fold-out chair. The squeak it gave under her full weight gave her a moment of concern. Thankfully the chair held its own.

Anna threw a most welcome blanket at her and then scrabbled in the picnic basket, extracting a bottle of chilled champagne and two glasses.

A smile swept across Katherine's face. "Okay, I could get used to camping if it comes with a bottle of champagne."

"I'll remember that!"

With champagne in hand and the slowly setting sun on her face, Katherine watched as Anna impressively erected the tent. She pumped the air bed to near its popping point, knowing Katherine liked a firm mattress, and then made several trips in and out of the tent, making her final preparations.

Katherine held the glass of champagne between her thighs and stared up at the reddish hue of the sky as she tried to clear her mind and absorb the tranquillity of the moment. There was only one thing missing: her best friend by her side. Would she ever be back there beside her? Or was this to be one of those moments where neither side backs down and twenty years passes without another word? She took a gulp of champagne at the thought. Their bond was too strong to let that happen.

After two rounds of Anna's sandwiches and another glass of champagne, Katherine finally started to relax. They had pitched the tent behind a crop of trees with full sight of the chapel wall. The sun was on its final descent behind the ruined abbey and the birds were beginning to settle into silence, ready for the owl to begin its turn.

"Shall we go for a romantic walk in the ruins before we settle in for the night?"

It was the best idea Anna had produced all day; she could do with clearing her head before bed.

They walked in silence towards the abbey. The light breeze was unseasonably warm. Katherine had originally been worried about being cold whilst camping out; she now feared being too warm.

"I guess this area will be full of archaeologists soon," Anna said finally, her hand scooping up Katherine's.

"Next week in all likelihood. Sophie sent an email this morning to say she had the results from the burial. We'll know more on Monday when she comes over to do some prep work. She'll leave her team to pack up at Halsey, and then they'll join her."

"I hope they don't leave a mess. The last thing we need is a patchwork of dead grass."

They reached the chapel and made for their favourite spot by the window.

Katherine sat with a sigh. She hadn't meant to; the tranquillity of the chapel pulled it from within her.

"You all right?" Anna asked, taking a seat beside her and rubbing her leg.

"Yes. No," Katherine changed her mind. Why she always felt the need to respond with a yes to that question she'd never know. It was okay to share. "I just feel there's no time to breathe. Every day brings some new hurdle I have to climb over. It's relentless. Everything is just on top of me, squeezing the life out of me."

She held back the tears she could feel forming in her eyes. She'd cried enough in the last twenty-four hours; she didn't have the strength for more. If crying was supposed to make you feel better, then why was it so exhausting?

"I think I underestimated how much responsibility the abbey would be. And not just the abbey — the staff, the weight of customer satisfaction that needs to be constantly met."

Anna's head popped up. "You're not thinking of giving up, are you? I know you'll get your license back in a few months, but I think we make a good team."

Katherine sensed a slight panic in Anna's voice. "Who knows what the future holds." It wasn't exactly reassuring, but it was the truth.

"I'm not sure this is the time to start getting philosophical," Anna said. "Things will improve; the build will be completed; the archaeologists will come and go. Becks will speak to you again."

Katherine started to speak, rethought her phrasing, then realised there was no kind way to say it. She tried to keep her tone gentle as she pointed out, "Harry won't improve."

"No." Anna pulled in her bottom lip and chewed on it. "He was never going to, was he?"

"No, he wasn't. This new diagnosis may lead to a swifter progression of his Parkinson's."

"You're sure you want to tell him tomorrow?" Anna asked. "We can just leave it to his GP to tell him on Monday if you can't face it?"

"It's best coming from us; we both know that. I'll be fine. I've given enough unwelcome news over the years."

"Not to people who are a father figure to you."

"We owe it to him to tell him." Katherine tapped

Anna's hand, which was still on her thigh. "Why do I suddenly feel the need for a peppermint tea?"

"It's the window ledge," Anna said, leaning back as she did. "I always crave it when I sit here. You brought it to me here the fourth time we met."

"Fourth time? Who was counting?" The fact that it had meant so much to Anna at the time caused an unprompted smile to cross Katherine's lips.

"Just me apparently." Anna nudged her. "Shall we go to bed?"

"Yes, I'm knackered."

Although she had gone to bed early after her disagreement with Rebecca, she hadn't slept well. Helena had entered her dreams for the first time in a while, and so she wasn't keen on sleeping tonight. She had brought her book and a sturdy reading light to their camping tent to keep her awake. Hopefully, she could summon visions of Carol Aird from *The Price of Salt*, instead of Helena from beyond the grave.

They made their way back to their tent in cooler air now that the sun had fully set. Rather than changing into pyjamas, they pulled on some jogging bottoms and sweatshirts. A quick brush of their teeth with a bottle of water to rinse, and they buried themselves under the duvet, finding each other's bodies for warmth.

"So, you had sex in a tent?" Katherine had to know.

"Yes. It was whilst I was on the Duke of Edinburgh's Award expedition."

"I'm not sure sex counts towards the physical activity section for D of E — or as a skill, come to think of it."

"Nor was pregnancy," Anna said with a wicked grin,

"but the daughter of our religious education teacher managed it whilst we were camping in Snowdonia."

"Oof, how embarrassing."

"Can I persuade you to partake in a little physical activity now?" Anna asked. "It's guaranteed to warm us up."

Katherine hesitated. "Do you mind if we don't tonight? My head is buzzing too much with everything."

"Of course not."

"Surely we should be on watch or something, anyway?" Katherine questioned.

"I think we're close enough to hear anything going on in the same place."

They lay in silence, Anna tucked into Katherine like a hot water bottle. Cuddling Anna always restored her equilibrium; she couldn't bear to think of a future without her. Which brought up a question she'd been trying to shove to the back of her mind.

"Are you sure you're okay about not having children? You don't feel you'll be missing out on a big part of life?"

"How will I be missing out on anything if I have you?" Anna replied immediately, squeezing the breath from her with her arms.

There wasn't a response that Katherine could find to that. It was all she could have hoped for — if it were true. Only time would prove that; for now, all she could do was trust it was.

Katherine waited until Anna fell asleep before extracting her book and torch. It wasn't long before she was putting the book down, though. Despite her best efforts at staying awake, her eyes were heavy.

The *ke-wik* of a tawny owl sounded nearby.

There was nothing better than the sound of an owl. It took her straight back to the old house in the city that she'd shared with Helena. It faced a small park with mature trees which several owls frequented. She and Helena would fall asleep to the sound of them hooting to each other outside their bedroom window. For a moment she allowed herself to imagine she was lying back in their bed, the warmth of the body beside hers Helena's, not Anna's.

She had often held hands with Helena as they walked through the park, dreaming of a day when they would be able to push their son or daughter around it in a pram, watch them kick the fallen autumn leaves as they grew. One day they would watch their grandchildren play as their child had, as they grew old and grey together. They'd called the house their forever house, the first and last house they would buy together. It was a little corner of the world to call their own, until one day it wasn't. Helena was never to return, and Katherine was left alone with the memories of what would never be.

She choked out a silent cry, a cry of guilt that she'd been harbouring for Helena all these years, a cry of guilt that momentarily she wanted the warmth of the body beside her to be someone else's, not Anna's, someone long lost to her. Her throat tightened and ached as she restrained the sob.

She had been lost once, then found by Anna, but now she was realising that that lost feeling had never left her. She was still wandering, floundering. She could hear a voice calling for her in the distance, telling her everything was okay. She couldn't make out if it was Anna's or Helena's.

She opened her eyes; a figure was leaning over her. Damp from sweat, she shivered.

In the darkness, she felt the softness of a hand against her face and then the sweetness of Anna's voice.

"Hey, are you okay? You were having a bad dream."

"What time is it?" Katherine asked, her mouth dry.

Anna looked at her phone. "Two thirty."

She had fallen asleep. Her senses were dulled in the darkness, but as she regained consciousness, she realised she could hear something right outside the tent.

"Are you all right?" Anna asked again.

"Can you hear that?" Katherine replied, not wanting to answer the question. Not able to answer it.

Anna listened for a minute, then nodded. "There's something outside," she whispered. "I'll take a look."

"Don't! It might be dangerous." Katherine gripped her wrist to prevent her from leaving.

Anna caressed Katherine's hand before easing it off her. "I'll be fine."

Katherine sat back and watched as Anna slowly unzipped the tent. Visions of axe-wielding lunatics roaming the abbey irrationally entered her head.

There was a moment's silence, and then Anna gasped.

"Oh, it's you! What are you doing here?"

Katherine's heart raced. Was it friend or foe? And what was anyone doing on the site at this time of night if they were up to no good? Her questions were immediately answered when Anna sat back, and Virginia waltzed in.

"Oh, Virginia!" Katherine turned on her torch and

pointed it at the cat, only to realise she had a mouse hanging from her mouth. "She's brought us a bloody present," Katherine whispered.

Anna squealed. "A mouse! Let's get out of here."

"No. She may drop it if we make any sudden movements. Can you try and shoo her out?"

They both made hissing noises and flicked their hands in her direction. It had the undesired effect of scaring Virginia from the tent, leaving her wriggling present behind.

Katherine spotted the mouse as it dived into the duvet. She screamed.

"Out, get out, quick. It's in the duvet!"

Anna moved at speeds Katherine had never witnessed before. With quick foresight she scooped up their phones and grabbed her house keys before matching Anna's speed and direction. They gave the tent a good twenty-metre clearance before stopping.

"Home?" Anna suggested.

Katherine couldn't help laughing. "I thought you'd never ask!"

CHAPTER 19

*T*wo faces peered into the tent the following morning to find Virginia curled up in the centre of the duvet pile.

"Charming, Virginia! Did you deliver a mouse just so you could have the bed to yourself?" Katherine said. "Don't you even think about pulling that one at home."

The cat opened one eye and then closed it again.

They stood up and reassessed the situation. "We'll have to get her out," Anna said. "The abbey will open soon; we can't leave the tent up."

"We'll do just that. It will still deter vandals, regardless of there being two middle-aged women hiding in it."

Anna drew her lips down and nodded. "You might be on to something there." Half a night in a tent was enough to remind her why camping was best left to those under twenty.

"I'm not just a pretty face." Katherine winked.

Anna wasn't going to argue with her on that. "So where do we think the mouse went?"

"I'll take a guess: in her stomach."

Anna scrunched her face. "Eww!"

"She'll have to come out, though," Katherine said. "I'm not leaving everything in it."

Anna quickly replied, "In you go then."

"Me?" Katherine rested her hands on her hips. "All this was your idea, may I remind you!"

She had a point, but there was still no way Anna was going in there. She didn't want to risk stepping on a mouse carcass.

"She wouldn't be asleep if there was a mouse in there, would she? I'm sure it's fine."

Anna wasn't going to fall for that. "If you're so sure, in you go."

"Oh, fine then." Katherine knelt and crawled into the tent.

Anna couldn't help herself. She drank in Katherine's rear end as it hung out of the tent.

"You better not be staring at my backside, Miss Walker."

"Nope, not at all," Anna lied through her smirk. She continued watching as it wiggled. "Any sign of a mouse?" she asked, leaning down just as something shot from the tent. She stepped back, nearly tripping over a guide rope. "Virginia!"

"No, doesn't appear to be," Katherine replied as she reversed out of the tent, clutching the duvets. "Unless it's caught up in this lot. You'll have to get the rest."

Anna packed up the rucksack, scooped up the picnic basket and pillows as quick as she could, and took them outside for a thorough inspection.

"Let's take this to the house," Katherine suggested. "We'll have to deal with it when we get back later."

As usual, Anna took the driver's seat as they made their way to Baycroft to visit Harry. She was tired after their disturbed night, and her thoughts fell to Katherine showing her vulnerability again. She was pleased Katherine felt able to be more open and share everything with her, but it also brought a weight of fear to her. She simply hated to see Katherine struggling.

They had barely spoken about Katherine's revelation about not wanting to have children; after all, there wasn't much to say. If Katherine didn't want to, and Anna could understand why she might not, she wasn't going to push her or be without her, so it was a matter of acceptance on her part. She wasn't going to deny that she was disappointed — she genuinely believed they would make great parents — but today, they needed to focus on Harry.

"I've been thinking," Katherine said, interrupting Anna's thoughts. "As the weather improves, we should try and spend more time with Harry. Take him and Mabel out to places."

"Mabel! Why does she have to come?"

"If she is important to him, then she's important to us. He's going to need all the help he can get going forward."

Anna couldn't disagree with Katherine. As much as she was unsure about Mabel's sudden friendship with her dad, it made sense.

The receptionist paged Lucy on their arrival, and

within minutes she was walking them round to Harry's room.

"Thanks for doing this," she told Katherine. "It's better coming from you, I think. Did you have any questions from the report?"

"No, it was pretty thorough and clear. I won't go into too much detail. Just make him aware," Katherine assured her.

Lucy nodded her agreement. "His GP is in tomorrow morning, so if he has any more questions or wants to go over it again, he can. We'll talk him through his treatment plan too. Call me if you have any concerns."

"Thanks, Lucy," Anna replied, holding her fist close to the door yet unable to knock. This was one of those moments in life where you wished you could turn and walk away but knew you couldn't. It was happening whether she liked it or not, and it was her duty to be there for Harry every step of the way, as he had been there for her on her journey into the world.

She felt Katherine's warm hand slip into hers, and a light squeeze gave her the strength to knock and enter. Harry was in his usual chair in front of the television.

"Hi, Dad," she greeted him.

"Morning, Harry."

A smile spread across his face at the sight of them, and he reached for the remote, accidentally knocking it onto the floor.

"Sorry we couldn't come yesterday. Becks was visiting," Anna said as she bent down to pick it up. She turned off the television and placed the remote back on the arm of his chair.

Harry nodded his understanding. "It's nice to see you anytime. She all right?" His words were slow and fractured.

"Yes, she's fine," Katherine lied.

Anna let Katherine take the nearer chair this time as she was going to be the one explaining his diagnosis.

"How have you been, Harry?" she asked.

"All right, doc, yeah."

"Are you being good for Holly? Doing all your exercises?"

"As much as I can. They had me doing some tests this week. I doubt I passed." Harry lifted his finger to his head and poked it. "It's not what it used to be."

Katherine looked over at Anna for support. She responded with a nod and a smile to urge her on.

"The test showed you have Parkinson's dementia, Harry." Her voice quavered, and she cleared her throat to steady herself. "Do you know what that is?"

"I understand, doc. I'm losing my marbles," Harry replied.

Anna noticed his expression didn't change. Had he already realised his mental ability was in decline?

"I can't remember things like I did." He chuckled. "Funny how you can always remember that you can't remember."

"There's no set progression with dementia, just progression. It can take any route over any time."

Harry nodded and lowered his head. "I know doc, que sera sera."

Anna sat with his last words for a moment, *Que Sera Sera* was a song her grandmother adored. Harry would put it on the record player whenever she visited them, and everyone would join in singing.

"We thought we'd try and get you out a bit more, Dad, as the weather improves," Anna said, pushing the happy yet sad memories away. "Maybe take you and Mabel on a few day trips."

Harry lifted his head and furrowed his brow. "Who?"

"Mabel, your — "

Harry chuckled before Anna could finish her sentence.

"Dad, that's sick."

"Sorry, love. Couldn't help myself. There's not much I can do about it but see the funny side."

"I'm not sure there is a funny side," Anna replied, looking to Katherine who was just managing to hold in a laugh.

"Well, you know me. I'll always find one, love."

He was right; she'd always admired her dad for his optimism and resilience. After her mum had died, he just got on with things. He was noticeably sad but made do. She supposed he was a product of his generation, who had seen hardships and horrors the generations since could only read about. Or more likely it was that his generation kept quiet about what they had gone through.

"If that helps you, Harry, then you do that," Katherine encouraged him with a pat on his hand. "I've been meaning to ask you: Did Anna ask a lot of questions when she was little?"

"Oh yes, right little chatterbox she was! And always with her head in a book. Who was it?" He raised a hand as if it would help him think more clearly; it trembled uncontrollably.

"Jane Austen?" Anna replied, guiding his hand back down to the chair.

"Yeah, that's the one, writes all those sloppy romances. Not proper books like crime."

"I won't argue with you there, Harry," Katherine said, "but even I appreciate a gooey romance at times."

"Why'd you ask, doc?"

"An old friend of Anna's has moved back to the village with her children."

Anna interjected. "Laura, Dad. Do you remember her? Jean's daughter, lived at the cottage at the bottom of the high street?"

He nodded. "Oh, yes."

Katherine continued. "She has a daughter, Abi. Full of questions and seems quite taken by the abbey."

"Sounds just like Anna. She was obsessed with the place when she was younger. Didn't you and Laura use to hang around there?"

"Yes, Mum would always tell us not to. She was worried it would fall on us."

"That's right," Harry confirmed.

Anna sensed her dad was beginning to tire of talking; he only had so much in him, so she told him about their week — a lightened, happier version at least. She started with Sunday's Easter bunny trail, then dinner with Laura and the children midweek. He listened intently to her. It saddened her that she'd never been able to and would never make him a grandfather. He really would have been one of the absolute best, just like he had been a father. He'd never once mentioned it to her as an adult, placed no pressure on her; neither had her mum. They'd probably given up on the idea when they found out she wasn't interested in men. A tingle in her face told her she needed to focus on something else before she cried. She moved on to their nocturnal escapades with Virginia's less-than-helpful assistance, which made him laugh until he coughed. They took their cue and left him to rest.

"That was easier than I thought it would be," Anna said as she steered the car to the main road.

Katherine answered with a simple smile.

Having dealt with the Harry situation, Anna had hoped Katherine might be in a better mood on the journey home. Instead she appeared lost in her thoughts. There was so much worrying her, and little Anna could do to fix things or help her. She hoped that tomorrow wouldn't be the start of more problems. Although Katherine was behaving normally, Anna could sense she was trying to contain her worries. From what she'd told her, she had never been at odds with Rebecca before. It came as a surprise to Anna, considering they were both strong, independent women, although it was more likely that the letter from the prison was still playing on her mind.

CHAPTER 20

Katherine woke early on Monday morning. Unable to get back to sleep, she decided to use the time productively by going to work. But after spending the last thirty minutes playing with a pen at her desk, she didn't feel she was quite living up to her own expectations of productivity. Her mind was overactive whilst her body was sluggish and annoyed at having been dragged out of bed before it was necessary.

It was yet another example of how she felt unable to focus or do anything properly these days. Most of the time she felt as if she were going through the motions or watching herself from a distance. As much as she tried to push the letter from her mind, she was angry and growing angrier that it had been sent in the first place.

The injustice of Harry's diagnosis played on her mind too. Not only was he suffering from one of the most debilitating illnesses, now he had the most dehumanising disease to contend with at the same time. Even so,

Katherine held more concern for Anna than Harry. She would have to witness it whilst Harry would become increasingly less aware of what was happening to him.

Feelings of guilt had been weighing on her since they'd spent Saturday night in the tent. How she could hope Anna was Helena was beyond her, even if it had been a dream. It was certainly not a thought she'd had in real life. She checked the schedule on her phone and was relieved to see the day was clear. The word "Pilates" stared back at her. She would be too tired for that at the end of the day; skipping another week would do no harm.

As she finally opened her laptop, she was relieved to see an email with a subject line of 'venue licence approval'. Although being able to hold events at the abbey was a relief for the organisation's bottom line, it would bring a new set of stresses and challenges to the abbey, and to her personally. She was tempted to keep the good news to herself for a little while. The last thing she needed right now was to organise a wedding. She would much rather wait until she could give it her full attention.

Another email held less good news. It was from Mark to say the glass order for the outside of the visitor centre extension had been delayed and wouldn't arrive for another week. Katherine would feel a lot better when there were fewer people on-site and some normality was restored. It now looked as if that was going to be pushed back. Again. At least Sophie would be back on-site this morning; the sooner her team started, the sooner they would be gone.

Anna appeared suddenly in front of her desk. She'd not heard her come in.

"Hey, missed you this morning."

"I woke early. I thought I might as well make myself useful here," Katherine replied, refraining from the truth of being unable to sleep for fear of worrying Anna.

"Has the licence approval come through? It's been twenty-one days, and I'm starting to get anxious."

Katherine gave a quiet sigh and followed it up with a smile. She should have known that Anna would have been counting the days on her calendar.

"Yes, the confirmation just came through."

"Great, because I've just had our first confirmed booking for the end of the summer. One of the couples from the opening, and thankfully only forty or so people invited."

"That's good news, finally."

Anna approached her and perched on her desk. "It also means we can set a date."

Carrie tapped at the open door. "Morning! Sorry to interject, ladies. I just wanted to check that the tent is staying up."

"Yes," they both answered.

Carrie laughed. "Okay."

"Did you get any comments yesterday?" Katherine asked.

"A few people wanted to know if we'd opened a campsite."

"Now there's a thought," Anna replied.

"No!" Katherine and Carrie replied sharply, causing them all to laugh.

Katherine met Anna's eyes and smiled at her. This, if she ever did contemplate leaving and returning to medicine, was what she would miss the most. Anna had been right; they did make an effective team. She wouldn't be half as balanced without it.

Working at the abbey stimulated her in ways being a village doctor hadn't. It reminded her of working in the urgent treatment centre where no two days were the same, keeping her body and mind active. Sitting in a consulting room day-in-day-out gave her no physical stimulation and barely any mental stimulation.

"The venue licence has come through, Carrie," Katherine said.

"Fantastic!"

"And we have our first booking," Anna added.

"Eek! Wedding fever!" Carrie spun on the spot. "Anna, if you're heading back to your office, would you mind grabbing a box or two from my office. The new restaurant manager will be arriving shortly and I'm sure he doesn't want to be tripping over my belongings."

"Sure." Anna answered as Carrie disappeared down the corridor. "So a date?" Anna said, returning her attention to Katherine.

"A date," Katherine repeated.

"I was thinking late summer?"

"Anna," Katherine began but then stopped, unsure how to continue. "Do you mind if we discuss this another day? I just can't think about it now. I've so much on, and to be honest, I don't need another deadline looming."

"Deadline looming? That is honest."

Katherine realised immediately it was a poor choice of words. "Sorry, I don't mean it to sound like that. I'm just constantly firefighting, and I'd rather be able to focus properly on our wedding."

Anna was quiet for a moment. "You're not having second thoughts?"

"Of course not."

Was she having second thoughts? Knowing that Anna wanted children, even if she had tried to reassure her she was happy to not have them, was plenty of reason to be reconsidering. If they married, Katherine would always feel like she was holding her back. Was it even right to marry her knowing they wanted different things?

Although she felt awful doing it, delaying would also give Anna some breathing space to decide whether she was happy with a life that didn't feature children, whether she appreciated it or not. As it stood, she had no one to even invite to a wedding other than Carrie, and she expected she was on Anna's list too. Would Rebecca get back in touch? Or should she reach out first, even though she hadn't changed her mind on what they disagreed about? No, she decided. It was up to Rebecca to accept her decision, regardless of whether she agreed with it or not.

Katherine spotted Sophie approaching the door. "Ah, Sophie, come on in," she said, slapping on her professional happy face. She gave Anna a weak, apologetic smile in the hope she realised this wasn't the best time to have a deep and meaningful conversation about their future.

"I bring news on our skeleton," Sophie said.

"How exciting, take a seat."

Sophie set herself down, opening a folder on the table between them. Anna took a seat beside her, and Katherine wheeled herself over in her chair.

"As we know, the abbey dates to around 1180 and was occupied up until the dissolution of the monasteries in the sixteenth century. Well, the carbon-14 dating puts our remains to 1240."

Anna's eyes widened. "Golly, as early as that?"

"Give or take twenty-five years," Sophie added. She consulted her notes and continued. "He was about fifty years old, five feet six in height with a waistband to match. Here comes the exciting bit."

"It gets more exciting?" Anna smiled. "I'm already on the edge of my seat."

Sophie grinned. "We believe he was an abbot."

"An abbot? How can you possibly tell that?" Katherine asked in disbelief.

"Do you remember when we excavated him? We found this ring," Sophie pointed to a photograph of a gold ring in her folder. "It tells us he was a man of status. It's copper alloy, but it has been gilded, and behind it, there's a point." Sophie pointed to another photograph which clearly showed a sharp point on the inside of the ring.

Anna leaned forward to get a closer look. "It looks beautiful all cleaned up, but ouch."

"Why on earth was that there?" Katherine asked, baffled as to why anyone would make a ring like that, let alone wear it.

"We believe it's to remind them of their position and devotion to God. Arthritis in his kneecaps tells us he spent a lot of time praying, and there was evidence of diffuse idiopathic skeletal hyperostosis from extensive bony growths on his spine. So he was likely obese, which tells us he had a full and rich diet."

"Wow. Anything else?" Anna sat back in her seat and smiled. "Favourite band or flavour of ice cream?"

Sophie laughed. "You'll need a psychic medium for those questions, not an archaeologist. There is more. It will all be in the report. I thought I'd just give you the highlights. My surveyor is on-site today. We're going to mark up the areas for the test pits so when my guys come tomorrow, they can crack on."

Sophie turned another page in her folder, pulled a pencil from her top pocket, and began pointing at areas on a black-and-white, blocky map.

"These are the results from the geophysical survey. As you can see, this square area to the side of the abbey shows clearly where the foundations of the cloister are and where we expected them to be. These dark outlines here are two of the outbuildings. Over here we have a few interesting anomalies we'd like to investigate. There's a large, circular area there and the outlines of something here, which could be more buildings. They aren't on any of the plans we have for the abbey."

"Great, well, we look forward to seeing what you come up with," Katherine replied half-heartedly.

Sophie closed her folder and stood. "We'll keep to the same hours as before and cordon off any areas necessary. We'll be away from the main area of the abbey, of course, but just in case anyone wanders over to have a nose."

"Thank you, Sophie, and just to warn you, there is an empty tent up there. Just move it if you need to. We can remove it if it's a nuisance. We've been using it as a deterrent for unwelcome guests."

"That's a great idea. We'll keep it up, even if we need to move it."

"Just be warned there may be a grumpy cat sleeping in it."

"Ah, how I've missed Virginia." Sophie rolled her eyes as she left the room.

CHAPTER 21

*A*nna played with the end of her pen, unable to focus on her work. She clicked the nib in and out as she stared at the office wall. The atmosphere at Abbey House had changed since Katherine's revelation that she didn't want to set a date just yet, or at all, which was what Anna was reading from the situation. Work had kept them occupied all week, but the situation was now beginning to stress her out.

Her Apple Watch had confirmed her heart rate was up, causing her to reach for her trusty beta blockers to quell her shortness of breath, tight chest, and racing pulse. It was how she had discovered that some of her pills were missing from the box in her dressing table drawer. Katherine was a qualified doctor. Self-medicating was hardly an issue, but the fact that she had taken them without asking was a worry. That she needed them at all was of more concern.

The following day Anna was due to look after the children for the weekend at Laura's cottage. She'd taken

Friday and Monday off work to ensure she could take Laura to the hospital and collect her. Now she was worried about leaving Katherine, who would be picking up the slack at the abbey with Carrie whilst she wasn't there.

She just didn't know what to do for the best. Giving Katherine more time was one option, but time for what? Time would bring a restored abbey, perhaps a restored friendship with Rebecca, but Harry was only going to get worse. These weren't the issue; the letter was — what it had brought with it, what it had opened in her at a time when she was already at breaking point.

Anna understood more than anyone that people came with pasts, and Katherine's was one hell of a past. Experience had taught her that once they let their pasts dominate them, control them and the ones they loved, it was a downward spiral.

A glance at the clock on the office wall told her she had thirty minutes before her potential clients were due in for a tour of Abbey Barn. Enough time to reach out to the only person who could help her. She scrolled through her contacts until she found what she was looking for. Her phone only gave a single ring, as a panicked voice answered almost immediately.

"Anna?"

"Hi, Becks."

"What's happened? Is she okay?"

"What? Oh, no, she's fine. Well, no, she's not fine."

"Anna!"

"Sorry. I don't know why I've called you; I just didn't know what else to do. I hope I haven't called at an inconvenient time."

"For the love of..." Rebecca huffed. "Anna, will you just tell me what's happened?"

"Sorry," Anna replied, sensing her vagueness was irritating Rebecca.

"You've said that."

"Oh, sorry. Oh."

Another exasperated huff came down the line.

"She's not herself, Becks," Anna said, finally finding her words. "She seemed fine initially... after the letter came." Anna was about to say 'after you left', but didn't want to draw attention to the way Rebecca had walked out of the situation. "Since then, she's gradually withdrawn. She has no interest in planning our wedding, let alone setting a date. She's been having nightmares; she doesn't know I hear her at night. I gently wake her and she settles, but it's been almost every night this week. She's been taking my beta blockers and not told me. She's missed Pilates for a few weeks. Her public face is fine, but I know her. Behind that she's crumbling."

"Okay, okay, I get it. Of course she's not herself; what did you expect? She has the best public face in the world. Underneath she's choux pastry held together with thirty-year-old Sellotape."

"I'm sorry for not backing you up last week. She was upset, and I just wanted to support her."

"It's fine, I get it. I was in your shoes once. I'm grateful you called me. I've been worrying about her all week. It's a good sign that she's reducing her workload, and I'm sorry to call your wedding a workload, but at least she's doing something proactive to help herself. It's not good she's feeling the need to do that, but you have to support her in that."

Anna toyed with the handle of her desk draw for a moment. "What if she's so consumed by the past that she can't face a future with me? That's what it's starting to feel like. She won't consider kids because of it. I think I'm losing her, Becks, and I don't know what to do. I can't talk to her… I think she'll end up pushing me away." Tears were now flowing. She hadn't phoned Becks intending to break down, it was the last thing she wanted, but the reality of everything was leading her to fear the worst.

"I understand more than anyone that you want to ease Kat's pain, and the easiest answer is to brush it away and move on. She needs to face it head-on. This is what she was like after Helena died. She seemed to pull herself together a few months after. She hadn't, though. It was merely a loose stitch with some incredibly old thread. It's my fault, I know that now. She refused to get help, she convinced me she was getting over it, and then she broke. That's when I put my foot down and forced her into a fresh start. If you want any hope of children — fuck, even a future — you need to persuade her to get the closure she needs. She has to go to the prison; I fear it's all we have left."

Anna nodded her agreement and then realised she was on the phone. "Okay."

An exasperated growl came back down the line. "Sorry, I know none of this is your fault. I'm just angry at her for taking so much on."

"It wasn't her intention. Everything just been going

wrong, what with the build and then the graffiti, then Dad… The letter was just too much."

"What's happened with Harry?"

"He's been diagnosed with dementia."

"On top of his Parkinson's? I'm sorry to hear that."

"Thanks. He hasn't forgotten you, though. He was asking after you the other day."

"Send him my regards, won't you?"

"Of course."

An awkward silence fell over the conversation.

Rebecca finally spoke. "You know what to do. Good luck. Let me know how you get on."

"Will do."

"Anna?" Rebecca paused for a moment. "Thanks for ringing."

Anna was about to reply when the line went dead.

It felt good to have an ally. It didn't feel great to be working with that ally against Katherine. Rebecca was right, though; she was sure of it.

No more hiding. It was time for Katherine to confront her past.

How on earth she was going to convince Katherine was one problem; what it would cost Anna in doing it was another. Katherine's wellbeing went well beyond their relationship, though, and that was what she would need to focus on.

CHAPTER 22

*A*nna's chat with Rebecca the previous day was still playing on her mind as she woke. It had kept her awake until at least one o'clock in the morning, which was part of the reason she found herself dragging herself through to her dressing room. She slumped into her Chesterfield chair at the dressing table. Her fingers found their way to one of its many depressions and fiddled with the sunken buttons.

She didn't need to get to Laura's for another hour or so, and she'd already packed her bag for the weekend the previous night in the hope it would distract her. It hadn't.

How was she going to raise the letter again without upsetting Katherine? Was there even a way to prevent her from getting upset? Unlikely. She couldn't put it off forever, as much as she wanted to. It was another hurdle standing in the way of their happiness, and it needed to be jumped over, or most likely crashed through, if they were going to get on with their lives. Rebecca was right: It was an opportunity to heal, if Katherine could just find the courage.

She pulled open the top drawer to extract her brush, reminding her she needed to put it in her bag when she was finished with it. The box of beta blockers had moved again, or had opening the drawer simply caused it to move? Opening it revealed that more had gone. There were very few left in fact. She let out a breath, not realising she had been holding it.

The sound of Katherine unpacking the dishwasher in the kitchen below resonated through the floor. There was never going to be a right time to persuade Katherine to visit the man who had killed her wife and child, so surely now was as good as any before Anna lost her nerve completely.

She dressed, keeping it casual since she wasn't going to work, packed the brush into her bag with a new packet of beta blockers, and took it downstairs. She placed it by the front door and headed to the kitchen, half-empty box of tablets in hand.

"Morning," Katherine said through a mouthful of cereal. She smiled up at Anna, who let out an internal sigh, and returned her attention to her phone.

If Katherine was cheery, it was only going to be harder. Anna sighed softly and approached the work surface, her heart beginning to pound in her chest. She placed the packet of pills down in front of Katherine.

Katherine's eyes moved from her phone to the box. She placed the spoon that she was about to put in her mouth back into the bowl.

Anna waited for some response.

Katherine pushed her stool back and carried her bowl over to the sink and placed it down. Her hands gripped the butler sink, and her frame stretched up as she inhaled deeply. "What do you want me to say?"

"Nothing… anything… everything? I don't know. What I do know is I can't live in the shadow of Helena."

Katherine turned in a flash. "You don't!"

"I don't; *we* do. I don't want you to forget Helena, but I do want you to remember me. I'm here; she's not. I know I said I understand why you don't want to go to the prison, but I'm not sure I do. I can't see why you don't want to go when it could help you."

"It sounds like you've been talking to Becks."

Anna drew in her bottom lip and chewed at it. She cursed herself; it was enough to tell Katherine the truth.

"You have." She nodded accusatorily. "You two have been conspiring behind my back, haven't you?"

Anna folded her arms across her chest. "I called her, yes. I didn't know what else to do when I realised you'd been stealing my pills."

"Stealing!"

"It's hardly borrowing, is it? I'm assuming you don't have plans to give them back."

Katherine turned back to face the window.

"Should you even be self-medicating?" Anna continued.

"I'm a — "

"Doctor," Anna finished her sentence. "Yes, I know. Should you be doing it?"

"I know what I'm doing. They helped me after I had

the heart attack. I've not taken them for years. I feel I need them now."

"Do you think you'll have another attack?" Anna had to admit she hadn't given Katherine's medical history an ounce of thought.

"No. They just help me switch off, level me out a bit."

"Since the letter came?"

Katherine ignored her question.

"Will you please reconsider?"

"It will just bring it all back," Katherine replied.

"It hasn't gone anywhere, Kat. It's right here, consuming us and our everyday lives. Our wedding shouldn't feel like a looming deadline."

"You know I didn't mean it to sound like that," Katherine hit back, taking a seat at the island.

"We can chase a time when we feel we can say we are over it, yet none of us get over it. We just learn to live with it better. I've experienced it with Mum, and I let it influence how I cared for Dad. You made me realise that! If this can help you live with your grief better, then why not try it?"

"What if it doesn't? What if going there opens me up to more pain? I can't take anymore, Anna. I've existed with my grief for the last few years. Facing my wife's killer on top of this and with everything else going on is not something I need, thank you."

"But what if it does help?" Anna pleaded. "Do you even want closure? Because sometimes I don't think you do. Maybe you enjoy wallowing in self-pity. Helena wouldn't have wanted you to hold yourself back and not live your best life or enjoy your future."

Katherine's mouth fell open in shock. "How do you know? You didn't know her; how would you know what she would have wanted?"

"Because we have something in common: we've both loved you. I know this struggle you're going through is not what I would want, and if she was half decent enough, she wouldn't want it either. Sometimes we have to go back a little to go forward in the right direction. You can't just plough on in the wrong direction and hope you end up where you want to be. Won't you take a risk? You took a risk with me after you lost her. Why not take a risk again with this letter? With a child? I really think we'd make great parents, Kat."

She'd opened the floodgates, and now everything was pouring through when she really should have focused on the task at hand, getting Katherine to the prison.

Katherine took a long while to respond. "The loss of a child is unbearable," she finally said. "They didn't get their life, or to share it with me. I didn't even get to meet them or hold them."

Anna nodded fiercely. "And this is your chance to tell the bastard that did this what they did to you — what they took from you. If you don't want them to feel better, then make sure they don't. I don't think doing it means both parties agree to make each other feel better, but I believe it could make you feel better."

Katherine shook her head and pulled a tissue from her pocket to wipe her eyes. "I'm sorry, I'm just not brave enough."

"You're the bravest woman I know; me being here is

testament to that. I'm just asking you to remember how to be brave again."

"Look." Katherine rose from her stool. "You're clearly great with children, and I don't want to be the one to stop you from having them."

Anna drew in a breath, unsure where that comment was going to lead, hopeful it wasn't where she thought it was going. She reached out. "Kat."

"No, please." Katherine shrugged her off and backed away. "There's no point moving forward until we know where we are moving forward to. Maybe we rushed into all this, I don't know."

"Kat, please?"

"Go to Laura's. We'll talk after. I think we both need some time apart." Katherine opened the patio door and shut it behind her, her way of closing any further conversation.

Katherine had pushed her away when she needed Anna the most, and without Rebecca to fall back on, Anna regretted ever calling her.

CHAPTER 23

*A*nna wound down the car window and inhaled a lungful of fresh Nunswick air as she waited outside Laura's cottage. She was still trembling from her heated discussion with Katherine. She couldn't bring herself to call it an argument. Whatever it was, it had left her feeling more drained and exhausted than her night of tossing and turning had done.

She jumped as Laura opened the back door of the car and placed her bag on the seat.

Time enough for one last, deep inhale and exhale before she would be in the seat beside her. This was not the time to break down; the last thing Anna wanted was for Laura to think she was in no condition to look after the children.

"Hi," Laura said as she clicked in her seat belt.

Anna gave her a broad smile and drove out of Nunswick.

"So I've tidied the house top to bottom," Laura said.

"The fridge is full. The spare room is made up. My room is ready for me to fall into when I get home."

"You've thought of everything. Shouldn't you have been resting?" Anna asked.

"I have the next few days to rest. It will be weird not having the kids around — though I have to admit that part will be sort of blissful."

"Jeez, thanks for the reassurance," Anna replied flatly.

Laura laughed. "Sorry, I'm sure they will be fine for you. I had words with them this morning about behaving."

That didn't add much reassurance, and it didn't help her trembling. She turned the knob to crank up the heat, hoping some warmth in the car would calm her. Taking on the sole responsibility of two children she barely knew for a whole weekend — what the hell had she been thinking? Admittedly she hadn't been thinking. Laura needed her, and she was there; it was what friends did.

"You all right?"

Anna nodded. "Yes, I'm fine, thanks." She could feel Laura's gaze burning into her.

"You don't look all right. You're very pale. Not more trouble at the abbey, I hope?"

"No, Kat and I just had a bit of a disagreement, that's all."

"I'm sure you'll work it all out. You two are an adorable couple."

Anna raised a false smile of appreciation. "Thanks."

"Want to talk about it?"

"Not really…" Anna meant to stop herself, yet found

her lips had kept moving. "It's just, a letter came from the prison, and the person who killed her wife wants her to join them in some restorative justice programme."

"What's that?"

"They meet, they talk, they move on."

"Sounds a little simplistic."

Anna shrugged. "That's the basics of it. I guess there is a lot more to it."

"And Katherine doesn't want to go?"

"No. Becks — her best friend — and I think it could help her. She thinks she's doing fine. She's been saying that for a few years."

"Whilst not being fine?"

"Yep."

"I can't say I blame her for not wanting to go."

"Would you have if you could have?"

"You mean if they hadn't shot the bastard dead right after he shot Steve?" Laura shrugged. "I don't know. I'm not sure I'd be brave enough. I can see how it might help. If I could give the son of a bitch a piece of my mind, that would have made me feel better, if temporarily. I'd like to ask why he did it, why he ripped a family apart. My counsellor said I shouldn't spend the rest of my life searching for answers I was never going to get."

"Counsellor. See, Kat's never had one."

"Really? For the kind of trauma she experienced. And after a heart attack too. They say doctors make the worse patients, but that's taking it to the extreme."

"Hmm. She's also said she doesn't want kids."

Laura blew a big breath out. "Oh gosh, sorry. That's a bit of a knock."

"Yes. I just feel like sometimes we're moving backwards, not forwards. She's got too much on to plan the wedding, let alone set a very simple date. She said she didn't want another deadline looming."

Laura winced. "Ouch."

"Yeah," Anna exhaled with some gusto. It was good to get it off her chest.

"Grieving can make us very selfish people. We can't cope with the things we can't cope with, and we don't often know what it isn't we can't cope with until we aren't coping with it. And it can happen at any time, even years later."

"I get that; I've lost someone too. When it's affecting your ability to cope in the present day and there could be a solution to help you, shouldn't you take it?"

"Who can say? We're all different, and we all grieve differently. We just have to hope that with the love and support around us we can get through it as we see fit."

That made Anna gulp. Had she been as supportive with Katherine as she could have been? Shouldn't she be pushing Katherine towards a counsellor rather than a face-to-face meeting with her wife's killer?

"Don't worry," Laura said. "You just have to keep talking. I'm sure you'll work it out. You love each other, and that's what matters."

"We're pretty shit at talking actually. We're in that stage of our relationship, you know, where you sort of tiptoe around issues because you don't want to cause an argument. Then things don't get said, and then they build into bigger things, and then, before you know it, she's saying we need some space." Anna stopped and caught her breath.

Laura reached out and placed a hand on her leg. "Start talking and don't stop. That's my advice. And my spare room is yours as long as you need it."

"Thanks," Anna replied. She hoped she wouldn't. The thought of being away from Katherine for any longer than the three nights she'd agreed to was heart-wrenching.

They arrived at the hospital a lot quicker than Anna had realised; she barely remembered the journey. It was always a strange feeling arriving somewhere yet not remembering how, more scary than strange. She was relieved her autopilot had delivered them safely.

Laura insisted that she was fine to be dropped outside the main entrance. She'd keep in touch and be available by phone when she was able to be, and she'd tell the hospital to keep Anna updated.

Once Laura had gone through the automatic doors, Anna found she couldn't face going back to Nunswick just yet. Although her friend had stocked the fridge, she wanted to pick up a few extra supplies for the children, so she headed off to the nearby supermarket.

Anna waved at Abigail as the bus pulled up beside her. She spotted Tom two rows back, but he immediately looked away as if he were going to die of embarrassment. He proceeded to keep ten paces ahead of her and Abigail as they walked back to the cottage. Tom had already let himself in by the time they reached it and had disappeared, she assumed by the thud of bass coming from the upper floor, into his room.

"Have you heard if Mum's okay?" Abigail asked as she passed her pink jacket to Anna to put on the peg.

"Not yet. They'll ring soon," Anna replied with a reassuring smile. She had hoped they would have rung before the children returned so she could put their minds at rest. When Katherine had explained to her what Laura was going to go through, she suggested it would only take a couple of hours to complete the procedure, and then Laura would need time to come round from the anaesthesia. It was too soon to start worrying.

Abigail was insistent that she wanted to complete her homework, so Anna prepared her a snack and watched over her as she worked away at the dining table. The girl reminded her of herself in so many ways. Her mum had always instilled in her the ethic of work first, play later, so she, too, would get her homework done as soon as she got home from school. She hated having things hanging over her, as they were now. Being at odds with Katherine made her feel misaligned. Every time her mind had a moment to stop, it would turn to her and consume her. She was going to need to keep busy this weekend.

Tom appeared within half an hour, in search of food, just as Anna's phone rang on the dining table. Everyone looked at it.

Anna scooped it up. "I'll take it in the garden."

Two sullen faces and pairs of eyes stared at her through the patio door as the nurse explained that everything had gone as expected and Laura was doing very well. She gave a thumbs-up at them to put their minds at rest.

Abigail wrapped her arms around Anna's waist as she stepped back into the kitchen. "Mum's okay?"

"She's all good. The operation went well, and now she's resting," Anna replied, giving her a little squeeze.

Tom grabbed a snack from the cupboard and disappeared before Anna had the chance to gauge his reaction and check that he was okay.

Anna had promised Katherine she would let her know how Laura was, so she tapped out a brief message on her phone. She was angry at Katherine for pushing her away and didn't feel like engaging in anything other than the basics until she had calmed down.

Operation went well. Laura is fine.

A response followed immediately.

Thanks for letting me know. I hope the children are okay.

After dinner, Anna became embroiled in board games with Abigail, who, as it turned out, was an exceptionally skilful strategist.

"Are you just getting me to play the games you know you can win?" Anna asked, narrowing her eyes at Abigail, who had just won the quickest game of Monopoly Anna had ever witnessed.

Abigail tried to disguise a grin behind her stash of pretend money. "Of course not. I just happen to be good at all of them. Can I sleep in your bed tonight, Anna?"

"Certainly not!"

"What about at the bottom?"

"At the bottom! No. I won't have you sleeping at the foot of the bed like a dog. Besides, I'm making the most of a whole bed to myself for a change. Katherine kicks me in the night."

Abigail giggled. "On purpose?"

"No," Anna laughed, then thought for a moment. "I don't think so."

There she was again, Katherine. Focus.

"Right, one last game and then to bed, Miss Abigail."

CHAPTER 24

*A*nna woke a little disorientated. The light in the room was different from normal, and the scent of the sheets was different. Warmth radiated from something beside her. She opened her eyes to see a pair of pink pyjamas and a long, chestnut ponytail. Abigail. The girl must have snuck in during the night.

Careful not to wake her, Anna rose, belted her dressing gown, and slipped from the room. Tom's door was ajar as she passed it. She cast an eye through to check on him only to find the bed empty. Opening the door fully she scanned the room.

Empty.

Hopefully he was just downstairs, having breakfast. She tried to contain the sense of panic spreading through her as she made her way down.

The kitchen was desolate.

She hadn't thought to check the bathroom, and the door had been closed when she passed it. The bathroom door wasn't locked. She gave a light tap and entered to find it too was empty. There was one room left she hadn't checked. Laura's.

The door was open enough that she could pop her head around to see in. Tom was wrapped up in the duvet. She smiled. It was nice to see that beneath the tough exterior he was missing his mum. Both children had been through so much; she was amazed it hadn't affected them more severely.

Midway through her cup of tea, she was joined by Tom and then Abigail. They proceeded to fight over a box of cereal. What was there to fight about over cereal, Anna would never know. If this was what it would have been like to have siblings, she was glad she had been without them. She could have used the help when her mum was sick, though. Would they have spotted that something wrong sooner than she? Perhaps they would have been the attentive son or daughter who would visit more regularly than she had. She stopped her thoughts before they escalated back into feelings of guilt.

"I thought this morning, Abi, that I would take you for a private tour of the abbey. Assuming I can remember all of my tour guide tales."

"Yes!" Abigail exclaimed, wiggling in her seat.

"Do I have to come?" Tom asked. "I wanted to go out on my bike."

"No. We'll only be an hour or so. Don't step outside the village and keep off the main road." Knowing Tom would ask for time alone on his bike at some point, Anna had already checked with Laura that it was okay to leave him to play in the village.

Tom nodded as he took another mouthful of cereal.

"We'll meet back here, and then I'll take you into town and treat you to whatever horrific fast food you want for lunch."

"McDonald's!" Tom put in quickly.

"Burger King!" Abigail shouted over him.

Pleased she had lightened the mood with her plan, she wondered if she'd set herself up for some issues later. Why had she thought they would agree?

"After lunch, I'd like to pop in to see my dad," she said. "I'm sure he'd be pleased to meet you."

Abigail wiggled again. Tom rolled his eyes and exhaled.

"We won't be able to stay very long. He has something called Parkinson's disease, which makes him shaky, and he tires very quickly. So it will be more of a quick hello."

"That's sad," Abigail said, dropping the sides of her mouth down like a clown.

"Yeah." Tom bit his lip in and chewed on it.

"Once we're done there, I thought we could watch a movie, make pizzas for dinner, and consume lots of popcorn and sweets."

A smile finally broke through Tom's lips, and he nodded.

Anna found it strange arriving at the abbey as a visitor, albeit one that jumped the queues in the ticket hall and headed straight into the grounds. Abigail had already seen some parts of the abbey when she helped stake out the Easter bunny trail, so Anna walked her round to all the top spots on her old tour and gave a more child-orientated version.

Tour completed, they swept Tom up from the high street and headed into town, where Anna agreed she would drive through both McDonald's and Burger King since they were within a mile of each other. She cracked the windows down a little; the last thing she wanted was to stink up the car with fried food. Katherine wouldn't approve.

She had hoped to bump into Katherine at the abbey. It would have been unlikely, as she would have been in her office or working from home. The initial anger Anna had felt towards Katherine for pushing her away had subsided, as she predicted it would. Just seeing her face would have lifted her spirits, which were rapidly descending into hopelessness. She had contemplated using the excuse of a forgotten item to pop home and see her, yet she couldn't bring herself to do it. Katherine had asked for a little space, and Anna needed to respect that. A little time alone might bring Katherine to the same conclusion about her well-being as everyone else.

Harry was overjoyed to see Anna and the children as they arrived in the reception area of Baycroft, where Mabel was wheeling him through.

"Anna, look! I've got a set of wheels," he said.

Mabel leaned forward and placed a hand on Harry's shoulder.

"He was so unstable walking and taking forever to get about, I insisted they give him a wheelchair. Now I can get him out and about a bit more rather than him being stuck in that chair." She beamed at the children. "Who are these two youngsters?"

"Dad, this is Tom and Abi, Laura's kids. I'm looking after them for the weekend. Do you remember I told you about them?"

"Yes, of course. Hi, kids."

Tom nodded in response.

Abigail stepped forward. "How old are you?"

"Abi! You aren't supposed to ask people that," Anna said, bulging her eyes at her.

Harry grinned and beckoned her closer. "I'm as old as my tongue and a little older than my teeth."

Abigail laughed.

"No doc today, love?" Harry asked, looking behind Anna.

"No," Anna replied. She hadn't even thought to have an excuse ready for Katherine's absence. "She's, erm... busy at the abbey today."

"Well, we were just heading to the craft studio to paint some pebbles for a new display in the garden. Would you like to help?" Mabel asked.

Before Anna could say they had just come for a chat with her dad, Abigail had answered for them.

"Please! I love painting."

Anna insisted she take over control over Harry's wheelchair, so Mabel led the way with Abigail at her heel.

The craft and hobby studio, as it was duly named on the door, was a large room that reminded Anna of her art room at school. Large windows let in natural light and overlooked a small allotment, which some of the more able residents were busy tending.

Anna leaned down to Harry's ear. "You sure you wouldn't prefer to be in your room watching television, Dad?"

"Oh no, I like to watch Mabel paint. It's therapeutic."

Mabel led them to an empty table where Abigail and even Tom took a seat. Mabel then furnished them with several large pebbles to choose from.

"Anna, will you take part?" she asked.

She was about to automatically refuse when she realised it might be fun. "Okay, thank you." She parked Harry across the table from them and took a seat next to Abigail.

Tom chose the largest pebble, Abigail a small, almost spherical one. Anna perused the pile and extracted one that was heart-shaped. As the children and Mabel were busy with the paints and brushes, Anna picked up a nearby box of acrylic paint pens and outlined the heart shape with white dots, filling the centre with a flood of red. It was nice if a little on the bland side. She'd wait for it to dry and then add more.

Abigail had created a very rudimentary outline of the world and was colouring the ocean parts in blue.

"That's nice, Abi," Anna complimented her.

"It's not really big enough for any detail."

"I've been all around the world, Abi," Mabel said.

Abigail twitched in response to this news, as if she were full of so many questions she didn't know where to start.

Mabel stepped in. "I was a singer on a cruise ship for thirty years. I've been everywhere."

Well, that explained her appearance. She would have

needed to look after herself if she had a career in the spotlight. Age wasn't going to defy her.

"You should hear her sing, Anna," Harry said. "She's a belter."

"Thirty years on a cruise ship. Did you not get sick?" Abigail asked.

"I did a little to start. My body soon got over to it."

"Did your husband go with you?"

"No, I've never married. I couldn't tie myself down to a life like that; I've always been a free spirit. Until I checked myself in here, that is." Mabel smiled thoughtfully and shrugged. "I had to stop at some point."

"Do you not have any children or grandchildren?"

Mabel shook her head. "Which makes it even more delightful when youngsters like you visit us."

The corner of Abigail's mouth lifted. "Do you miss being at sea?"

Mabel contemplated the question for a moment. "No, I don't actually. Obviously, I enjoyed it at the time. The problem with cruise ships is you never stop anywhere long enough to make friends, and the people on the boat always change, even the staff. Don't get me wrong, I made a few lifetime friends. Most of them have dropped off the earth now, so it was time for me to stop and find a new family. Which I have here." She smiled and winked at Harry.

"What is your favourite place in the world?"

"Now that's a tough one. When you've sailed through the Fjords of Norway and along the Nile; illuminated yourself with the bright lights of New York City; walked the Great Wall of China and then the Inca Trail, how can one choose? If I had to…"

Abigail was wide-eyed in awe, her bottom on the edge of her seat.

"I'd choose Cairo."

"Good choice," Abigail agreed with a firm nod. "Have you really been to all those other places?"

"And more. I don't think there is anywhere I haven't been."

"Antarctica?"

"Ah yes, you've got me there. Too cold. I did fly over the Arctic Circle once, though. Perhaps if you come again, we could borrow an atlas from the library, and I can show you all the places I've been."

"I have an atlas at home. I'll bring that." She was all business as she turned to her mother's friend. "Anna, when can we come back?"

Anna smiled at her enthusiasm. Was there anything this girl wasn't interested in?

"We'll have to ask your mum."

Abigail twisted her lips and turned her attention back to her painting.

The first coat had dried on Anna's heart-shaped pebble. She chose a light pink and added a smaller heart within the red heart.

"Where would you like to go, Tom?" Mabel asked, trying to draw Abigail's big brother into the spotlight.

"Whistler."

"Canada, right?"

Tom's face lit up. "Yeah."

"So you must be a skier or a biker?" She narrowed her eyes at him. "I'm thinking a biker."

"Of course."

"I've only been as far as Vancouver. We stopped there when I was on a tour of the West Coast of America."

Tom picked his pebble up and showed it to Mabel. "This is me shredding a jump."

"Goodness me, you're upside down."

Tom sniggered. "Maybe one day I'll be able to. If I keep practising."

"That's the spirit."

A young man arrived with a trolley and dished out tea for the adults and juice for Abigail and Tom. The room fell into silence as they drank and finished painting their pebbles.

"Harry, you look as if you're about to doze off," Mabel observed. "I should get you back to your room."

"If you wouldn't mind, Mabel."

Anna stood. "I'll take you, Dad." She wanted a few moments alone to check in with him.

Mabel opened her mouth to speak, then closed it again.

"Back in a minute, kids," Anna said.

"I'll take them into the garden to place their pebbles," Mabel said. "I'm sure the other residents will love them as much as I do."

Anna pushed Harry back to his room and settled him in his chair.

"You okay, Dad?"

"Yeah, love. Just quick to tire these days."

"It looks as though Mabel's looking after you."

"Life without her here would be very dull, love. She doesn't half liven the place up."

"I can see that. Abigail certainly seems taken with her," Anna said, tucking his blanket on his legs.

"Mabel has far more interesting stories than I do."

"You rest. I'll see you soon."

"Okay, love. Make sure you bring the doc next time. I miss seeing her cheery face."

Anna hesitated and gave him a kiss on the head. "I will."

She wanted to tell him that she missed it too, but that would let on that she and Katherine were at odds. She barely wanted to admit it to herself, let alone worry her dad. That would lead to crying, and if that happened, it may never end. She sucked in a breath and headed back to reception to find Mabel and the children waiting for her.

"All done and ready to go."

"Thanks, Mabel. Right, come on, kids. Let's go home."

They said their goodbyes to Mabel, Abigail promising that she'd be back with her atlas soon. As Anna turned to leave, Mabel pressed something cold into her hand.

"You keep this. I think you made it for someone special. Make sure you give it to her."

It felt like her pebble. She gripped it tight. Mabel was right, and Anna was glad to keep it. She flashed Mabel her first genuine smile and herded the children outside.

"I like Mabel," Abigail said, "and your dad is funny. Do you like her? Is she his girlfriend?"

As always with Abigail, you never knew which question to answer first. One thing Anna did know was to get her answers in quick before she asked more.

"Yes, she is, and I think I might be starting to," Anna said, turning to look at Baycroft, where Mabel was still waving from the entrance.

Abigail and Tom argued all the way back to Nunswick about whose pebble was the best. Already exhausted from the day's activities, their spat was something Anna could have done without. At least the rest of the afternoon would involve crashing out in front of the television to watch a movie. She hadn't quite appreciated how tiring entertaining two children could be, especially with the weight of responsibility for them added.

The spring sunshine was beaming down on Nunswick as they drove into the village and past Abbey House. Anna glanced over for any sign of Katherine, to no avail. It was still early when they pulled up outside Laura's cottage. It would be a shame to coup them up to watch a movie just yet.

"Shall we play in the garden for a little while? Whilst the sun it out."

"Can I go out on my bike?" Tom asked.

"Yes, of course. Just don't step outside the village —"

"And keep off the main road," Tom huffed as he finished her sentence. "I know. You're beginning to sound just like Mum."

They all made their way through to the garden, where Abigail suggested they play swingball. Tom unlocked the shed door and extracted his bike and helmet first, allowing Abigail to scramble about further to find the swingball in the overfilled shed.

"Found it!" Abigail said as she reversed out of the shed, swingball bag in hand. It knocked something inside, which rolled out onto the grass, stopping shy of Anna's feet. She looked down to see what it was only to see a can of spray paint with a purple lid.

Abigail bent down to pick it up when Tom pushed her back and swooped in to grab it first. He shoved it into his back pocket, clambered onto his bike, and was off down the side path before Anna could even blink. More concerned with Abigail to process what had just happened, she helped her up.

"Are you all right?"

"Yes," she replied, getting up. "Stupid twit," she yelled loudly after her brother. "That's the paint Dad used for my bike."

Anna knew it was also the paint that had been used to tag the abbey, and now she knew who by.

Abigail set up the swingball and went on to win every game, but Anna's mind was elsewhere. Should she have gone after Tom? She couldn't leave Abigail alone. Katherine would know what to do in this situation.

Anna decided she'd give Tom an hour or two and see if he showed up when he was hungry. It would give her some time to think about what the hell she was going to say to him. As the light began to fade and Abigail tired of their outdoor games, Anna returned the swingball set to the shed only to spot a metal detector leaning against the side.

CHAPTER 25

atherine flipped back a page in her book, realising she hadn't taken any of it in. She wasn't a stranger to feeling alone, sitting by the fire with a book and a cat on her lap. This time, though, something was different. She was truly alone. In the time after Helena and before Anna, she would have had Rebecca checking in on her every day, if not twice a day. Although they were only in contact once a week now, she hadn't heard from her since she'd stormed out a week ago.

Katherine closed the book and set it aside. It was no use continuing; she was too tired. Successive nights of restless sleep were catching up with her, and she was unable to stop her brain from churning over its worries. Virginia stretched a leg out on her lap. Was she destined to become a lonely, old, cat lady?

She had only spent one night apart from Anna, and yet her body ached for her, and her mind wandered without her. A tear had even formed in her eye that morning at work when she'd placed a cup of tea on the coaster Anna had bought her with the Virginia Woolf quote: "Just in case you ever foolishly forget; I'm never not thinking of you." Was Anna thinking of her now? If she was, what was she thinking? Probably that she could do better than this old lady who can't get over the past and move on with her life.

Had Anna been right? Was she wallowing over Helena? She didn't feel like she was. She had thought she was doing well; she just didn't want to go to the prison and face the person that had killed her wife. As for children, it was perfectly normal for people to change their minds after once wanting them. If it was so important to Anna that children featured in her life, then she didn't want to stand in her way. She'd noticed Anna and Abigail at the abbey that morning. The girl was enamoured by Anna; she had so much to teach a young person, and she would clearly make a great mum.

On that thought, Anna's name flashed up on her phone with a photograph of the two of them at the Palladian Bridge in Bath. Katherine hesitated before answering it. She wasn't really in the mood for the conversation they needed to have. She would tell Anna she didn't want to talk just yet and answered it in case it was an emergency.

"Sorry to ring. I know you wanted space," Anna said immediately.

Katherine was about to object that she didn't want space, she just felt they could use it, but Anna continued, her tone more serious than before.

"Tom's run off."

Katherine sat bolt upright. Virginia shot off her legs.

"I thought he'd be back when it was time for dinner, but he's not. I'm really worried. What if something has happened to him? What on earth would I tell Laura? I can't leave Abi. Could you come over to watch her whilst I look for him?"

"You stay with her. I'll find him," Katherine replied. She was about to hang up when Anna continued.

"Katherine, wait," Anna added in a softer tone.

"Anna, this isn't the time."

"No, it's not that. There's something you should know about Tom. The reason he ran off was because of a can of purple spray paint in the shed… and a metal detector. He ran off with the spray paint."

"That little…!" Katherine sighed heavily. "Do you think he intends to use it now he's been found out?"

"I would hope not. Perhaps check the abbey first, though."

"Will do." Katherine hung up and, grabbing her coat from the understairs cupboard, was out the front door within minutes. She retraced her steps to the abbey that she'd only locked up an hour before. There certainly hadn't been any sign of Tom when they closed; they always carried out a security sweep before the gates were locked for the night.

The light was fading fast. Wherever Tom was, she needed to find him soon. If he had made his way over to the abbey once it had closed, she could bet where he would be. Out of breath, she finally reached the far end of the site and rounded the end of the chapel to find Tom sitting against the wall next to his bike.

"I thought I might find you here," she said. "Anna is very worried about you. You really shouldn't have run off like that."

Tom didn't answer.

Something was off about the way he was holding his hand.

"Are you hurt?"

Tom nodded.

"Let me look. I'm a doctor." Katherine knelt beside him in a flash.

Tom held out his hand to her. "I thought you worked at the abbey."

"I was a doctor; you never really stop being one."

She examined his palm; it was bleeding from a cut. Thankfully it didn't look too serious. "I need to clean this and cover it. Let's go to Abbey House; I have a first aid kit in there. Have you hurt yourself anywhere else? Did you fall off your bike?"

Tom winced as Katherine helped him up. "Yes, I think I bruised my leg when I fell."

"Let's see how you do at walking. Follow me. I'll bring your bike."

Tom hobbled a little as he followed Katherine back across the site. As they reached Abbey House, she leaned his bike against the wall.

Inside the house was now in darkness; the light had faded completely since she left. She switched on the hall light to see Tom was already removing his shoes. Impressed that he'd remembered, Katherine slipped her boots off.

"Come through to the kitchen."

She pulled out a seat at the kitchen island for him and fished out the first aid kit from the cupboard under the sink.

Tom took a seat. "You don't like me, do you?"

"I don't know you, Tom, so how can I not like you?"

He shrugged and placed his bleeding hand in her waiting hand.

"I don't like Anna," he confessed. "She's bossy. She's trying to be our mum."

"You don't like her because she doesn't let you run rings around her," Katherine said firmly. "And she's not trying to be your mum. She's trying to give you some stability and continuity whilst your mum can't be here. And that's Anna all over, giving." She cleaned his hand none too gently with an alcohol wipe.

Tom flinched and sucked in a breath.

"Sorry." Katherine stopped and looked at him. "She didn't have to be here for you this weekend, you know. She could have left you to a stranger's care. Instead she gave up her weekend and annual leave to be here for you and Abigail, so you could stay at home in familiar surroundings. I know sometimes when you're young, and even when you're an adult, it's hard to see what others are doing for you. If I know Anna, and I do, better than anyone, I'd bet she's tried her hardest this weekend to do what she can for you, to make you feel as settled as possible."

He considered this, then admitted, "She bought us popcorn and sweets, and we're making pizzas for dinner. That's my favourite."

Katherine nudged her shoulder into Tom's. "See? Anna isn't even that keen on pizza. That's for you."

A little smile teased at his lips.

Hopeful it was a sign she was breaking through his

defences. It was time to confront the issue, as tenderly as she could. She returned her focus to cleaning his hand rather than intimidating him with eye contact.

"Did you spray-paint the abbey, Tom?"

His leg fidgeted and he looked down at his hand.

"Can I ask why you did it?"

Tom shrugged. "Bored, I guess. The bloody can fell out of my back pocket when I jumped up the kerb. It went into my back wheel and threw me off. I hope it hasn't broken my bike."

"Never mind the bike, Tom! You're lucky the can didn't explode or cause you to break a bone." Katherine stopped herself. She hadn't intended on raising her voice; it never helped in these situations, especially with children. "You're really into riding, aren't you?"

"I used to ride my bike at the BMX track every day where we used to live. Then Mum decided she couldn't be there anymore because it reminded her of Dad, so we ended up in this boring village where there's nothing to do."

"I understand that. A fresh start can help people, though. It helped me when I lost someone."

Tom looked at her. "Who?"

"My wife and our unborn baby."

Any remaining colour washed out of his face. "Sorry."

"Thank you. What is it about biking that you like so much?"

"I like the adrenaline rush. I feel in control, focused. It kind of helps me let off steam." He paused. "It helps me forget things for a while. Then…"

She caught his eye. "It hurts when you stop forgetting

and start remembering again."

Tom nodded as he lowered his head to wipe his eye.

"Sometimes there comes a point when we have to move on, and sometimes we just need a little help to do that. I did. I have Anna now, but... I haven't moved on completely. I still feel the pain." Katherine thumped her chest with her fist. "A wise man once told me that to live is to lose, and if you're not losing, you're not living."

"What does that even mean?" Tom asked.

Katherine smiled at the boy. "I take from it that losing people we love is part of life; it's part of the bargain. We have to accept it. We also owe it to ourselves and the ones we've lost to continue living our best life after, for ourselves and them. It also means we must take chances to find love again and accept that we may lose it again. We can't control loss, but we can control how it affects us. There comes a point when we have to accept that something bad happened, and we have to decide if we're going to let it control the rest of our lives. It doesn't mean we should forget them, though, perhaps just hold them at a distance."

Her words sat with her for a moment, weighing heavy in her gut.

The past was controlling her, and she was allowing it. Did she need to take her own advice and hold Helena and the baby at a distance?

"Nothing will bring your dad back, but right now your mum needs you. So does your little sister. You all need each other. You're going to be the man Abigail looks up to, and so you need to be the best version of yourself. What would your dad make of all this business?"

A smile crept across Tom's lips. "He'd give me a right ticking off. I wouldn't have pocket money for, like, ever."

"Exactly. I know you're angry, and maybe doing this in some way helps you channel that anger, but there are other ways that don't hurt anyone."

Tom creased his forehead at the comment. "Who has this hurt?"

"Myself, Anna, the staff. We work tirelessly to look after the abbey, and to see it damaged is heartbreaking for all of us."

"I'm really sorry."

Katherine placed a hand on his back. "I know."

She rummaged in the first aid kit for a large enough plaster to cover the cut. "It's also a waste of police time."

His eyebrows jumped at that. "You called the police?"

"Yes, of course we did. What you did was a serious criminal offence."

Tom looked down and poked at his cut.

"I'm guessing you are responsible for the metal detecting as well?"

"I didn't find anything. I promise," he replied, fidgeting on the stool.

"I believe you." Katherine placed the plaster on his hand.

"Dad used to take me metal detecting. I found our old detector in the shed when I found the paint. Will you tell the police it was me? I promise I won't do it again."

"I'll see what I can do. But you need to start being the man your dad would be proud of."

"Is my mum going to die too?"

"Of course not, the operation wasn't for anything life-threatening, and it went well. She'll need a bit of time to recover, and then she'll be all better. She's going to need your help, though."

Tom nodded. "Will you have to tell her about what I did?"

"I'll leave Anna to decide that. Come on. Let's get you home, she'll be worried sick. Leave your bike here for the moment. Come and fetch it when you're better."

They walked in silence down the poorly illuminated high street. Katherine was distracted by the thought of seeing Anna after twenty-four hours without her. Tom scuffed at the pavement with his shoes, hands stuffed into his pockets.

"So, what do you like other than riding your bike?" Katherine asked, finally breaking the silence.

"I like cooking. I used to bake with Mum when I was younger, but then Abi came along and she stopped. You're a great cook," he said. "That shepherd's pie was really nice."

"Thank you. I can teach you if you like. Then you can cook for your mum and Abi."

"Really? I'd like that," Tom replied, just as his foot caught something on the path. He picked it up.

Katherine could just make out the spray can.

They walked the remainder of the way in silence.

Tom stopped at the cottage door and patted his trousers. "I haven't got my key."

He knocked. Anna opened it in seconds.

Tom turned to Katherine and gave her the briefest of smiles before passing the dented spray can to Anna. "I don't need this anymore." He disappeared into the house.

"Okay." Anna scrunched her face and took it from him. "Is he all right?" she asked Katherine.

"He fell off his bike. It seems the can fell from his pocket and into his back wheel, throwing him off. He's cut his hand and bruised his leg, and his ego."

"Karma." Anna looked around. "Where is his bike?"

"I told him to leave it at ours. I don't think he'll be riding it for a few days. One of the gardeners rides a bike; I'll ask him to check it over for him, make sure it's safe. I think it's important he has it back soon. It helps him let off steam."

Anna nodded. "Will you come in?"

"No. I won't, thanks. Don't be too hard on him; he's a good one, really. He's just worried about losing his mum, as well as his dad. There's no harm done. I'll contact the police and tell them the case is solved; we just have to hope they don't want to take it any further."

Their eyes caught each other's and held their gaze. Katherine wanted to reach out to Anna, to tell her that she missed her and that she was suffocating without her.

Now wasn't the time.

She flashed her an apologetic smile and walked back down the path. She still had things she needed to think over before she spoke to Anna. Following her chat with Tom, she was beginning to see things differently.

The lack of amenities for youngsters in the village had also set her upon an idea. Although she didn't need anything else to add to her to-do list, she was too excited for how the idea could benefit Tom to give it up. With any luck it would only take a telephone call, the hard work would be down to Tom.

CHAPTER 26

The rain was easing as Anna pulled into the pickup point outside the hospital on Monday morning. It hadn't stopped since Saturday night, keeping them all inside. Sunday had been spent with the children finishing up their homework, then all of them cleaning, watching movies, and consuming junk food. The children were happy with that, so she considered her job done.

Laura was waiting in a wheelchair beside the automatic doors.

"Am I glad to see you," she said. "Get me out of here!"

"Yes, ma'am," Anna replied, doffing an imaginary chauffeur's hat.

Hooking Laura's bag on the handle of the wheelchair, she pushed her friend to the car.

"Do you need help getting in?"

"No, I can walk. They just insist on taking you out by wheelchair for some reason. I wasn't going to complain," Laura said as she eased herself into the car.

Anna returned the wheelchair to the entrance and,

hearing a car horn in the queue behind her, ran back to the car. Some people were so impatient.

"How are we?" she asked Laura, buckling up her seat belt before driving off.

"Not too bad, thanks. They have me on some quite strong painkillers. I'll need to ease off them over the next day or two. I guess I'll feel it more then. There is some discomfort from the stitches when I move. I'm glad I opted for laparoscopic surgery."

"Well, the house is how you left it."

"Miracle."

"Less of a miracle, more two kids being forced to tidy up yesterday."

"Using them as slaves, I like it," Laura joked. "How have they been?"

Anna remained silent for a moment. She had been planning what to say when the question came, but now she didn't quite know if she could say it.

"Oh, that bad, eh?" Laura said.

"No. Erm. Abi has been a delight, of course."

"Of course. And Tom?"

Anna braced her arms against the steering wheel.

"Come on, it can't be that bad, surely?"

Anna decided it would be best to just spit it out, like ripping off a bandage. "He was the one who spray-painted the abbey. He ran off on Saturday afternoon when the spray can fell out of the shed in front of me, and then he didn't come home. Katherine found him later at the abbey, where he'd fallen off his bike and hurt himself. He's okay, though. Katherine sorted him out."

Laura took a moment to think and then sucked in her

breath. "He won't be when I get home. I'm sorry, I can't believe it was him. He'll be paying for any damage."

"You are his mother, so it's totally up to you how you deal with him, but I think Katherine really got through to him. He's apologised. He was as good as gold yesterday. He was nice to Abi, and he helped me around the house."

"Did he say why he did it?"

"He and I had a good chat once Abi went to bed. He said he was sorry and promised he wouldn't do it again. He doesn't seem overly happy about moving; he spoke about a BMX track he misses. I think it's just a case of a bored teenager acting up. He was also very worried about losing you on top of his dad."

"I knew moving would be tough on the kids, but it was for the best. I hadn't quite appreciated that, although it helped me, it may not have helped them."

"From what Katherine said, it seems biking helps him let off steam."

"And I took him away from his BMX track, and his friends, and all the memories of his dad," Laura replied, turning her attention to the scenery. "This is my fault."

Anna bit her bottom lip. "It couldn't have been an easy decision, whatever you chose to do. There was no right or wrong choice, so don't beat yourself up. He'll adapt; kids do, just look at Abi. Tom just needs a little extra support, I'm sure, and possibly something to focus on."

"Thank you for saying that. It wasn't an easy decision." Laura blew out a heavy breath. "I'm sorry for the trouble he's caused. Like I said, I'll pay for any damages. You know, I never even thought about the paint in the shed. Then I'd never had reason to think it could be

Tom. I'm guessing he used Steve's metal detector as well?"

"It's fine, all water under the bridge. The important thing is that he doesn't do it again. He said he won't, and I believe him. Katherine will contact the police and update them. I'm hoping she can convince them we've dealt with it; defacing an ancient monument is quite a serious crime."

Laura seemed to steel herself before saying, "He'll have to face whatever punishment they see fit. Now I'm fixed, I can do more with them."

Anna laughed. "Quite literally 'fixed'."

Laura's mouth dropped open.

"Too soon for jokes?"

A grin formed on Laura's face. "Trust you to make one! Anyway, how are things with Kat?"

"The same. We haven't really spoken this weekend, except for our little Tom emergency. I just feel I've backed her into a corner that she's not going to see a way out of."

"Katherine is a sensible woman. I don't think she's going to do anything drastic either way."

"I hope you're right," Anna replied, exhaling a breath she felt she'd been holding in all weekend.

"At the end of the day you have to ask yourself: do you want kids, or do you want Katherine?"

"I want Katherine," Anna said without any need for thought. "Kids with Katherine would be great, but just Katherine is more than enough. She's everything to me."

"Tell her that. Let her know she has your support, and then show her that support every time a memory of her dead wife comes and pulls the rug from under her. Because it always will — a smell, a saying, anything can trigger a memory, and nothing can tell us how we'll handle it when it does."

"Is this you telling me I'm the arsehole?"

Laura burst into laughter and then clutched her abdomen. "Ouch. Definitely too soon for jokes."

"Sorry," Anna said through clenched teeth.

"So, what does the rest of the day look like for you?"

"I have the day off, so I'm going to make you guys dinner, I'll walk up and collect the kids from the bus, sort them a snack, and head home, I guess. Unless you want to be alone?"

"Having a servant for a few hours sounds like sheer bliss."

Having settled Laura onto the sofa, found her favourite blanket, and positioned the remotes next to her, Anna headed to the kitchen to scour the fridge for the ideal sandwich filling.

"What about ham salad?" she called through to Laura.

"Perfect. Anything would be after that hospital food," Laura shouted back.

The sound of the doorbell echoed through the house.

"I'll go. I need the loo anyway," Laura continued.

Anna could make out voices in the hallway and then the click of Laura closing the front door.

"Anna, you have a visitor."

Katherine appeared in the doorway of the kitchen with a suitcase, which she set down beside her.

Anna froze. A cold chill swept through her body. She leaned on the worktop for support, trying desperately to hold herself together.

"Hi," Katherine spoke softly.

"Have you brought me my things?" Anna asked, nodding at the suitcase.

"What?" Katherine looked down at it. "Oh, yes… no, not like that; it's mainly my things."

Anna shook her head in confusion.

"I'm hoping I can get a bed for the night," Katherine explained.

Anna put the knife down and approached Katherine, her legs steadying at the realisation that she'd misread the situation.

"You want to stay here for the night? Why?"

Laura reappeared.

"It seems the archaeological team have dug something up after all," Katherine replied. "A bomb."

"You're joking? Surely?" A laugh escaped from Anna's lips. This had to be a joke.

Laura looked to Katherine and then to Anna. "I don't think she is joking."

Katherine shook her head; a slight glaze covered her dilated pupils.

"Shit. Is everyone okay?"

"Yes. They've evacuated the abbey and the top of the high street, including Abbey House. They gave me five minutes to pack a bag. I didn't know what you needed, so I just grabbed you a few things. I'm sorry if it's wrong. I don't want to put you out, I could go to a hotel, but… I'd like to be close by in case anything happens."

"You want to watch Abbey House and the abbey get blown up you mean?"

Katherine's face drained, and Anna realised she wasn't in the mood for humour.

"Of course you can stay. Anna's in a double." Laura shot a look to Anna and then continued, "Or you can have the sofa. It's quite comfortable."

"I'm sure Anna and I can squeeze in together. We're well practised. Thank you."

The relief that swept over Anna made her a little lightheaded. This must be a good sign. In the space of two minutes, she'd gone from thinking Katherine had packed her belongings and kicked her out to knowing she'd be sleeping beside her that night.

"Can I sit? I'm a little shaken up." Katherine took the nearest chair before either Laura or Anna could answer.

"I'll make you some tea," Anna said, rushing to fill the kettle.

"No, thanks, I can't stop. I need to go to the pub."

Laura chuckled. "I'm not surprised."

"No — well, yes, I could use a whisky. But they're setting up an operations centre there to coordinate everything from. I need to be there."

Laura looked to Anna and furrowed her brow.

Anna got the message. "I think they can wait ten minutes for you to have a cup of tea. You look like you need it. Have you had lunch?"

Katherine shook her head and then rubbed it.

"I'll make you a sandwich. I'm just making us one."

"Okay, thank you."

Laura slowly lowered herself into the seat beside Katherine.

"I'm sorry, Laura," Katherine said. "How are you?"

Anna made them all sandwiches whilst Laura filled Katherine in on her operation. By the time Anna joined them with a pile of sandwiches, Katherine appeared less bewildered than when she had entered. She tore through Anna's perfectly crafted ham salad sandwiches in minutes.

"Thanks for that," she said. "I feel a little perkier now. Though I could still use that whisky."

Anna swallowed the last mouthful of her sandwich. "I'll come with you to the pub if that's okay?"

Although it was her day off, she wanted to be there. The situation sounded serious, and she didn't want to leave Katherine to deal with it alone. In an emergency, it was all hands to the pump.

"I'd like that. I could use the support."

A little mayonnaise sat on Katherine's lower lip. Anna leaned forward without thinking and wiped it with her finger. Their eyes met as their lips twitched into smiles.

"Laura, are you okay without me?" Anna asked as she cleared their plates from the table. "I don't want to abandon you."

"I'll be fine. I think I'll go for a lie-down before the school bus descends."

"I'll make sure I'm back for them in case you're still asleep. Give me a minute to grab my laptop. I'll take the suitcase up to our room, Katherine."

The prospect of sleeping beside Katherine again sent a tingling sensation rushing through her. The thought that they still needed to talk through and resolve their issues dissipated it sooner than she would like; talking would have to wait.

CHAPTER 27

Katherine examined the open-plan kitchen diner whilst Anna ran upstairs. There were several photos of Laura and her family dotted around on the windowsills. How Laura could have photographs of her late husband lying around baffled her.

"Laura, if you don't mind me asking, how did you move on from the death of your husband? You seem to be dealing with the loss better than I have mine." She looked up and made eye contact. "I assume Anna has filled you in on my past."

"She has yes, and I'm sorry."

"Thank you. Likewise."

Laura clasped her hands together and leaned her chin on them. "You have to want to move on, or at least allow yourself to. It's natural to cling on to grief, it's our connection to the past. I was told to think of it as a bridge. We use that bridge to walk back to another time. As time passes the bridge always remains but we move further away from it, well some of us do, others sit by it…"

"Wallowing?" Katherine interrupted.

"Unable to move," Laura corrected her with a smile. "You have stand up and start walking. I spent a lot of time feeling guilty that I'm here and he's not, experiencing the things with his kids that he wouldn't get to. I've been through a lot of therapy, and I suppose one of the things my counsellor made me realise was that I had a responsibility to make sure I enjoyed that time, and all my time, for him too. That's when I decided to move house and try a fresh start."

"I did too. It just followed."

"Grief isn't a task to be completed; it's an alteration to yourself." Laura stopped a moment to yawn. "As much as we try not to, we'll always carry it with us in some form. I just realised I had to carry it differently."

Katherine nodded. She could understand Laura's feelings of guilt. It was something she felt daily.

When Laura yawned again, she said, "I'm sorry, I'm keeping you from your rest."

Laura rose from her seat, wincing as she used the table to help herself up. "I'm going to head back to the sofa. I don't fancy attempting the stairs just yet."

"Thanks again for letting me stay. I really appreciate it."

"You and Anna are welcome anytime. I really can't thank her enough for what she's done for me this weekend. Well, both of you, from what I understand."

Katherine smiled. "Anna truly is a wonder, and *I* was more than happy to help. There's a good lad underneath all that angst."

Laura tapped Katherine on the shoulder as she passed her. "Thank you for reminding him of that."

"Ready?" Anna called from the doorway, her laptop bag over one shoulder.

"As I'll ever be," Katherine replied as she followed her to the front door.

She drew in deep breaths of crisp air as they made their way up the high street to the pub, where anything could be awaiting them. She sensed a pair of eyes on her; Anna was clearly worried about her. She'd given her a lot to worry about over the last few weeks and would no doubt continue to be a cause of worry. There was so much she wanted to say to Anna, but she couldn't say it all on the short walk to the pub.

"Are you okay?" Anna asked. "The discovery of the bomb must have been quite a shock."

Katherine exhaled with a partial laugh. "One minute I was writing an email, the next I was being escorted into Abbey House by two policemen to pack some knickers. It certainly wasn't what I envisaged for the day," she replied, trying to keep it light-hearted.

Anna gave a light laugh in response and then stopped suddenly. "Shit! What about Virginia?"

"They told me to lock her indoors; she's safer inside than out."

"Makes sense, I suppose," Anna replied, catching up to Katherine again. "Are they sure it's a bomb?"

"Yes, I managed to speak to Sophie before I left. One of the less experienced archaeologists was making good headway uncovering it before Sophie spotted what she was exposing and called the police."

As they neared the pub, they could see the entrance to the abbey and Abbey House were cordoned off and being patrolled by three police officers. A stout man, dressed in military camouflage, with a large moustache resting on his upper lip, was speaking to a local resident. His voice grew louder as they approached.

"We have worked as quickly and diligently as possible to limit the disruption caused, madam. As you can expect with an incident of this nature, public safety has to be our primary concern."

The woman huffed and walked off.

"It's not like anyone else was evacuated from their homes. Only we were within the radius," Anna whispered as they passed.

"People like to have something to complain about, Anna. I would have thought you would know that by now, especially living in a village like this," Katherine remarked as she stepped into the pub.

The pub was a hive of activity. The right-hand side of the bar had been taken over by police officers; on the left-hand side, they found Carrie and Sophie at a table, being served coffee by Chris.

"Ladies, what can I get you?" he asked. "On the house of course."

Katherine resisted the urge to ask for a double whisky; the last thing she needed was to talk to people about such an official matter with whisky breath. They ordered coffee and joined the others at the table. No one spoke for a few minutes as they removed their coats and greeted Moose, who'd appeared between Katherine and Anna's chairs.

"Bloody hell," Anna said, blowing out a breath as she sat.

"Indeed," Carrie replied, taking a sip of her coffee.

The door was opened with a bang. Mark approached them, his eyes bursting with rage.

"You said you'd find nothing that would shut the site down," he shouted at Sophie.

Katherine noticed Sophie pull herself back a little at Mark's manner. She instinctively rose from her seat to create a barrier. "No one could have envisaged finding a bomb, Mark. Calm down, please."

He exhaled deeply and collapsed into a chair at a nearby table, folding his arms over him like a cross child.

The man with the moustache entered the bar. "Katherine Atkinson?"

"Yes, that's me," Katherine said, half raising her hand.

"I believe you hold overall responsibility for the site?"

Katherine nodded, despite her wish at this moment that she'd never set eyes on it.

"I'm Major Terry Martin, retired. Shall we take a seat?"

Katherine retook her seat as the major sat beside Mark. Chris appeared with their coffees and lingered with interest.

"We've carried out an examination of the ordnance and believe it to be a five-hundred-pound device from World War II. I understand Abbey House and the entire site was used for military operations during the war, so it's likely to have been deactivated and reburied, but we need to wait for a unit to confirm before we stand down. Until then, a four hundred and fifty metre outdoor exclusion zone will remain in place. We've got some chaps checking the archive in London to see if there is a record of its deactivation."

"Likely to be deactivated," Mark put in. "Can't you be sure? I've got a ton of glass I'm halfway through installing. If a bomb goes off, it will shatter the lot."

Katherine rolled her eyes. "Mark, glass shattering will be the least of our problems if a bomb goes off. There won't be any abbey to attach it to."

Mark leaned back in his chair as realisation washed over his face.

"Do you know what the military used the site for?" Anna asked.

The major spread his legs a little and crossed his arms. "I believe it was a communications post. They were often tucked away in remote villages like this to avoid the threat of bomb damage."

"How did one end up right next to it then?"

"The Germans might have suspected there was a post here and dropped one, or they could have just been emptying their planes before they returned home; it's on the way. About ten percent of the twenty-four thousand tonnes of explosives they dropped on us didn't explode. They either have faulty fuses or some other defect, and we're still dealing with it over half a century later, thankfully with no casualties."

That was reassuring for Katherine.

"Though they had some casualties in Germany a few years back. A digger caught a British bomb that killed one and left four wounded. World War II is still claiming her victims."

Katherine wanted to refute the use of 'her', if women

had been in charge there would never have been wars. Women didn't fight with guns they fought with words. The Major started up again before she could object.

"My teams detonate approximately sixty a year. The Germans commonly used electrical fuses in World War II, and they stopped functioning when the battery expired." He chuckled to himself and continued, happy to have a captive audience. "Clearance efforts after the war were extensive. Some unexploded devices were either deemed of no risk or too inaccessible for practical removal."

"What will happen if it is deactivated? Will you just cover it back up?" Katherine asked.

"Either way we'll want to get it off-site and detonate it with modern explosives. If conditions allow, we'd detonate an active bomb in situ. Conditions here certainly don't allow for that, assuming you want the abbey kept upright."

Katherine nodded. "Very much so, please."

A noise rang out from a walkie-talkie attached to his belt. "I better get this. I'll send one of the chaps in to get some contact details from you. We'll keep you updated."

"Thank you," Katherine said, standing and offering her hand. The major had a firm grip.

He disappeared, and within minutes a younger man entered with a notebook.

"If I can just get the contact details for a Katherine Atkinson, please."

Katherine stepped forward and relieved him of his notebook. "I forgot to ask the major how long is this going to take. He said you were waiting for a unit?"

"They're the best guys for the job. Considering what's at risk here, it's best left to them."

"Timescale?" Katherine repeated.

"They may not be here until the morning, I'm afraid."

"Backlog of bombs, is there?" Mark muttered as he stood. "Keep me posted, Katherine. I'm going to have to try and put stops on deliveries before we have a lorry car park on the high street."

"Will do, Mark," Katherine said as pleasantly as she could. She was pleased to see the back of him.

He exited the pub as loudly as he'd entered it. Sophie disappeared shortly after to confirm with her team that they were to go back to the office until further notice.

Katherine, Anna, and Carrie remained in the pub to go through the logistics of a site closure for the next day or two. With great foresight, Katherine and Carrie had grabbed their laptops as they were directed out of the abbey. They agreed Anna would update the website and contact the few suppliers they were expecting deliveries from. Carrie was to contact all booked ticket holders to inform them and issue refunds or new tickets. Thankfully it was always quieter at the start of the week, so that didn't involve much work. They agreed it was best for the boss to inform everyone directly, so Katherine would contact all the staff and make the dreaded call to the trustees.

The major reappeared a little later. "The press has got wind of it, I'm afraid, and they're looking to interview someone in authority at the abbey. I'm assuming they want you, Katherine."

An uneasy feeling rose from the pit of her stomach. "I'm not sure I want to appear on camera. I'm not even dressed for it," she said, looking down to remember what she was wearing. She grabbed a mirror from her handbag and then felt a hand on her arm.

"You look beautiful, as always, and you'll be fine," Anna assured her, giving her arm a little squeeze.

Anna's comment brought her a moment of calm. She was right; she could do this. A lot of things were mind over matter. Just get on with it and it will be over within ten minutes. She stood and followed the major outside. Anna and Carrie trailed behind to see what was going on. He pointed to an area down the road that had been cordoned off for the press. There was a crowd of at least twenty people standing there with numerous cameras between them.

She turned to Anna and Carrie. "Buckle up, ladies. This one's going to be a team effort! Stick to the facts and don't be afraid to keep repeating them, and don't let them put words in your mouth."

By the time they had finished talking to what turned out to be three national news stations and two local ones, Gloria had joined them with three of her green slime shakes. Though she was clearly after any extra snippet of gossip she could glean, the drinks were gratefully received after all their talking.

Katherine looked at her watch. "Oh, is that the time? Aren't the children due in soon, Anna?"

"Yes," Anna replied in a tone that could have carried more subtlety. "They might be a little worried by what's going on, especially when they find themselves routed around to the bottom of the high street."

"I'll keep you posted, Carrie," Katherine called over

her shoulder as they strolled off down the high street. "Now go home."

"Will do."

They left Gloria handing out her business cards and speaking to anyone who would listen about the trauma the villagers were going through with the discovery. Katherine found herself picking up her pace as the school bus came into Nunswick. Children's faces were pressed to the window as they took in the scene of police cars and media vehicles.

Tom and Abigail were off the bus in a shot.

"Anna, Katherine." Abigail stopped. "Is Mum okay?"

"Yes, she's inside. Come on."

"What's going on?" Tom asked as soon as he could get a word in.

Anna tried to answer all the questions the children threw at her whilst attempting to herd them down the path to the cottage.

Laura was waiting at the door. "I saw the bus come past. Come here, my babies. I've missed you." She threw open her arms.

They ran towards her, and her eyes widened with panic. She raised her palms. "Whoa, maybe just one at a time and very gently."

Abigail wrapped her arms around her mother's forearm and squeezed it. Tom copied his sister with the other arm.

"Come on in," she said. "I'm sure I can manage cuddles on the sofa much easier than this."

"We need to get some work done before dinner," Anna said as she stepped into the hallway.

"Which I'm making!" Katherine interrupted from behind. "Perhaps you could help me, Tom?"

He beamed. "Can I?"

Katherine winked at him.

"So we'll leave you to it. Shout if you need anything," Anna said.

"Snacks!" Tom and Abigail yelled before disappearing into the sitting room.

"Okay, I'll see what I can rustle up," she replied.

"What have you two done to my kids?" Laura asked with a grin.

Anna and Katherine looked at each other and shrugged.

"I'll have to go away more often, though somewhere more glamorous than the hospital next time. Barbados. Can I book you two for a fortnight in July, please?" She giggled to herself as she followed the children into the sitting room. "Help yourself to the kitchen."

"I'll get the kettle on," Katherine called back.

"I think we're going to need something stronger," Anna said, following Katherine into the kitchen. "It's a shame we don't have any champagne."

"There's at least six bottles in the suitcase."

Anna gawped at her.

"What?" Katherine grinned. "I may have been panic packing, but I wasn't going to forget that."

"Six bottles!"

Katherine shrugged. "I didn't know how long we'd be away. Pop one on ice, won't you? I need to call the trustees."

"Yes, boss," Anna replied on her way up the stairs. "It's no wonder I struggled to get the suitcase up the stairs."

Having only just called all the trustees to relay the news about the graffiti artist being identified, Katherine didn't relish calling them again to tell them about a bomb on the abbey grounds. The only certain thing about the future was that it was unpredictable.

CHAPTER 28

a tray laden with popcorn, biscuits, crisps, and juice was lowered onto the sitting room table by Anna. Tom and Abigail were barely noticeable, sunken into their beanbags in front of the television.

"Keep an eye on the local news, won't you? They said we would be on tonight."

She was immediately bombarded with questions asked through mouthfuls of popcorn.

"You'll have to wait and see," Anna laughed as she tried to extricate herself from the room.

Laura caught her arm and whispered, "Have you two sorted things out yet?"

"No, we haven't had a moment to talk," Anna replied, the laughter falling from her face as quickly as it had risen moments before.

"Well, she's here and she's sharing your bed. That has to be a good sign."

Anna nodded, a smile breaking through. "I'm taking it as one."

Abigail leaned backwards on her beanbag so she was upside down. "Are you both staying here tonight?"

"Yes, we aren't allowed home."

"Is Virginia staying too?"

"No, she has to stay at home and indoors, where she'll have the bed to herself and an all-she-can-eat buffet. Don't worry, she'll be safe there."

Abigail pouted, and then pulling her lips to one side turned her attention back to the television. Anna was about as convinced as she was that Virginia was safe at Abbey House.

Returning to the kitchen, she placed herself opposite Katherine at the table. A welcome cup of tea was waiting for her. Her cold hands reached for it, and she sipped it whilst her laptop woke up. Katherine was already tapping away furiously on her own computer, her tongue clenched between her teeth, a sign of her concentration mode. The tapping stopped briefly, and Katherine picked up her tea. Their eyes met.

"I'm pleased you're here," Anna said. "Well, I'm not, obviously. I'd rather neither of us were here. I'm happy you're here with me, I mean."

A smile twitched on Katherine's lips. She lowered her gaze down to her laptop and then back to Anna over the rim of her glasses. "Me too."

Anna's insides melted into a fuzzy mess of tingles.

An hour later, screams resonated through from the sitting room and Abigail came skidding into the kitchen on her socks.

"Katherine's on our television!" She disappeared as quickly as she'd appeared.

Anna shot up and grabbed Katherine's hand. "Come on!"

"I'd rather not," Katherine protested.

Anna didn't care. She wasn't letting go of her hand, and she was heading in only one direction; Katherine was coming, too, whether she liked it or not.

Three pairs of eyes were glued to the television as they entered the sitting room. Katherine hung back by the door, hand to her blushed face as if ready to cover it.

Anna beamed with pride as they watched Katherine confidently answer all the questions fired at her. She really had the gift of the gab.

"As I said, I don't think we should speculate until we have all the answers," Katherine responded firmly to the journalist. "Once we reopen, I do hope you will all visit Nunswick Abbey and take advantage of our delightful new event space Abbey Barn where…"

The journalist interrupted her with a thank you and turned to the camera to sign off. The room filled with cheers.

"You were brilliant, Katherine," Laura remarked. "They weren't going to get anything out of you."

Anna grinned, impressed by the performance. "Great sales pitch, I wish I'd thought of that."

"Cool as a cucumber."

"Thank you, Tom. Now I think it's time we made dinner. I had a scout about, Laura, and I think you have everything for a spaghetti bolognese."

"Perfect. Thank you for cooking."

"Thank Tom. He'll be doing the hard work."

Tom followed them back through to the kitchen, where

Anna retook her seat in front of her laptop. There was still work to be done, yet she achieved little of it as she couldn't tear her eyes from Katherine as she instructed Tom in the food preparations. He was so engrossed in the process he was even making notes on his phone. He was a changed character to the petulant teenager of a few days ago, and she could state with confidence that that was down to Katherine. She had already and was continuing to prove she would make a good mother. Anna blinked away a moistness in her eyes and focused on her work.

Following what was a delicious meal, courtesy of Tom, they realised they had missed the local news. Anna had no wish to see herself on television. She would only feel the need to pick holes in her performance, so it was best left unseen, if it had even aired at all. The rest of the evening was spent with her teaching Tom and Abigail to play draughts whilst Laura and Katherine watched a nature programme. There was little watching from either of them, more dozing. It had been quite a Monday for Katherine.

Abigail insisted that Anna read her a bedtime story, and having done it for the last three nights, she couldn't say no. She tucked herself beside Abigail, who proceeded to fall out of bed in an overly dramatic fashion.

"Yes, thank you, Abi! My bottom is not that big!"

Abigail climbed back into the bed in a fit of giggles.

"What are we reading? Is it *The Worst Witch* again?" Anna sighed. "Haven't you heard of Jane Austen?"

"Who?" Abigail asked, passing Anna a book.

"Never mind. I'll have to have words with your mother."

The chapters in children's books were remarkably

short, and she soon realised she'd read through five of them. A yawn forced its way out as she turned yet another page. It was later than she had realised. If the creak outside the door was Katherine heading to bed, Anna would need to get her skates on if she wanted to catch her before she fell asleep. She checked beside her and saw that Abigail had already fallen asleep. How long has she been reading to herself? The book Abigail had picked had been one of Anna's favourite stories growing up, and she'd got quite carried away reading it again.

She extracted herself from the bed, nearly falling arse over tit as she did. She hadn't quite mastered the horizontal-to-vertical movement whilst not moving the bed. It was the kind of skill a parent would acquire very rapidly, she imagined.

A faint light shone from under the bedroom door; Katherine was still awake.

"You know what, I never realised how tiring it could be reading a story to someone," Anna said as she entered.

"Isn't Abi a little old for bedtime stories?" Katherine replied from the bed.

Katherine had taken the left side of the bed, which Anna had slept in the last three nights, leaving her the right side as they slept at home. Anna hadn't realised she had been sleeping on a different side to normal. Had it been a subconscious way to feel closer to Katherine?

"Is anyone too old for bedtime stories?"

Katherine tilted her head to one side. Anna had her there.

"I'm going to read for a bit. Do you mind?"

Katherine rolled over. "No, of course not. Night."

"Night."

Desperate for physical contact with Katherine yet deprived, she forced her attention to her book. Katherine was beside her; that was all that mattered. It must have been at least the twentieth time she'd read *Persuasion*, yet if anything could distract her, it was that. It was still in her opinion the best of Austen's books. Her last full novel, published six months after her death, was the most melancholic, most lyrical, most romantic of them all. Half an hour later, as she read the words of Captain Wentworth in his letter to Anne — 'I am half agony, half hope' — she closed the book. She too was half agony, half hope. Did she and Katherine have a future?

As she shuffled down in the bed to get comfy, the movement of the bedding wafted the scent of Katherine to her. It dissipated too quickly for her liking; she was like a drug, and Anna needed more. Leaning forward slowly, until she was an inch from Katherine's back, she inhaled.

"Are you seriously sniffing me?"

Anna nearly jumped out of her skin.

"Sorry, I thought you were asleep," she replied, bracing for further chastisement.

"And sniffing me when I'm asleep is better?"

Anna chuckled. "No. I've… I've just missed you — your warmth in bed, your face, your voice and, apparently, even your scent."

Katherine turned over to face Anna, squinting at the low light from the bedside table.

"I've missed you, too, but I don't want to hold you back from your dreams, Anna. I want you to be happy and have everything you desire from life."

She shook her head. "I don't just want kids, Katherine. I want kids with you. I think the weekend is proof I couldn't do it without you, and if I must do it without you, then I don't want to do it. You will always be enough for me. More than enough. I will be grateful for every minute of every day I get to spend with you. I can't see a future without you in it."

"Are you sure I'm enough?"

Anna fumbled for Katherine's hand underneath the duvet.

"Of course."

Their hands grasped at each other.

"I thought I'd moved past it," Katherine confessed. "I hadn't; I just pushed it deeper. After talking to Tom about losing his dad, I realised I've been letting my grief control me rather than me controlling it. I've decided that I will go to the prison. You're right: It couldn't make things worse, and it could help me get better. When you asked if I wanted closure, I thought about what closure meant. I don't want to forget about Helena and the baby, but I want to put them in a box in the attic."

Anna frowned at her. "Okay…"

"Metaphorically speaking, of course. They're here all around me, and I need them to be somewhere else. At a distance, but within reach, if I want to reach them. If going through with the programme will help, then I'll do it."

"We don't know if it will, though," Anna said softly.

"I'll try, for us. Becks was right."

"Of course she was. Don't you know Becks is always right? Just don't tell her that, eh?"

Katherine laughed. "She knows it already. There is one slight problem, though. I threw the letter away."

"Not a problem," Anna said. "I took a photograph in case you changed your mind."

"You did, huh?"

Their bodies moved closer together until they were tightly bound in each other's arms.

"Did you seriously think I'd kicked you out and dumped your possessions in a suitcase?"

Anna let out a small chuckle. "I might have done, but only for a fraction of a second."

"I'm sorry if what I said made you feel that could ever be a possibility. I just felt overwhelmed. I still do, to be honest. I think I need to work on not letting things overwhelm me. Focus on the things I can change and not those I can't. The abbey is currently out of my hands. I can't even set foot in my house, but I'm in bed cuddled up with you. Harry won't get better, so we have to spend as much time with him as we can and ensure he has some great memories to forget."

Anna spat out a laugh and covered her mouth with the duvet to deaden the sound.

"That wasn't meant to be funny, Miss Walker."

"Then why am I laughing?" Anna asked, poking her eyes over the hem of the duvet.

"Because you have a warped sense of humour, like your father."

"True."

"I'm going to call Becks tomorrow and apologise too."

"No doubt she's been awaiting your call."

Katherine tutted. "Most likely. Now turn that light out,

we've no idea what tomorrow will bring. It could literally be anything at this rate."

"One thing first," Anna said, placing her hand on Katherine's cheek and drawing her towards her. Their lips joined, folding into one another. Anna had missed this. Being physically and emotionally distant from Katherine had been exhausting. She'd felt like a pining puppy. The problem with Katherine was she was an exceptional woman. A woman that stimulated Anna physically and, more importantly, mentally. She could never be without her.

CHAPTER 29

*K*atherine opened one eye and then the other. The room was unfamiliar, yet the face in front of her was a welcome sight, one she had missed the last few nights. Virginia was no match for Anna, though she snored a little less. She slipped from the bed, ensuring she didn't disturb Anna, a technique she'd learned when she'd worked early and late shifts at the urgent treatment centre. She had prided herself back then on never waking Helena.

Dressing felt a little lighter this morning. A weight had been lifted overnight when Anna had reassured her that she was enough. She had felt emotional the previous night when she'd passed Abigail's room and seen Anna reading to the girl. She seemed a natural at it.

A message indicating a voicemail had been left on her phone popped up. She perched on the dressing table stool and listened to it. Staring at Anna, she listened to Major Terry's authoritative, booming voice say things were moving along rapidly this morning. He asked if she could get to the site as soon as possible. She had habitually put her phone on silent overnight and had missed the message when it came in an hour ago. She was going to have to wake Anna.

She leaned over her and stroked the soft skin of her arm that dangled out of the bed. Anna was what she called a messy sleeper; an arm or a leg was always hanging out. Anna turned on to her back, eyes still closed, so Katherine lowered herself over her lips and kissed them. Her eyes finally blinked open, and her lips widened into a smile against her own. Resisting the urge to lower herself on top of Anna and never stop kissing her, she pulled away.

"We're needed on-site now. Things are happening."

Anna leapt from the bed like a rocket and stripped her pyjamas off. It was amazing to Katherine how quickly she could wake up from a deep sleep. "Any idea what?"

"No, the major left a message to say to get to the abbey as soon as possible."

"Give me five minutes."

"I'll wait downstairs," Katherine replied.

She made her way to the kitchen to find Tom and Abigail immaculately dressed in their school uniforms and eating breakfast.

"Morning, you two. Your mum not up yet?"

"I took her a cup of tea earlier," Tom said. "I've packed our lunchboxes, and the bus will be here in five minutes."

"You are organised this morning, well done. I'm sure your mum will appreciate staying in bed."

Tom's eyes sparkled.

"We've been called to the site. Things are happening apparently."

"I wish we could stay and watch," Abigail remarked, placing her spoon into her empty bowl.

"I wish I could go to school and not have to deal with any of it. You must make the most of your youth, children. Never wish it away. Adulthood will come soon enough, along with the full weight of its responsibilities." Katherine let out a sigh.

"I'd love to have your job one day," Abigail said as she packed her bowl into the dishwasher.

"Really?" Katherine was a little taken aback.

"It must be so cool looking after the abbey. You're like the mother hen that keeps everything together."

Katherine laughed at her idealistic view. "It doesn't feel like that most of the time. It often feels like my chicks are all running around the farmyard out of my control."

"Chicks do that." Abigail nodded. "But they always end up back in the coop at night under the mother hen's wings."

Katherine was thrown off balance by this keen observation. Had she been too focused on the things that had been going wrong at the abbey and failed to see all the things she had achieved? Visitor numbers were on the increase, Abbey Barn had been successfully renovated, the visitor centre was on its way to completion. These were all remarkable achievements considering this time last year she was a humble General Practitioner. She inhaled a deep breath and remembered that none of this stood for anything if a bomb detonated that morning and wiped it all out.

"You can keep your job, for the time being," Abigail sniffed. "I won't need it for a few years yet."

"Why, thank you, Abi."

The girl flashed a cheeky smile and disappeared into the hall.

"Ready!" Anna's voice came from behind her. "What were you thanking Abi for?"

"She's after my job. I'm allowed to keep it a little longer until she's ready."

Anna tucked her shirt into her jeans. "You better watch out. I've played board games with her; she's ruthless. Let's see them to the bus and then head up to the site?"

The bus was just entering the village as they closed the gate; Tom and Abigail ran off to meet it. As they waved goodbye and passed back down the high street, Katherine felt Anna's hand slip into hers. She squeezed it, not ever wanting to let go of it again.

"Let's see what fresh hell awaits us at the top of the road," she said.

The top of the high street was as busy as it had been the previous afternoon. Gloria was clearing tables outside the tearoom as they passed.

She waved at them. "This bomb nonsense is great for business."

They smiled and nodded.

"Her business maybe," Katherine muttered. "I'm not sure it's doing ours much good."

"You never know," Anna said. "This might have put Nunswick Abbey on the map, what with all the press coverage. I can see it now, on our website: 'As seen on BBC One'."

"You might just be right. I knew there was another reason I was marrying you other than that pretty face."

Katherine realised as soon as she spoke the word that, although things appeared to be back on track, they hadn't yet discussed marriage. Luckily, the major waved at them before the conversation could continue.

"Please tell me you have good news," Katherine asked him.

He nodded. "The disposal team came in at first light and confirmed that it had been deactivated. They've just loaded it onto a trailer, and — oh, here it comes now."

He rushed off under the cordon and started bellowing for everyone to keep back as an old Land Rover left the abbey car park, pulling a trailer covered in a tarpaulin. Several other vehicles followed, leaving the abbey car park empty.

"Bomb voyage," Katherine shouted as it passed. Laughter spread through the small crowd, which quickly dispersed as the major began to remove the cordon.

She turned to be met by a stone-faced Anna.

"Bomb voyage, seriously? How long have you been waiting to say that?"

Katherine ignored her. "Shall we go and examine the damage?"

"Do you even know where it was?" Anna asked, following her across the car park.

"No. I guess we just look for a large hole."

What they did find five minutes later resembled a small crater rather than a large hole. It was located within a few metres of the tent.

Anna peered down into it. "Wow. I think that's a little more than the gardeners had bargained on."

"I'll call them and see if they can come today. I'm not

happy leaving a hole this large exposed when we reopen tomorrow."

"I guess we can take the tent down now. Virginia will be so disappointed. Can you imagine if we had got up to anything that night we slept in there? The earth might have literally moved for both of us."

It sent shivers up Katherine's spine to think about it. "I'll ask the gardeners to take it down. It seems crazy that we'll be closed today. It's going to take some work just calling around to mobilise everyone again."

Katherine's phone rang out from her pocket. The name told her it was a call she had been anticipating.

"I have to take this; I'm hoping it might be a bit of good news for a change."

"I'll head back to Laura's to pack our belongings, then take them home and deal with Virginia. You get to work."

"Thank Laura for me."

Katherine picked up the call and watched Anna's behind as she walked away. What an epic wobble.

CHAPTER 30

The high street was transformed by the time she reached it. There wasn't a media van or police car in sight. Pedestrians were ambling, going about their usual business. It was as if nothing had happened over the last twenty-four hours. It was astounding how quickly things could change. She'd only been back in Nunswick for just over a year, and within that time her life had been turned upside down.

Those days had felt as stressful as the current ones, though it was a different kind of stress. It just went to show that no one could live a stress-free life; there were just different types of stress and different ways to deal with them.

Katherine finally appeared to be tackling hers head-on. A tingle in her stomach reminded her of the worry she was carrying about that. How would Katherine cope with going to the prison? What if it did make things worse for her? She had to think positively, one of them should, and it wasn't going to be Katherine.

Her gaze was drawn to the old house as she passed it, as it always was. A smile tugged at her lips as she thought of the times Katherine had visited them there. Whether it was to spend time with her dad, cook them a meal when she could see Anna's workload was heavy, or support her on the day she closed the door for the final time. A tightness caught her around her throat as she realised she'd probably never step inside her family home again. Although she carried some memories with her, it felt like there were memories trapped inside the house that she could not access. Blowing out a hard breath, she crossed over the high street.

Anna let herself into Laura's cottage and headed straight to the guest bedroom to pack. Although it was a comfortable room, it didn't beat Abbey House. She was looking forward to snuggling up with Katherine back in their bed, falling asleep in awe of the feature wall before them.

Laura popped her head around the door after a few minutes.

"Sorry, did I wake you?" Anna asked. "I was trying to be quiet."

"I was only dozing." Laura covered her mouth as she yawned. "What's going on?"

"The bomb was already deactivated and had been reburied. They've just removed it, and we have the abbey back."

"Yay."

"So thank you for your extended hospitality, but we'll be heading home."

Laura leaned against the doorframe. "I can't thank you enough for what you've done for me and the kids."

"It's fine, honestly. They were a pleasure — well, Abi always, Tom eventually."

"He's transformed, Anna. Treating Abi with kindness, waiting on me hand and foot. Though I think I'll have to send him up to Abbey House to learn a new recipe. He's already insisting on making spaghetti bolognese again tonight. Not that I'd complain really, as golly, that woman of yours can cook."

"I'll tell Katherine, and it's her you need to thank with regards to Tom. She returned him to me like that. I think maybe she reprogrammed him."

"Good, he needed it."

"I think whatever she said to him did some good for her too. We talked through some things last night, and although we've agreed kids are out of the question, she's decided to go through with the restorative justice programme."

Laura shook her head and folded her arms. "She's brave. Let's hope it gives her what she needs."

"It better. Otherwise I just don't know where we go from there."

"I'm sorry it hasn't turned out as you hoped with kids. You are welcome to borrow mine anytime."

Anna grinned. "Thanks. You head back to bed; I'll let myself out. Do you need anything before I go?"

"No, I'm good, thanks."

"Ring us if you need anything, anything at all, night or day, okay?"

Laura pulled Anna into a tender hug. "I will, thanks."

As she entered the hall at Abbey House, Anna was greeted by Virginia, who was just coming down the stairs.

"Sorry, Virginia. Did I wake you?" A quick tickle under the cat's neck enticed her chin out. Anna hated it when she did that. Either she'd have to commit to a few minutes of petting or leave Virginia disappointed with her chin out, which was never a good look for a cat. "I bet you've slept through all of this — and no doubt on our bed."

She left their belongings in the hallway, hoping she wouldn't receive a telling-off from Katherine later. There was a mountain of work awaiting her at the office, and she was desperate to get to Abbey Barn to get it cleared. She was followed back out the front door by Virginia, who shot across the gravel drive and onto the high street.

Mark's team were pulling into the car park as Anna reached it; Katherine must have called him immediately. She hurried along the path to her office in the hope she wouldn't have to talk to him.

When she finally settled into her office with a cup of peppermint tea, her phone pinged. It was a text from Katherine to say that as the abbey was staying closed for the day, she was going to work from home and deal with some personal matters. Anna hoped they would include contacting the prison; she'd texted Katherine the photograph of the letter she had taken. Katherine suggested Anna stay on-site in case any visitors turned up not realising they were closed and to deal with the gardeners who were on their way to confront the enormous crater on the grounds. So much for a day spent hiding in her office and clearing a backlog.

She finally kicked off her shoes in Abbey House at five o'clock, pleased to return to a familiar routine and surroundings. Katherine was in the kitchen, filling a teapot.

"Hey. It's nice to be home. Did you manage to get much done?"

Katherine rubbed at the side of her head. "My ear is literally burning from the number of phone calls I've made today. Everyone has been informed we are back to normal tomorrow, and I called Becks."

"What did she say?"

"That she had been expecting my call."

Anna chuckled. "I told you so."

"Hmm." Katherine twisted her lips as she placed two mugs on the work surface. "Tea?"

"Please."

"I've responded to the letter from the prison too. There was a phone number on there, so I thought it was best to ring."

"So you couldn't back out."

"Something like that... perhaps," Katherine said, narrowing her eyes at Anna. "I got through to the facilitator who's dealing with it, and we had a very long chat. She talked me through everything, what to expect, how things work. She asked me lots of questions. We went over what I wanted to get out of it and what *he* wanted to get out of it."

"That all sounds promising."

Katherine nodded. "It doesn't stop me feeling incredibly nervous about it."

"Well that's to be expected. And you have these if you need them." Anna tapped the half empty box of beta blockers that was still on the work surface. "I have more."

"Thank you, but I think I will book an appointment at the surgery."

Anna nodded her agreement. This was progress.

"She said she needed to weigh up everything we'd spoken about before confirming if she thought a meeting in person was the right way forward. She said she'd let me know in a few days."

"Can I ask what his name is? We've never really spoken about him before." She held up a hand. "But only if you're okay with that."

"I'm okay with it. Jeremy," Katherine replied, taking a stool at the island. "Jeremy Thacker is his name. There's not much to know... not much I wanted to know. He was a retail manager of a shopping centre. Wife, one child, I believe. He got blinding drunk after an argument with his wife and decided he hadn't had enough and needed to go out for more. Then he killed my wife and child."

Anna placed a hand on Katherine's shoulder and watched as she picked at her fingers. She didn't know what to say in response. With nothing forthcoming from Katherine, she decided it might be best to change the subject.

"What was the call this morning when I left? Was it good news?"

"Oh! Yes," Katherine replied, her voice suddenly full of excitement.

Anna took a stool beside her.

"I've been so busy looking out for the older generation in the village, what with the exercise classes and walking routes, that I've neglected the younger. They're just as bored and more troublesome, as we found out."

Anna tried to hold in the smirk that was crossing her face. Was there any problem Katherine wasn't trying to solve?

"What?"

"Nothing, it's just, haven't you got enough on your plate already without trying to solve youth boredom?"

Katherine steamrollered ahead, too excited to rebut Anna's legitimate concern. "You know that piece of land by the playground, where the village hall once stood?"

Anna nodded; she knew it well. It was a piece of ugly wasteland between Laura's cottage and the churchyard.

"I did a bit of digging over the weekend and discovered it's owned by one of the trustees who used to live in the village. After a lot of persuading, they've agreed I can get a covenant drawn up so they can donate it to the parish council. They only bought it to prevent it being developed into housing, and the plan I have for it will only enhance the village."

"What are you going to do with it?"

"I'm going to get Andy, you know, the tall, lanky one of the gardeners, to build a BMX track for all the children in the village, and Tom's going to help. I assume he'll jump at the chance; I haven't mentioned it to him yet."

"I'm sure he will. I'm not sure the likes of Gloria will see it as an enhancement."

"Tough. If she doesn't want them riding on the road

and outside her tearoom, she'll have to accept they need somewhere purpose-built. It's at the bottom of the village and slightly set back. We can even landscape it to hide it if there is that much dislike for it. We'll set some restricted hours like from eight a.m. to eight p.m. for it. That way the old folks won't be disturbed."

Anna shook her head at Katherine. "You're just like Nunswick's fairy godmother. You swoop in, wave your magic wand, and make everything better."

Katherine smirked. "I like to think so."

"I might just have the perfect name for it," Anna said, stretching her arms out and making the shape of a rectangle with her fingers.

"This is going to involve a sign and a trip to the printers, isn't it?"

"I couldn't possibly comment," Anna replied, leaning forward, and planting a kiss on Katherine's lips.

CHAPTER 31

Katherine lay back against the headrest and closed her eyes. She was not normally one to feel car sick as a passenger, but she was certainly feeling it today. It was unlikely a result of the car's movements, more likely where the car was taking her. The prison's restorative justice programme's facilitator, Sheila, had called a week ago to confirm she was happy to arrange a face-to-face meeting between Katherine and Jeremy.

If she could just get through today, everything else on her agenda was improving. Sophie was finishing her on-site work in a matter of days, having confirmed the location of further buildings in the grounds, including what would have once been an impressive cloister. Mark had pulled out all the stops on the visitor centre and was about to start the final internal fittings. Some impressive merchandise was pouring in for the shop, and Daniel, their restaurant manager, was making a delicious start, having already produced a very welcome afternoon tea for herself, Anna, and Carrie as guinea pigs. Everything was finally coming together at the abbey. It was just her personal life that continued to plague her.

"Are you sure you don't want me to come in with you?" Anna asked as she pulled the car up outside the prison.

"Anna, for the umpteenth time, yes, I'm sure. It's something I need to do alone. I appreciate that you feel you need to be with me, but I don't need to be thinking about you in there, how you're reacting to what you hear."

Anna nodded and reached across the centre console. The warmth of her hand against her leg was welcomed by Katherine. It was a cool morning, and the nerves for what lay ahead were physically affecting her.

"You're shaking."

It was typical of Anna to notice. She thought she'd been hiding it so well.

Katherine rubbed at her arms. "I'm fine, just cold."

Anna raised her eyebrows at her.

"Okay, I'm cold and fucking petrified," Katherine snapped.

Anna turned to face her. "I'm not going to say don't go in there. I'm going to say get in there, get it done, and get out. Say everything you need to. Scream it if you like."

"We're not allowed to scream apparently. The facilitator said they won't tolerate any behaviour that could be seen as combative and unhelpful."

"Okay, let's go with internal screams then," Anna said, taking Katherine's clammy, cold hands in hers. "I just wish I could do this for you."

"I know you do. This is all mine to bear." Her heart pounded in her chest as it had done for the days leading up to this moment. "I could have used those beta blockers today."

"Then why didn't you?"

Katherine shrugged. "I want to feel everything today, whatever it brings."

She opened the car door and slowly got out, straightening the creases in her long, black coat. It was the coat she'd worn to Helena and the baby's funeral. She leaned back into the car for her handbag, which she had preemptively stuffed full of tissues.

"I'll see you in a while then."

"I'll be waiting. Good luck."

Katherine made the short walk to the prison door, forcing one leg in front of the other. Being a city prison, it was built in a traditional style, with high, brick walls and an archway with enormous, wooden doors. She headed for the security booth at the entrance, where she gave her name and was escorted by a guard across a courtyard and into a Victorian-style building.

The guard left her in a reception area where another guard asked if he could search her bag. She handed it over. It hadn't crossed her mind she would be searched. He rummaged through the contents, handed it back to her, and then pulled a flat wand from a strap on his legs.

"Can you lift your arms, please?"

Katherine followed his orders, hoping she didn't smell of sweat. He ran the wand over her body and, content that she wasn't carrying anything questionable, led her to a waiting area. What the guard didn't know was that she was carrying a pencil sharp enough to open anyone's carotid artery, should she choose to use it. A woman could get far when equipped with the correct stationery.

A short lady with a grey bowl cut approached before Katherine could rest her trembling legs.

"Katherine? I'm Sheila, the facilitator." She held her hand out.

"Hello," Katherine replied, shaking it firmly in the hope Sheila wouldn't feel the tremble.

"Come through. We'll have a quick chat, and then we'll start when you're comfortable, okay?"

Katherine followed her into a room with bare walls and worn carpet tiles. A table sat in the middle of the room, two boxes of tissues and some small bottles of water in the centre. She shivered despite the warmth radiating from the back of her neck and under her arms. It wasn't exactly a welcoming environment considering what was about to happen in here. She would certainly mention that if there was a feedback form. Internally she rolled her eyes at her thought; this wasn't a training course.

"Now I suggest you sit here." Sheila pointed to the nearest chair. "It being closest to the door and all. I'm going to suggest Jeremy is seated opposite you, over here. I'll sit between you at the end of the table. A guard will be with us at all times, and he'll sit opposite me. Are you happy with the arrangement, or would you prefer it without the table?"

"It's fine, thank you." The table was her protection, a barrier between them. She didn't feel threatened by Jeremy; it was more a lack of trust in herself to not do something stupid. In truth, she didn't know how she was going to react when she saw him.

Taking a seat where Sheila had suggested, she placed her bag under the table and took out her notebook and her deathly sharp pencil. It was more out of habit that she'd brought them with her. They had added to the false belief that she was just going to any other meeting, that and the formal business attire, another layer of protection.

"Can I get you a tea or coffee?"

Fearful she wouldn't be able to hold the cup steady, she politely refused, and Sheila took her seat.

"Following our conversation, I've typed up some notes with a list of questions you said you'd like to ask. Jeremy has a couple of questions he'd like to ask too."

Jeremy. She just made it all very real with one word. This wasn't any meeting; it was a meeting with him.

"Have you thought of any other questions you'd like to ask?"

Katherine shook her head.

Sheila passed her a sheet of paper which included some basic 'house rules' including that she should listen, be respectful, and not interrupt, followed by a list of the bullet-point questions they had discussed.

"Now, before we start, remember you are free to leave at any time. If you need a break, ask. You don't have to ask or answer anything you're not comfortable with. I will lead the conversation to start with, though you may find you begin to engage with him more independently."

Katherine nodded.

"Are you ready for him to come in?"

Katherine nodded again, wondering if her voice would come to her when he arrived.

Sheila unclipped a walkie-talkie from her belt and spoke into it.

The door opened a few minutes later, and a guard entered, followed by Jeremy. Her breath caught in her throat at the sight of him, she cleared it with a cough. The last time was in court, where she'd listened to him describe that night and how he'd killed Helena. She had thought about him over the years, but now realised she had been imagining someone quite different. Although his height was the same as she remembered, the man before her was much older, greyer, and more forlorn. He had never aged or withered in her mind. Then in a suit, his grey jogging bottoms and plain navy sweatshirt diminished his stature. Her heart rate picked up again, going into fight or flight mode. She took some slow breaths to calm herself.

Jeremy took the seat opposite Katherine and made eye contact with her. She looked down at her notebook, not ready to engage with him just yet.

Sheila went through the rules again. Katherine zoned out, imagining she was walking through the fields of sunflowers on the cover of her notebook.

"Would you like to go first, Katherine?"

Katherine nodded. She remained silent, unable to get her words out.

"Would you like me to speak for you, Katherine?"

Katherine closed her eyes and shook her head. Taking a deep breath, she forced her head up and opened her eyes to see Jeremy still sat there, most definitely not an illusion — as much as she wished it. She swallowed hard, hoping to keep whatever was sat at the top of her stomach where it was.

"Why did you request to see me now?" she began.

Jeremy leaned forward on the table. It was at this point Katherine noticed he wasn't wearing any kind of restraints. Was this normal?

"At the time of the accident, I was thinking about the impact on my life, not others, so I wanted an opportunity to say sorry. I understand how important it is for the word to be said, and I wanted to say it to you, face to face." Jeremy stared into Katherine's eyes. "I am sorry, and I want you to know that I think about it every day, as I expect you do. I don't think there will be a day when I don't think about what I did."

With no words with which to respond, Katherine nodded. It wasn't an acceptance of the apology so much as an acknowledgement that he'd said it.

A glance at the sheet in front of her helped her focus on the next question. She wanted to get through them as quickly as possible and get back to the safety of the car, where Anna was waiting for her. "What were you thinking when you got in the car in that state?"

"I ask myself that a lot, and the only conclusion I've reached is I wasn't thinking." Jeremy scratched his forehead. "I can't believe I did it, that I would be so stupid. But I'd done it before, and nothing had happened. I guess I thought I was in control."

The room fell into silence. Visions of the man in front of her driving into Helena's car replayed in her mind. The sound of an impact she never heard, the hissing of the engine, wasn't that how it played out in the movies?

Sheila stepped in to re-establish the momentum.

"Katherine, what else would you like to ask Jeremy?"

Katherine looked to Sheila, and she urged her on with a nod.

"Can you tell me" — Katherine took a breath and then looked at Jeremy — "what happened that night?"

"Jeremy, are you happy to describe to Katherine your recollections of the night?"

He sat back in his chair and scratched at the tops of his legs. "I'd had an argument with my wife that night. She'd been threatening to leave me and take my daughter. I'd already had a lot to drink... too much to drink. I wanted more. So I got in the car to go to the all-night off-licence near to my house. They probably wouldn't have served me anyway." Jeremy shifted uncomfortably at his words.

This information, facts Katherine already knew, reminded her what a needless and senseless waste Helena's death had been. It wasn't like Laura's husband's death, where he'd slowed an attacker down, physically used his body to prevent harm to others. An intoxicated man wanted to get more intoxicated and decided to drive to an off-licence that probably wouldn't have served him anyway, and it cost Helena and the baby their lives.

"I didn't see the red light... I just didn't see it. I kept going, and then the car suddenly stopped. It all happened so fast, and then everything happened really slowly," Jeremy rambled, his hands jerking as he spoke. "I came round with my head against the airbag. I remember thinking that someone would come and help, someone would have seen it happen. No one was there. No one came. I looked over the steering wheel, but all I could see was the bonnet squashed up, so I didn't realise I'd hit someone. I thought it was a lamppost or something, you know."

Katherine sniffed and gulped.

"I got out, and then I saw the car, and… and your wife with her head against the airbag. The window was broken… I leaned in to see if she was okay."

His pace finally slowed. Katherine bit her lips together to control her trembling chin, fighting back the tears that were resting in her eyes, threatening to cascade at any moment.

Jeremy continued. "She opened her eyes and looked at me. Then, just before she lost consciousness, she…"

Katherine held her breath.

He frowned. "She called out for her cat."

Katherine gasped in a lung full of air and clutched her stomach. She covered her mouth with her hand, and the tears coursed down her face. A coolness swept over her trembling body, and her throat tightened, restricting her ability to draw in another breath. She had to get out of the room. She stood and was instantly swept up by Sheila as she crumpled under the weight of his words. Sheila guided Katherine as she staggered towards the door.

"It's too much, it's too much," she choked the words out as Sheila led her through to the room next door.

"It's all right, let it all out," Sheila said, passing her a handful of tissues. "Sit down."

Katherine took some shallow breaths to try and calm herself, mopping her face with the tissues.

"I… was… her… Kat," Katherine said between sniffs and breaths.

"I thought as much," Sheila replied, passing her a bin for her wet tissues and handing her clean ones.

"I can't go back in there. I can't," Katherine said between gasps.

"Breathe, Katherine. Take a moment, and then when you're calmer, we'll talk, okay?"

Katherine nodded and blew her nose.

"I'll be back in one second. Don't go anywhere."

Sheila dashed from the room.

Katherine sat back in the rigid plastic chair, slowly inhaling and exhaling. Why on earth had she come? This wasn't helping; it was making everything harder. To know that the last word on Helena's lips was her name tore her apart. She must have been so scared. All alone, with just her killer staring at her through the window.

Sheila returned with a bottle of water and opened it before passing it to Katherine.

"Thank you." Katherine sipped at the water. Her throat was tight and achy from crying, making it difficult to drink.

Sheila pulled a chair up in front of her and sat. "I won't pretend this is easy, Katherine, but it's a process. You've heard the hard parts. I know it hurts, trust me, but next comes the healing. Katherine, look at me."

Katherine looked up and met Sheila's intense gaze.

"Trust me. This is my job; I know how this works. You're not the first person to sit there saying you can't go back in, and you won't be the last. If you walk out now, and I'm not going to stop you, you will only ever wonder what might have happened if you'd just pushed yourself that bit more and walked back into that room. You need to see this through; you owe it to yourself and those who care about you."

Her thoughts turned to Anna and Rebecca; they wouldn't let her leave. She had come this far, and already she had learned something, something heartbreaking yet important. What else didn't she know? What else could she learn from staying?

She dabbed her eyes, wiped her nose, and inhaled a deep breath. "Okay. I can do this."

"Of course you can," Sheila said, patting her hand. "If you need to leave again, then do. I'll be right behind you."

Sheila stood, yet Katherine remained seated. She needed a question answered before she could go back in.

"Why isn't he wearing any handcuffs?"

Sheila sat back down.

"He's not a threat, Katherine. We have no need to restrain him. He made a mistake, and he's paying the price of that every day by being held in here. He has a clean prison record and appears to be a model prisoner. He's retraining. He's already completed a degree whilst he's been here and is starting a master's degree shortly in psychology. He wants to help others. Not all prisoners are bad people; sometimes they are good people who just made a mistake."

As much as she wanted to refute it — Helena's death wasn't just a mistake to her — she understood what Sheila was saying. She had mixed feelings about Jeremy's achievements. Was it good that he was doing something worthwhile with his time in prison, or did it make it worse? Would she have preferred to see him in chains, beaten up from ill treatment by his fellow inmates, addicted to drugs and suicidal? She didn't think so, although temporarily it may have brought her some satisfaction. What punishment was enough punishment for someone who'd killed her family? She didn't know the answer.

"Ready?" Sheila asked.

Katherine stood. "As I'll ever be."

CHAPTER 32

*J*eremy and the guard were sitting in silence when they returned to the room. Jeremy bit his bottom lip and lowered his head as Katherine retook her seat.

"Now, Katherine, you wanted to know how this has affected Jeremy, so perhaps that would be a good place to restart."

"Well, being in prison gave my wife the ammunition she needed to divorce me finally," Jeremy said. "She couldn't get past what I'd done and decided she was going to move on with her life."

Did he mean for her to feel sorry for him? It wasn't working.

"Our daughter, she's twelve now," he continued, a smile pulling at his lips. "I don't get to see her very often. I haven't seen her for a few years. After all the arguments about my ex taking her away, ultimately it was me that left her to grow up without a dad." Jeremy bowed his head, his smile washing away with his thoughts.

Katherine clenched her fists under the table. He'd had a child, and although he rarely got to see her, she was alive. It clearly saddened him not to see her, but why should he be able to when she hadn't been able to see her child grow? Wasn't this justice? She pondered what was worse, losing your child before you could meet them or having one you could never see? The thought of the latter pained her as much as her own loss.

She noticed his eyes were pinched tightly together, something she herself did when she tried to prevent herself crying.

"Jeremy, are you okay to continue?"

Jeremy nodded. He took a deep breath and sniffed.

"Perhaps you can tell us what you've been doing to improve yourself since you've been in here," Sheila asked.

"I've retrained as a psychologist." He tried to contain a proud smile as he spoke. "I've started to help people in here. They connect better with one of their own, you see."

Katherine nodded. She could understand that.

"When I get out of here, I hope I can continue coming back. Help people turn their lives around, make a difference somehow." He looked directly at her before continuing. "Then it doesn't all feel so senseless."

Katherine didn't react. It would never stop feeling senseless to her, regardless of what he thought he was doing to make it less so.

"Now, Katherine," Sheila said, "I hope you don't mind me sharing that when we spoke, you mentioned feelings of guilt that were preventing you from moving forward with your life?"

Katherine nodded. "I do feel guilty. As much as I've

tried, I can't get past the guilt. It was my fault she was there at the time. It was me in a hospital bed that she was rushing to get to in the middle of the night. If I'd just slowed down, looked after myself like she kept telling me to do, she'd never have had to leave the house. Sometimes I wish I'd just died and never responded to the first aid treatment. If I were dead, would she have still come to the hospital or would she have stayed at home? Even a few minutes later would have spared them from you."

She allowed her eyes to fix on Jeremy as he looked up and intensely met her gaze.

He shook his head. Voice raised; he finally spoke. "Seriously? You feel guilty? You didn't kill her. I did. It should be safe for someone to drive to a hospital in the middle of the night without fear of being killed. I know we'll both have to live with this the rest of our lives, but we can't both feel guilty. I was guilty, which is why I'm in here locked up. You're free. You need to allow yourself that freedom."

Katherine pushed herself into the back of her chair as Sheila put her hand out to calm Jeremy.

He grasped his hands together on the table, his fingernails turning from pink to red. Exhaling a long breath, he continued more calmly. "Live your life because I can't, and she can't, and your child can't. It's up to you." He shook his head. "Don't feel bad because you're living and they aren't. Feel bad because you're not living when they can't."

Katherine's gaze dropped to the table. She closed her eyes tightly, as Jeremy had done. He was right; as much as she didn't want him to be, the bastard was right.

"This is my guilt to bear, Katherine, not yours," he added, looking directly at her. "You must be exhausted carrying it."

"I am." She wiped a tear away.

Jeremy reached out across the table but, thinking better of it, immediately withdrew his hand.

"Do either of you have any further questions?" Sheila looked between Katherine and Jeremy, both of whom had lowered their heads.

"Katherine, have you got out of this what you wanted to?"

Katherine paused before speaking. "He's apologised and shown remorse for his actions. I know he didn't set out with the intention to kill Helena and our baby, so we have common ground in that we both wish it didn't happen. I understand what led him to do what he did. It doesn't make it any better, but I understand why you were in that state."

"Jeremy, is there anything you'd like to say before we finish?"

"I am sorry for what I did to you. If I could take it all back, I would in a heartbeat."

Katherine nodded. He did appear to be genuinely remorseful for what he had done, and she couldn't imagine living in his shoes, but it was time to think beyond him now. "I'm ready to accept that, and I'm going to forgive you, not because you deserve my forgiveness but because I deserve it. I need to heal. I can't hold all this in me anymore, or it will destroy me."

"Thank you," Jeremy responded blankly.

"Don't thank me. Thank the person you killed,"

Katherine replied firmly. "It's her that's asking me to give it to you. To be honest, I feel she would have asked me to give it to you a long time ago because that was the type of woman she was. I just haven't wanted to. Now I have a chance at a future with another amazing woman, and I'm sure as hell not going to allow you to rob me of that chance, so yes, you have my forgiveness. I will *not* forget what you did to her, to us."

Jeremy nodded. "I understand."

"For what it's worth," Katherine continued, breathless, "I'm pleased you're managing to turn your life around. I hope your daughter can reconcile with what you've done and that you can have a relationship with her one day."

"Thank you. I don't deserve your kindness."

Sheila stretched her arms out, placing her hands on the table in front of them. "We have no follow-up planned, but if anything changes, you both know how to reach me."

"Thank you," Jeremy replied as he stood, taking a cue from the prison officer, who was now looming over him.

"I'll be in to see you later, Jeremy, so you can sign the paperwork."

He nodded at Sheila and then looked directly at Katherine one last time. "Goodbye, Katherine. Thank you for coming to see me."

She said nothing and simply watched as he left the room.

"Feel free to sit for a moment and compose yourself," Sheila said, scribbling some notes on the papers in front of her.

"Thank you." She did need a moment. Her head was

spinning with everything they had spoken about, and her face and body ached.

Sheila popped her pen down. "I hope you don't mind me saying, Katherine, but you've spoken a lot today about guilt. Do you feel by holding on to this guilt that it gives you control over a situation that was ultimately out of your hands? Does the pain make you feel like part of what happened?"

Katherine thought for a moment. Was that what she was doing, clinging on to it still in the hope of changing what happened? Did the guilt make her feel closer to it, part of it?

"Perhaps," she replied softly.

"The universe is hectic and chaotic, Katherine. We have no control. You hold on to your guilt to give yourself hope that you could have changed the outcome. It was a horrific accident — preventable, but an accident, nonetheless. Nothing is going to bring your wife and baby back now. You can work through every scenario in your head to bring about a different outcome, but nothing will change the fact that they've gone and you're still here. You need to allow yourself to move on. You've grieved enough. Remember them, but don't let them haunt you."

That was all well and good to say, but —

"How?" Katherine spluttered, trying to contain her frustration.

"There's no magic switch. You must start by accepting that you cannot change anything. You need to understand that it's okay to move on. Then you'll find you start to allow yourself to, and then it will start to get easier. Lost loved ones want us to live our lives because then they live on. What would Helena say if she could see you?"

"She'd tell me to snap out of it." Katherine laughed. "I think I have; then I realise I haven't. I've just been pushing it deeper, hoping it will eventually fall out of me."

Sheila nodded. "It's a common mistake. The only way out is to confront it. You seem like a woman who likes to be in control, and this is something that needs to be taken charge of. If anyone can do it, I'm sure you can. To fully embrace your future, you need to let go of the past. Stop punishing yourself for something you cannot change. From what you've told me, I understand you have quite the future ahead of you if you can just allow yourself to take it. Love doesn't often come around twice; that much I know."

Katherine's lips curled into a smile at the thought of Anna. "I'm incredibly lucky to have Anna. I don't think I was ready for her to show up in my life when she did, but…"

"She did anyway," Sheila finished when Katherine lapsed back into thought. "Worry about the things you can control, not the ones you can't. I'm a grief counsellor, so if you'd like to talk further, email me. We can set something up."

Katherine nodded. "I'd like that, thank you. I better get going. Anna will be wondering where I am."

Sheila led her out into the courtyard and back to the main gate.

"I hope this experience will bring you some closure, Katherine. I really do."

"Thank you for your support. I'm not sure I would have got through it without you."

Sheila flashed her a smile in response and disappeared back into the courtyard. The guard opened the door for Katherine to the outside world, an outside world that looked and felt a little different. Helena wouldn't have wanted her to live as she was. Anna, Rebecca, Sheila, even bloody Jeremy, they were all right, as much as she hated to admit it. It was time to start looking forward, not back. She felt a profound sense of relief as she stepped out into the sun, a relief that couldn't hold itself in.

CHAPTER 33

Katherine had been in the prison for over an hour, all alone. Anna wished she'd tried to be more persuasive, insistent even that she shouldn't go in by herself, but she had to respect her wishes. She placed her book down on the dashboard and stretched. A yawn forced its way from her mouth as she checked the wooden doors at the end of the road again for signs of Katherine.

The car door opened. Anna jumped an inch off her seat. A figure, who was most definitely not Katherine, sat in the passenger seat.

"Becks, what the…? You scared the shit out of me."

"Sorry." She craned her head to peer out the window at the main gate. "She still in there?"

"Yes. What on earth are you doing here?"

"I cleared a few hours of my schedule to be here for my best friend."

Anna checked the rear-view mirror to see a cab disappearing back down the road. "I'm sure she'll appreciate it."

"Here." Rebecca thrust a takeaway cup at her. "I wasn't sure what you liked, though I assumed living with Katherine you'd be addicted to peppermint tea by now."

"Thanks. It's perfect."

Anna wrapped her cold hands around the welcome cup to warm them. Running the engine of a car to keep warm wasn't something she approved of, not in spring anyway.

"How's she been?" Rebecca asked, taking a sip from her cup.

"She went in a shaking wreck. No doubt she'll come out as one."

Rebecca extracted her phone from her pocket and began tapping at it furiously, so Anna returned her attention to her book. Rebecca was an unexpected but welcome surprise. She had a way with Katherine that Anna just couldn't fathom, though she supposed it came with their years of friendship. She calmed her more easily, and she always said the right thing. Anna was learning slowly, picking up what she could from Rebecca. When Katherine had said she was petrified, every part of Anna wanted to just drive her away from the source of her pain. She hadn't. Instead, she tried to empower her and give her the strength that Rebecca would have.

Rebecca placed her phone on the dashboard and turned to Anna. "Thank you for getting her here."

Anna was about to speak when Rebecca continued.

"I know we may not always see eye to eye when it comes to Kat, but I'm glad you're —"

"Coming around to your way of doing things?" Anna finished with a sly smile.

Rebecca spat out a laugh. "Yes, something like that. I'm sorry, I should have been more open with you, helped you. I suppose I didn't want Kat to replace me. I'm used to being the one she comes to, and if she could come to you for everything she got from me, well, she wouldn't need me anymore."

Anna snorted. "Seriously, you think Kat could ever be without you? And yes, you should have seen me more as an ally than a threat. We both love her and want to help her. We need to start working together and supporting each other to do that. It will only serve Kat's interests more."

Rebecca nodded her agreement. She picked at her red-varnished nails as she took in the surroundings.

"You know, it was me that introduced them."

"I didn't know that. I've tried not to ask too many questions for fear of upsetting her."

"Helena worked at an art gallery in the West End. I'd bought some pieces from her over the years, and we'd become friends. She invited me and a plus one to an exhibition, so I took Kat. I hadn't even realised Helena was into women. I knew she had an ex-boyfriend, so I'd ignorantly assumed she was straight. I'd have introduced them earlier had I realised, and things… things may have been different." Rebecca's fingers became agitated, and her hands trembled slightly. She rubbed them together as if warming them.

Anna finally understood Rebecca. Having introduced the two of them, she felt the weight of responsibility for Katherine's heart being ripped apart when Helena was taken from her. Had she spent the last few years replaying everything in her mind, wondering if she could have done something to make the outcome different?

Rebecca wiped a tear away and sniffed. "Anyway, I'm here for you as much as I am Kat, okay? I'm pleased you called me that day. It must have taken a lot of guts after the way we left things. I know I'm not the most approachable of people. It comes with the job, I'm afraid."

Anna nodded. She couldn't find any words. It was strange to see Rebecca lowering her walls.

Rebecca returned her attention to her phone. Assuming that was the end of the conversation, Anna returned to her book once again, only to realise she wasn't taking any of it in.

On what felt like the hundredth time she'd glanced up to check the road for signs of Katherine, she finally saw her emerge from the prison walls.

"She's coming."

Rebecca shoved her phone back into her pocket and opened her door. Realising Rebecca was going to meet Katherine, Anna extracted herself from the car and followed. Rebecca was one of those annoyingly confident people who knew just the right thing to do and when. In short, she was a leader. Like Katherine.

Katherine made it a few metres away from the prison before she spotted them and stopped, holding her hand over her mouth. Reaching her first, Rebecca wrapped her in a hug as Katherine fell into her arms. Feeling like a spare part as she often did when Rebecca was around, Anna approached the two of them slowly. The two sobbing women opened their arms to her and pulled her into the hug with them.

As they eventually pulled apart, Katherine was almost unrecognisable, her face puffy and red from crying. Anna held her face in her hands and wiped under her eyes with her thumbs before placing her lips on Katherine's.

"I'm so proud of you," she said as she pulled back. "We both are," she added, nodding to Rebecca.

Katherine gave them a crumpled smile. "What are you doing here, Becks?"

"Where else would I be today? Now, shall we get pissed?"

Katherine shook her head and dabbed a tissue at her eyes. "No, I'd like to go and see Helena." She looked to Anna. "If that's okay?"

Anna ran a caring hand down her arm. "Of course it is."

"And then I'd just like to go home to bed. I've never felt so exhausted."

Rebecca put an arm around her and guided her to the car. "Whatever you need, Kat. We're here for you."

Katherine walked away from the car. She knew the route far too well and she'd always walked it alone. Today would be no different. Anna's and Rebecca's concerned faces stared at her through the windscreen as she glanced back. Thankfully they'd understood she wanted to visit Helena on her own.

She followed the recently mowed path down three rows and across six headstones to the left, to the tree with a bench in front of it. It was one of the better spots in the cemetery.

Katherine looked down at Helena's final resting place. She pushed away the mental image of her body, with the tiny body of their baby inside it, lying six feet below. She would have preferred Helena to have a cremation — then she could have spread her ashes somewhere meaningful. They could have been free to roam the earth instead of being trapped beneath it.

There were no flowers or pots beside the headstone. Helena had thought it was depressing to see dead flowers and plants left at gravesides. "What's wrong with simple grass and a few weeds?" she had once remarked.

Katherine looked at the familiar wooden bench where she always sat when she visited, where she always wept. Having drenched it with tears over the years, she felt like it was part of her.

Resisting it this time, she turned back to the grave. "I won't stop long, and I'm sorry I haven't been for a while. I was trying something new this year for the anniversary." Katherine bit at her lips. "It backfired, as the best plans always do. Becks says she popped by to see you, though. She came to see me after. We had a bit of a falling out… over Jeremy of all people."

Taking a deep breath she continued. "I went to see him today. He asked for forgiveness… I gave it to him. I know you would want me to — for my benefit, not his. He made me realise that we make our own ghosts. We haunt ourselves."

Anna hadn't been wrong when she'd accused Katherine of wallowing. She had allowed grief to become a familiar friend over the years, embraced it even, as reflection of the love she lost. It had given her purpose when she had nothing else.

"You're always there in the back of my mind. I hear you telling me off when I do things differently to how I know you would have done them. Then I hear Anna's voice." Katherine exhaled, closing her eyes briefly. "None of this has been fair on her, but then, I didn't expect her. She appeared from nowhere and…" Katherine looked back to the car to see Anna was now out of it and leaning against it. They made brief eye contact before Anna turned away. "…and she consumed me."

Katherine's gaze fell back to the headstone.

"I seem to recall I referred to Anna as an annoying tour guide on my last visit. Since then I've come to love her as much as I love you. Loved you," Katherine corrected herself. Although her love for her was still present, Helena was very much in her past. She knew she needed to start changing her mindset if she was going to move on with her life. Minor changes like this would be a start.

She looked up to the sky as she wrapped her coat around her to contain her trembling, though she knew it wasn't the cool air that caused her to shake.

"I need to take you from my mind now, but you'll always be in my heart, Helena, both you and the baby. I have a lot of work to do emotionally, and I don't know where that will leave me, so I can't say when I'll visit again… or if I'll be able to."

She blew out a slow breath, blinking away the tears in her sore eyes.

"I won't forget you. I'm just going to try hard not to remember you so often, if that's okay?"

Katherine placed her fingers to her lips and then rested them on the headstone. "Goodbye my loves."

She retraced her steps to the car, where her future was waiting for her with open arms to embrace her.

CHAPTER 34

*A*nna woke the next morning, pleased to find Katherine still asleep beside her. The journey back to Nunswick from the prison had been quiet. Katherine had fallen in and out of sleep on the way. When she was awake, Anna left her to her thoughts as she stared out the window. She must have been given a lot to process, and Anna didn't want to push her into talking about it if she wasn't ready.

At the graveyard she'd half expected Katherine to break down, so she was surprised to find she was calm and resolute. She was even more surprised that Helena had a burial rather than a cremation. Katherine had said Helena wanted to feed the worms and be reabsorbed into nature.

Rebecca had made Katherine promise to call her when she felt able, and then they had left her to get a taxi back across the city.

The only words Katherine had spoken on the matter came before she fell asleep. She promised to tell Anna everything when she was ready. Anna hoped that would be soon. She hated walking on eggshells around Katherine.

With an easy day ahead of them, she was in no hurry to wake Katherine. Instead, she left her to sleep whilst she checked her emails and then wrapped a birthday present she'd bought for Abigail. She was assisted by Virginia, who insisted on sitting on the wrapping paper she had rolled out on the kitchen table.

"If you don't move, I shall wrap you and gift you to Abi."

Virginia tucked her front paws under herself and settled more comfortably onto the paper.

Blowing out an exasperated breath, she pushed her scissors along the paper and started again.

She took Katherine a cup of peppermint tea an hour later and found her stretching whilst trying not to disturb a sleeping Virginia, who was now tucked into her side.

"I'm going to run you a bath," Anna said. "Then I'll make you a BLT for brunch and insist we watch some trash on television."

"Sounds perfect. Thank you."

"We can take a walk later if you like. I need to drop Abi's present to her."

"Shall we let Tom in on our little BMX secret whilst we're there?"

"Yes, let's. I can't wait to see his face."

Later that afternoon they made their way down the path to Laura's front door. Anna reached forward and pushed the doorbell, then took a step back. If the noise emanating from within was anything to go by, Abigail was having a party.

As Laura opened the door, the noise washed out around them.

"Do you want to come in?"

Katherine and Anna looked around Laura to see lots of small people bouncing about to the music.

"It rather looks as if you have your hands full already," Katherine replied.

"We just wanted to wish Abi a happy birthday," Anna added.

Laura smirked and shouted over her shoulder. "Abi!"

She appeared in the hallway, skidding to a halt in stocking feet.

"Happy birthday!" Anna and Katherine said together.

Abigail's eyes lit up as Anna extracted a present from her bag and passed it to her.

"Can I open it now?"

"Of course."

Abigail tore the paper off to reveal a book. "*Pride and Prejudice* by Jane Austen." She looked up at Anna. "You mentioned her."

"Well remembered."

"Thank you. I'll start it tonight."

A small girl arrived at Abigail's side and dragged her back to her party.

"Trust you to give a book as a present," Laura commented.

Anna beamed, taking it as a compliment.

"Is Tom about?" Katherine asked. "We thought we'd show him his surprise."

"Ah, yes. He's going to be over the moon. I really can't thank you enough for what you're doing for him. I'm not sure he deserves it after all the trouble he's caused you."

"He has a lot of hard work ahead of him, enough to keep him out of trouble for a while," Katherine replied.

"He's hiding in his room away from this lot." Laura extracted her phone and tapped on it, clearly sending her son a message. Tom appeared at the foot of the stairs a few moments later. "Pop your shoes on. These ladies have something to show you."

Tom did as he was told and followed Anna and Katherine down the path.

"Is this a rescue mission? Abi's friends are so loud. I can't even drown them out with my headphones."

"Something like that."

"Where are we going?" he asked.

Before long, they stopped beside the area of wasteland.

"Here," Anna said.

Tom frowned. "The playground?"

"No, the BMX track," Katherine corrected him.

Tom's eyes darted between the two of them. "What BMX track?"

"The one you're going to build here," Katherine said, leaning on the fence.

"Are you serious? I can build a track here?"

Anna nodded and pulled another package out from the bag. "And this is for you."

Tom twitched his eyebrows as he took it. "It's not my birthday. It's Abi's."

"I know. I don't think she'll mind. Open it."

Tom tore at the brown wrapping paper to reveal a metal sign that read 'Steve's Acre'.

"I thought you could put it on the fence somewhere," Anna continued.

Tom nodded as he stared at the sign. "I can't believe it. Thank you. I can't wait to get started."

"Well, don't get too carried away," Katherine added quickly. "Andy, one of my gardeners, is going to help you with it. He'll come and talk it over with you and make a plan. He has a lot of experience building these things, and he's great with a spade."

Tom nodded and wandered off over the rough grass, working out potential routes with an imaginary bike.

Katherine held her arm out for Anna to link into. "Miss Walker, would you care to take a turn with me to watch the sunset over the abbey?"

"I don't mind if I do."

As they ambled back up the high street, Anna noticed the front door to her old house was open. She strained to catch a glimpse inside and then stopped, setting her sights on the top of the high street where Abbey House dominated the view. It was time to look forward, not back, as she'd been telling Katherine.

"The visitor centre looks great now all the scaffolding has come down," she remarked as they passed it.

Katherine sighed. "Was it worth all the effort?"

"Things that take the most effort are often the ones worth having. Like us." Anna squeezed Katherine's arm.

"I hope that's not really how you see our relationship," Katherine replied.

"Sorry, I don't mean it's an effort being with you, just that we've had to battle a lot of external forces."

"That we have," Katherine agreed.

They made their way across the abbey site to a bench which was perfect for watching the sun set behind the abbey.

"The gardeners did a remarkable job filling that bomb hole," Anna said. "It will be nice when Sophie has filled in all her trenches too. Just think, by next weekend we could have normality restored at the abbey."

Katherine collapsed onto the bench beside her. "That is a time I look forward to."

A scratching noise drew their attention to the nearest trench. They furrowed their eyebrows at each other and then glanced back to the trench to see Virginia jump out.

"Virginia, have you been using that as a litter tray? What a surprise for Sophie on Monday." Katherine chuckled.

Virginia approached them, rubbing herself against both their legs before disappearing under the bench.

Anna shook her head. "You'd never catch a dog doing that."

"No, they don't even try to bury it."

Anna nudged herself into Katherine, and they fell into silence. The abbey was such a peaceful spot to while away time. She didn't believe there was anywhere in the world she felt happier, especially with her gorgeous fiancée sitting next to her. Assuming Katherine still had that intention.

"Katherine…"

She turned to face her. Anna sensed she already knew what she was about to ask.

"You want to know what happened at the prison?"

Anna nodded. "Only if you're ready to talk about it."

"I am."

Anna took her hand and listened as Katherine described her initial impression of the prison. The depressing shadows the high walls cast over the courtyard. The smell: a combination of the disinfectant of a hospital ward and the sweat from a gymnasium. The bare walls. The feeling of claustrophobia despite knowing she could leave at any time. How she'd only just held herself together as Jeremy had entered. Helena's last word.

Anna felt tears forming in her eyes. How had Katherine got through it? How was she holding herself together as she recounted it now?

"It felt like, for the first time, I was given a voice. A chance to be heard. Answers I've always needed." Katherine looked down at their joined hands. "I gave him my forgiveness and Helena's; it's what she would have wanted. She could never bear a grudge."

"I'm sure that's more than he deserved."

"It was," Katherine quickly agreed, looking up. "Yet it was important for me to give. I didn't go in there with any intention of giving it, but I could see that giving it would force me to accept what had happened. Once it was accepted, I realised there was no changing the outcome."

"I get that."

"That man deprived me of one future. I'm sure as hell not going to let him deprive me of another." Katherine turned to Anna. "I would like to have children with you but on one condition."

"We adopt?" Anna interrupted her with a hopeful smile.

"Yes." Katherine's face softened with relief. "Are you sure you're okay with that?"

"Of course. I know how difficult it would be for you to watch a pregnancy evolve and not compare it to the past. We're looking to the future from now on, yeah?"

Katherine nodded.

"So we'll do things differently," Anna continued. "Hopefully, this way we can help some kids who need it. There is a point I'd like to raise, though."

"Go on."

"I sense that a weight, albeit small, has been lifted since the visit, but I think you have PTSD. I'm going to insist you get therapy." It was something that had bugged her since she'd first become acquainted with Katherine. The woman had experienced the worst trauma imaginable yet had received no professional emotional support in dealing with it. If any blame was to be laid for it, it was to be laid at Rebecca's door. Not that Anna had the intention of airing that fact.

"Okay," Katherine replied softly.

"No arguments?"

"No, I think you're right. I am feeling lighter, but I don't think it will hurt to talk it through with a professional. I feel stupid for not doing it sooner."

"Doctors make the worst patients, I hear."

Katherine nudged her shoulder into Anna "Sheila offered her services, so I think I'll get back in touch with her. She was nice, and she knows my history. It makes sense."

Anna nodded. "One other thing, actually."

Katherine rolled her eyes at what was becoming a list of demands. "Yes?"

"Back to Pilates, and I'm going to join you."

"Oh," Katherine said cheekily. "You in Lycra…"

"I might need to borrow a pair of yours."

"I'm sure that can be arranged. I'll even help you into them."

A smile spread across Anna's face, yet one thing remained unresolved. "Do you think we can set a date and plan our wedding?" she asked, hoping she wasn't pushing Katherine too much.

"To be perfectly honest, Anna, I just want to marry you. I don't want to plan and wait. I really don't care about flowers, dresses, or invitations. I don't have anyone to invite anyway."

Anna chuckled. "Me neither!"

"Then why were we looking at samples?"

"I thought you would have a huge list."

Katherine shook her head. "You, Harry, and Becks are all I have in the world."

"Then we better work on making us a bigger family."

"All in good time. Let's get married, get the abbey back into some semblance of a routine first. Shall I ring the registry office and see when the next registrar is available?"

Anna turned to face Katherine with her eyebrows raised. Although it was the best answer Anna could have hoped for, she still couldn't believe it. "You're serious?"

"More than I've ever been. We can give the barn a trial run."

A smile radiated from Anna's face. "Yes, okay, yes," she replied, pulling her into a hug and then placing her impatient lips against Katherine's.

atherine stood in the hallway of Abbey House and admired herself in the full-length mirror. She rearranged a few strands of hair from the loosely finished up-do that she'd chosen specifically because she knew it made Anna weak at the knees. Anna had also let on that morning that she would wear hers down, so the hairstyle would also add some contrast between the two of them.

As she smoothed out her ivory, knee-length dress and straightened her matching jacket, her eyes caught the necklace that lay delicately around her neck. Twiddling the diamond pendant between her fingers, she thought back to Christmas when Anna had given it to her. Her heart had skipped when she'd unwrapped it, only to find the box was identical to the one Margaret had given her. Thankfully the contents of Anna's box were far more to her taste. A flush of coolness swept over her as she remembered Margaret's betrayal. She shivered and pulled her thoughts away, determined not to muddy her gorgeous necklace with memories of Margaret or her own ignorance of the woman's actions.

The front door opened, and Rebecca stepped into the hall in an A-line, floor-length dress in dusky pink. She placed two bouquets on the hall table and then hitched up the gown's V-neck. "Right, I've taken the flowers to the barn and left Gloria fussing over them. Carrie was showing the registrars through to her office as I left. You've really have worked wonders on that building; it's quite transformed."

"Thank you."

"Where's Anna?"

"Upstairs. Laura's giving her a hand. Harry and Mabel are entertaining the children in the sitting room or possibly the other way around. Thanks for picking them up on the way."

"No problem, his carer said she'd arrange to collect them later on."

"How is my little gift for Anna?"

"Safely hidden away in her office. Carrie said she'd keep an eye out."

Rebecca picked a bit of fluff off Katherine's jacket. "Decided not to go for a traditional dress then?"

"I thought I'd let Anna have that pleasure since I've already done the elaborate wedding dress."

Her thoughts fell back to her first wedding; it had been quite the big, traditional event. Katherine would have been happy with a small ceremony, yet Helena insisted on the full works. She'd said at the time that they were only getting married once, so they might as well do it in style. Katherine took in a deep breath. Here she was doing it again, which was fine. Helena was gone, and Katherine deserved every happiness she could find with Anna.

"She'd be proud of you if she could see you now," Rebecca said, smoothing the material back down with her fingers.

"I know she would." Katherine's heart warmed at the fact that Rebecca's thoughts had drifted to the same place. She checked her watch as she had been every few minutes since she'd got up. "Right, it's two forty. That gives us a few minutes for champagne. There's a half-full bottle left that Laura and Anna started, and you know me, I can't have a half-finished bottle in the house."

"Damn right." Rebecca chuckled as she followed Katherine through the sitting room to the kitchen. Four faces were staring at two presenters on the television as they warmed the audience up for an impending football match.

"I'm intrigued," Rebecca continued as they reached the kitchen. "How did you get a registrar at such short notice?"

"I offered them a lifetime membership to the abbey."

Rebecca's face fell flat. "You bribed a government official?"

"Of course not." Katherine rolled her eyes. "They had a cancellation."

"A cancellation that so happened to coincide with your birthday?"

"Shh," Katherine hissed, checking if anyone in the sitting room had overheard. She extracted the open bottle of champagne from the fridge. "No one knows but you and Anna. I really don't want any fuss, reminders, or surprises, thank you."

Rebecca laughed at her as she fetched down two flutes. "Your secret is safe with me… if you insist."

"I do. I don't want anything to overshadow today."

"Not even your half-century?"

Katherine passed a glass over to her. "Not even that."

"In that case, happy birthday, my dear friend."

Katherine clinked Rebecca's glass. "Thank you."

Rebecca downed the champagne in one go. "Right, let's get the two of you wed."

"Yes, let's." Katherine followed suit and drained her glass. "You take everyone over, and we'll join you in a few minutes."

"Right, everyone!" Rebecca clapped as she entered the sitting room. "Off we go. We've got a wedding to attend."

Katherine watched as Rebecca herded everyone out. Harry was managed between her and Mabel. Once the house had fallen silent, Katherine walked through to the hallway where Laura was slipping out the front door.

Her breath caught in her throat as she looked up the stairs to see Anna in a floor-length, A-line, ivory wedding dress. Long curls cascaded over her shoulders and down her long, lace sleeves. Katherine drank her in as she descended the stairs. The small hint of make-up enhanced her bold, brown eyes, and her subtle red lips glistened, calling out to be kissed. How was Anna hers?

"You look… breathtaking," she said, the truth in this case. "It's a beautiful dress. Sadly, all I'm going to be thinking about is getting you out of it later."

Anna's gaze fell over Katherine. "You look amazing too. Somehow I knew you'd avoid the traditional gown."

"I wanted everyone to be looking at you. I know I will be." Katherine reached out for her hand as she descended the last step.

"I can't believe we're finally doing this. And on your fiftieth birthday."

"It's the best birthday present I can imagine." Katherine stroked Anna's face, unable to stop herself from touching her.

Anna squinched her nose. "I just want to kiss you, but I don't want to smear our make-up — which *will* happen if I kiss you."

"Then let's wait until after."

They scooped up their bouquets from the hall table. Rebecca had outdone herself with the flowers this time. Dusky-pink roses were mixed with white dahlias, thistle, and eucalyptus, all tied with rattan string. Had these come from her mysterious contact at the Covent Garden flower market?

Katherine kept to the newly laid path around the edge of the drive as they made their way across. It was a welcome change not to lose her heels to the gravel. Anna didn't seem to be having any trouble as she walked across it.

"How on earth are you managing that gravel?"

Anna flashed a pair of white Dr Martens from under her dress.

Katherine laughed. "Trust you."

"I wanted to be comfortable, and I can reuse them. What could be better? I might even paint them."

"That I have to see. The registrars are waiting for us in Carrie's office to go over the legal formalities, so we'll head there first."

Heads turned as Anna and Katherine made their way hand in hand across the car park towards the visitor centre. Some of the staff appeared from inside and clapped as they passed, drawing the attention of the visitors nearby, who joined in.

"Embarrassing," Anna groaned, hoping Laura's expertly applied make-up would cover her blush. She didn't know what she would have done without Laura's assistance with last-minute dress shopping. Her insistence on applying her make-up and curling her hair had no doubt prevented Anna from, at this moment, looking like she was going to work in a wedding dress.

Katherine squeezed her hand and spoke through gritted teeth. "Just smile."

Anna whipped a smile of gratitude onto her lips and flashed it at the crowd until they could turn away down the path to the barn. With only a small number of people attending the wedding, and thankfully no invitations required, an audience was something she wasn't prepared for.

A side glance at Katherine distracted her from her blushing as a lump formed in her throat. She swallowed it down, hoping it would crush the butterflies when it reached her stomach. How could she be so lucky as to be marrying this beautiful woman?

"Carrie said her husband would take some pictures for us. Apparently, he's a photographer."

"Yes, I know." Katherine smirked. "A scene-of-crime photographer."

Reaching Carrie's office door, Anna held it open. "Oh. Still, nice of her to volunteer him."

Once the legal formalities were dealt with, they left Carrie's office via the external door and walked around the side of the barn to find Harry beaming at them from his wheelchair, a rose in his lapel. Abigail wriggled with excitement beside him in her dusky-pink dress, swaying her smaller bouquet of white roses. Rebecca, with a matching bouquet, stood very much in watch over the two of them.

Dan clicked his camera and walked backwards as Anna and Katherine came towards him.

Leaning down together, they placed a kiss on each of Harry's cheeks.

"You both look… I'm lost for words." He wiped his eye with the back of his shaky hand.

Katherine was quick to extract a tissue from her jacket pocket and assist.

"Thanks, Dad. Ready, Abi?" Anna turned her attention to the young girl.

"You look like a princess." Her already wide smile widened further as she took in Anna's dress.

"Thank you, Abi." Although she was sure it was purely thanks to the dress, her cheeks still warmed at the compliment.

Dan let his camera hang from his neck strap. "Looking lovely, ladies. If it's okay with you, I thought we could take some shots around the abbey after the ceremony?"

"That's more than okay, thank you." Katherine flashed him a smile. They had only met once before, at the New Year's party, and then it was only fleeting. For him to offer — or at least to have been offered by Carrie — was very generous. Otherwise, it would have been left to Rebecca to snap some photos.

"It's my pleasure. Two beautiful ladies and one beautiful abbey, what more could a photographer ask for?"

Anna's stomach lurched a little as she spied Laura, Tom, Mabel, and Carrie through the glass window of the barn.

This was it. The moment she'd been dreaming of since she was a little girl, a moment she had thought would never come: her wedding day and the life that lay beyond. The journey that had brought them here hadn't been smooth sailing, yet they had arrived in one piece. She thought of the struggles they had overcome together. Katherine having lost her job for her. Margaret — a shiver ran up Anna's spine at the very thought of her. Then Katherine finally deciding to face her grief in the hope it would make carrying it more manageable. She'd given up so much, put herself through hell just to be with her, to get them to this moment.

Harry interrupted her thoughts as he scrambled to get himself out of his wheelchair.

"Anna, I want to walk — "

"You're fine in your chair, Dad," she said, concerned for his balance. "We'll manage."

"No. I'm your father. I want to walk you down the

aisle. It's not something I ever thought I'd do. Now I can, I'm not letting my failing body stop me."

Realising he wasn't taking no for an answer, she gripped him under one arm. Katherine stepped in and hooked herself through his other. The original plan had been for Rebecca to push him down the aisle between the brides. Carrie had placed the chairs far apart to allow for his wheelchair. It seemed the plan was shot.

"How about we walk you down the aisle, Harry?" Katherine asked. As ever, she was fantastic with him, leaving his pride intact. Anna's heart ached that much more.

"It would be an honour if you would."

Katherine turned to Anna, a shimmer in her eye. "Ready?"

Anna took a deep breath and grinned. "Ready."

Rebecca flashed a thumbs-up through the window to Carrie, and the doors to Abbey Barn opened for its first wedding.

CHAPTER 36

*K*atherine blinked away the tear that was forming in her eye as they walked with Harry, slowly but steadily, down the aisle to the soft tones of Pachelbel's Canon in D. Being walked down the aisle by a father figure was something she had never expected, having lost her father as a child.

"You okay, Dad?" Anna whispered, giving his arm a little squeeze against her own.

"I'm all right, love. You okay? There's still time to turn around." A smirk crept across his lips.

"Don't even try it, either of you," Katherine hissed under her breath as they neared the two registrars.

"As if I would." Anna grinned. "Give it fifteen minutes and you'll be stuck with me forever."

"And me," Harry chimed in.

Katherine's lips tightened. "I can think of nothing better."

The sound of stifled giggles came from Abigail and Rebecca behind them.

They reached the end of the aisle, where Mabel was waiting with Harry's wheelchair. After setting him back down in to it, Anna passed her bouquet to Abigail as Rebecca relieved Katherine of hers.

They grasped each other's hands as they made their final approach to the registrars together.

Silence fell as the music slowly faded away. Katherine took a moment to observe the simply yet beautifully decorated room. Two vases of dusky pink roses sat on either side of the table and white bunting strung across the beams.

The taller of the two registrars, a woman in her fifties with shoulder-length, ash-blonde hair, took her position in front of Anna and Katherine.

"Good afternoon, ladies and gentlemen, and welcome to the beautiful Abbey Barn for the marriage of Anna and Katherine. My name is Andie; I will conduct the ceremony, and Georgina" — Andie gestured to her colleague — "will complete the schedule, which is the legal record of the marriage. This ceremony will be in accordance with the civil law of this country. This requires the couple to declare their freedom to marry one another. They will then go on to make their marriage vows in which they promise to take each other as partners for life. These vows are a formal and public pledge of their love and a promise of a lifelong commitment to each other. Please be seated."

Katherine gave Anna's hand a light squeeze and received one in return.

"This place in which we are now met, has been duly sanctioned, according to law, for the celebration of marriages, and we are here today to witness the joining in matrimony of this couple and to share in their happiness. If there is any person here present who knows of any lawful impediment to this marriage, then they should declare it now."

"Meow."

All eyes turned to the aisle to see Virginia waltzing along it.

The room broke into a fit of giggles.

"Virginia!" Katherine chastised the cat. It was typical of her to crash a wedding and something they would need to consider for Abbey Barn's future clients.

The cat spotted Harry patting his legs and jumped onto his lap, twirled a few times, and then settled herself into a ball. Harry beamed at being reunited with his old friend.

"Shall we continue?" Andie grinned and stepped back. "Rebecca is now going to read a sonnet."

Rebecca stepped forward and placed herself where Andie had stood. She cleared her throat before reciting from her head, confidently and passionately:

"Let me not to the marriage of true minds
Admit impediments. Love is not love
Which alters when it alteration finds,
Or bends with the remover to remove.
O no! It is an ever-fixed mark
That looks on tempests and is never shaken;
It is the star to every wand'ring bark,
Whose worth's unknown, although his height be taken.
Love's not Time's fool, though rosy lips and cheeks
Within his bending sickle's compass come;
Love alters not with his brief hours and weeks,

But bears it out even to the edge of doom.
If this be error and upon me prov'd,
I never writ, nor no man ever lov'd."

Rebecca winked at Katherine and Anna as she passed them to retake her position.

The sonnet had been Anna's idea. It had taken Katherine by surprise when she'd suggested it. She had no notion Anna harboured a passion for Shakespeare.

"Thank you, Rebecca, that was lovely." Andie stepped back in front of Anna and Katherine and gave them a reassuring smile. "Before you are joined in matrimony, it is my duty to remind you of the solemn and binding character of the vows that you are about to make. Marriage in this country means the union of two people, voluntarily entered into for life, to the exclusion of all others. I am now going to ask each of you in turn to declare that you know of no legal reason you may not be married to each other."

"Are you, Anna, free lawfully to marry Katherine?"

Anna nodded. "I am."

"Are you, Katherine, free lawfully to marry Anna?"

Katherine turned to Anna and stared dreamily into her eyes. "I am."

"Now that you have both declared that you are free to marry, we have come to the part of the ceremony where you take each other as wife and wife. Anna, would you like to start?"

"Yes." Anna nodded eagerly. "I, Anna Walker, take you, Katherine Atkinson, to be my wedded wife. I promise to be your best friend, to respect and support you, to be patient with you, to work together with you to achieve our goals, to accept you unconditionally, and to share my life with you forever."

Katherine's body was awash with a fusion of passion for the woman before her and excitement for the future they would share. She took a deep breath to calm herself before she spoke.

"I, Katherine Atkinson, take you, Anna Walker, to be my wedded wife. I promise to cherish you every single day we are blessed with, to never take you or us for granted, to communicate with you no matter how hard things are, and, above all else, to love you immeasurably."

Anna's face crumpled at her words. Katherine could see tears forming in the corners of her eyes. If Anna broke down now, she would struggle to hold herself together.

"Do you have the rings?" Andie asked, looking to Rebecca and Abigail. They stepped forward and passed their rings to Anna and Katherine.

"A ring is the ancient and traditional way of sealing the contract you have just made. It is an unbroken circle, which symbolises unending and everlasting love, and is an outward sign of the lifelong promise you've just made to each other. Anna, please repeat after me: I offer you this ring as a symbol of my love and devotion."

"Katherine, Kat," Anna corrected, placing a gold band around her finger. "I offer you this ring as a symbol of my love and devotion."

Andie turned to Katherine and nodded.

"Anna, I offer you this ring as a symbol of my love and devotion." Katherine pushed the ring over Anna's finger and stroked the back of her hand before letting go.

"Anna and Katherine, you have now both made the declarations required by law and have made a solemn and binding contract with each other in the presence of your witnesses, guests, and the registrar of marriages. It therefore gives me great pleasure to pronounce you are now wife and wife. Congratulations! You may now kiss."

The joy on Anna's face and in her moist eyes melted Katherine's heart as she leaned forward and, wrapping an arm around Anna's waist, pulled her in. Their lips finally joined as a married couple.

CHAPTER 37

*T*he sun was beginning its descent by the time Dan had finished photographing them. Having been to the site the previous day, he'd scoped out various suitable spots for photos. This was above and beyond the call of duty, considering he'd been roped in at the last minute. He confessed he was trying to move into wedding photography and was hoping Katherine and Anna might allow him to use their photographs as a showcase. They agreed he could.

They added an additional spot to his list, requesting a photograph in the chapel window. Dan was more than happy to oblige and extracted a sheet from his roller case. He placed it in the window for them to sit on, arranging it as well as possible so that it wouldn't show, though he promised to edit it out if needs be. He couldn't have been more attentive. They then left him to it in the chapel; he wanted to catch some pictures of the sun setting over the abbey.

"What do we do now?" Anna asked, kissing the back of Katherine's hand.

"I thought we'd all head back to Abbey House and open a bottle of champagne. I'm sure we have a crate or two in stock."

As they approached the barn, crowds of people were making their way into it.

"Why does it appear half the village are heading into the barn?" Anna asked.

"Perhaps because they are. There are some of my Pilates ladies."

A group of older ladies with their husbands all turned to wave at Katherine.

She smiled and waved back. "This is a little strange."

Gloria met them along the path, her garish, magenta dress boring into their retinas.

"It seems the villagers got wind of a wedding and decided they were going to throw you a party."

"And I wonder how they got wind of that?" Anna smiled at Gloria, then narrowed her eyes over her shoulder. "Is that Chris wheeling a roast hog? I wondered why the village smelt so tasty all day."

"Yes, and I've laid on a buffet inside, my gift to you both."

"Gloria, I don't know what to say." Anna scooped the small woman into a hug.

"There we were thinking we didn't have anyone to invite to a wedding, and the whole village turns up." Katherine chuckled. "Thank you, Gloria."

"You're both very well regarded, you should know that,"

Gloria replied. She smoothed her clothing back down after her overzealous hug from Anna. "You've done a lot for our little village. It's only natural everyone would want to share in the happiness of your special day. I think the staff from the abbey are coming over, too, now the abbey has closed."

Moose wandered over to greet them, snuffling his wet nose into Anna's dress.

"Moose! Manners, please." She pushed the bear-like creature's head away.

"Oh, that reminds me. I have a gift for you in your office. We should check on it," Katherine said, taking Anna's hand.

"It?" Anna questioned. When Katherine kept mum, she turned to Gloria. "We'll join you all shortly," she called.

"Take your time, darling. We're not quite finished setting up yet."

Anna let Katherine guide her around the corner of the barn to her office door.

"Go on, in you go," Katherine gestured.

Anna entered her office cautiously, a mix of excitement and trepidation. She hadn't thought to get Katherine a wedding gift; they hadn't even discussed it. She'd been explicitly told she wasn't to buy a gift for her fiftieth birthday. Yet she did have something she had planned to give Katherine at some point. She hadn't bought it, so it fell within the rules. Now would be the perfect time to give it to her, and thankfully she'd hidden it away in her desk drawer.

Her attention was immediately drawn to a crate sitting in the middle of the room. She covered her gaping mouth with her hand and turned to Katherine. "Is that what I think it is?" She set her bouquet down on her desk.

"I don't know. What do you think it is?"

Anna edged closer to the crate to get a better look, crouching as much as she could in her dress. A little brown nose emerged from within a collection of blankets, followed by a pair of brown eyes staring back at her. A little mouth full of white, razor teeth yawned. Anna melted as she tickled a soft little ear through the cage.

"You bought me a chocolate Labrador puppy? I don't know who to hug first." She wiped the tear that ran down her cheek.

"Me. I've got a feeling once you cuddle him, I won't be getting a look in ever again."

Anna placed her hands on Katherine's cheeks. "Thank you. Thank you for marrying me, thank you for him, and thank you for being brave when I needed you to be."

"Thank you for giving me a reason to be brave, and thank you for marrying me," Katherine replied. "I'm the lucky one here, and I'm not sure I can wait much longer to tear you out of that dress."

"You'll have to wait a bit longer, I'm afraid. We have an audience awaiting us, it seems, and —" Anna reached over to her drawer and opened it. "I have something for you. It's silly, really. You probably won't like it."

Katherine twitched her face in response. "Of course I will."

"Here." Anna passed her a box tied with a silk bow.

Katherine opened it. "You made this for me?" She took out the painted pebble and examined it in the palm of her hand. "It's beautiful. Thank you. It shall take pride of place on my desk as a paperweight."

"Golly." A smirk crossed Anna's lips. "Repurposing it as an item of stationery, is there any higher accolade?"

"Indeed there is not."

Soft squeaks drew Anna's attention back to the cage. "Sorry, I'm going to have to cuddle my puppy now."

The puppy clawed up at the side of the cage, exposing his bald, pink belly.

"Look, he wants his mum." Anna opened the cage and lifted him out, wrapping him in a blanket so he didn't leave fur on her dress. He squeaked as he nuzzled her face. She was boiling over with love. "What on earth is Virginia going to say about you?" Anna said, swaying the pup lightly up and down as if she was settling a baby.

"If she has a problem, she can see me about it," Katherine replied sternly. "I nearly had another heart attack when she arrived during the ceremony."

"Typical of Virginia to show up and announce herself like that."

Katherine stroked the top of the puppy's head. "What about a name then?"

"Woolf."

"Are you serious? You're going to make me shout *Virginia Woolf* from my kitchen door to get the pets in?"

Anna bit her lips together to contain her smile. "Yep."

Katherine leaned forward and kissed her. "I love you, Mrs..." She pulled back. "What exactly are we calling ourselves?"

"Mrs Anna Atkinson-Walker?"

"Hmm, it has a certain ring to it. Dr and Mrs Atkinson-Walker."

Anna scrunched her face. "When you say it like that is sounds so…"

"Heterosexual," Katherine said, turning her mouth downwards. "We may have to think on that. Right now I need some champagne."

"Me too," Anna agreed eagerly. "Come on, little Woolf, let's introduce you to everyone. I'm sure Moose would love to meet you." She turned to her wife. "How did Woolf get in my office, may I ask? And how exactly have you managed to keep him a secret?"

"Becks, of course."

Anna rolled her eyes. "Is she in the puppy trade as well as the flower trade now? You do know you're going to have to have a conversation with the local paperboy, though. We've got a lot of toilet training ahead of us."

"Finally," Katherine exclaimed. "We find an appropriate use for the local newspaper."

CHAPTER 38

They made their way down the corridor and into the main part of the barn to find it heaving with people. Most of the village had turned out for them. A table along the back wall held Gloria's extensive buffet of finger food. It was a surprisingly impressive selection of nibbles, perfect for soaking up alcohol. The rows of bulb lights that Katherine had insisted be hung from the beams for such events created a warm, cosy, and inviting atmosphere in the large room.

Anna made a mental note to ask Dan to take some pictures inside. They would do wonders for the wedding brochure she was working on. Many of today's photographs were likely to make their way into it.

"Champagne, ladies?" Carrie welcomed them, holding out two glasses which she was swiftly availed of.

"Why does it always feel like you're handing us glasses of champagne, Carrie?" Katherine laughed.

"Hmm, probably because I am, and probably because

you always deserve it. Rebecca brought a couple of boxes over from yours; she said you wouldn't mind."

"Not at all."

"Most people have brought their own drinks, but we've opened the bar too. Chris brought his staff down and stuck a note on the pub door directing them here."

Everyone broke into a round of applause as they realised the happy couple had entered the barn. Anna and Katherine raised their glasses at them in return.

Anna's stomach rumbled as she eyed the buffet. A three-tiered wedding cake with floral decorations sat pride of place in the centre. She clasped her hand to her chest as her face crumpled; the puppy promptly nibbled at her fingers and champagne glass.

"Who made us a cake?"

Laura stepped forward. "That would be me."

"Of course it was." Anna winked at her. "Thank you."

"You're welcome. And who is this gorgeous little one?"

"Woolf."

Abigail stepped forward. "Can I hold him?"

"And me," Tom pleaded over his sister's shoulder.

Anna didn't want to part with her soft little bundle, but she had all the time in the world for cuddles with him. Katherine needed her attention this evening. She passed Woolf over to Abigail. "There's a lead on top of his crate in my office. Take him outside regularly tonight. He's not toilet-trained yet." The children wandered off to some chairs that had been placed at the side of the barn and drowned him in attention.

"I can't believe what everyone has done for us." Anna

narrowed her eyes at the DJ, who was setting up in the far corner of the barn. "Is that Chris?"

Laura chuckled. "Yes, Gloria said he used to be a DJ before he took over the pub."

Anna shook her head. "You learn something new every day."

Trays of steaming hog roast passed them and were added to the crowded buffet table. Once the table had been stripped of its gems and the cake was cut with a lot of posing for Dan, Anna heard a tapping sound come through the speakers. Her head whipped around to Chris, only to find Katherine holding the microphone.

"What can I say except thank you to each and every one of you for this, especially Carrie and Gloria, and of course Chris. You've all welcomed me to Nunswick, Anna back to it, and having found each other, after a rather shaky start" — Katherine winked at Anna, drawing a smile from her — "we begin our life together as a married couple. My beautiful wife, Anna, thank you for bringing me into your family" — Katherine's eyes searched for Harry and she raised her glass to him — "which is as dear to me as my own once was. The first time you walked into my consulting room, I thought you impertinent."

The words brought laughter around the room. Anna pursed her lips at Katherine.

"Not to mention rude." Katherine flicked her eyebrows up as she spoke.

Anna's mouth opened in faux horror as the laughter continued.

"How wrong could I have been!" Katherine raised her hand, whipping the crowd into a cheer of agreement.

"What I failed to see at the time — but quickly realised, I might add — is that you are a strong-willed, determined, supportive, and passionate woman, whose strength has — quite rightly — pushed me to find the very limits of my own strength. We have already achieved so much together, and I look forward to every day in our future when we will achieve more." Katherine raised her glass. "To Anna."

"To Anna," echoed around the room.

Anna's body tingled with warmth as everyone raised a glass in her direction. She'd never felt so loved. Katherine held out her hand for her to join her on the dance floor as Etta James's voice came over the speaker and 'At Last' poured forth. What a choice of song. It had only been a year since she'd first laid eyes on Katherine in her consulting room. The doctor had swiftly got under her skin and made a beeline for her heart. With hindsight, this moment felt like an inevitability, and they had walked the path towards it together. A few hurdles had been placed in their way, some had been stepped over, others had been crashed through and some of the worst they had fallen over, relying on the other to help them back up. With each hurdle they learned something new about each other, learned to trust a little more and love a little harder.

She wrapped an arm around Katherine's back and pressed her body into hers as they joined hands, swaying lightly to the music. The warmth of Katherine's face pressed against hers was like the warmth of the sun. Katherine charged her, challenged her, helped her grow, lightened her mood, and illuminated her life.

She spotted her dad wiping his eyes as he watched them dance, and she smiled at him. Mabel fussed over him and dug a tissue from her handbag. Weeks before, she had felt jealous of Mabel's closeness with her dad, but now she felt only gratitude towards her. The woman clearly adored him and for good reason. Someone else looking out for her dad was something to be embraced. Mabel was a good sort, and a welcome addition to their family, just as her new pup was. She spied it nipping and clawing at Tom and Abigail in a corner of the room. What had Katherine got her into?

Rebecca caught her eye and winked; Anna sent one in return. A once closed book to her and a frenemy of sorts, she was beginning to open her pages.

"I loved your speech," Anna whispered into Katherine's ear.

"That was the intention." Katherine's reply tickled at Anna's ear.

"I didn't get to make one."

"Oh, did you want to?"

"No. The speeches are best left to you. Anyway, I'd only bore everyone with what they already know."

"And that would be?"

Anna pulled herself back and looked at Katherine. "That you are an incredibly sexy, generous, intelligent, and strong woman, whom I adore. What they don't know is that you are vulnerable yet brave, hard yet soft, challenging yet the easiest person to be around." Anna slid her hand down to Katherine's bottom. Her lips found Katherine's, kissing her passionately as the song drew to an end. Their audience broke out into a fresh round of cheers, wolf-whistling, and clapping as Chris came over the microphone and encouraged everyone onto the dance floor with a more upbeat song than the last. They were soon lost amongst a crowd of enthusiastic, bouncing bodies.

Carrie touched her arm as they finally emerged. "Anna, your dad's carer has come to collect him and Mabel."

They made their way outside to find a weary Harry. He reached out his shaky hands to them, and they each held one between their own.

"I couldn't be prouder of you both, and I wish you all the happiness in the world."

Anna wiped a tear from her eye and bent down to hug him. "Thanks, Dad." To know she had made him proud touched her deeply. She had always been true to herself, made her own decisions about her life and how she was going to live it. Even when it had felt impossible to, she had found a way through, and all of it had led her here… to Katherine.

A tissue was placed in her hand as Katherine bent down to hug Harry. She was always one step ahead of Anna.

"You look after each other, won't you?" he said.

"We will, Harry. We'll see you soon."

Anna wiped her eyes and then hugged Mabel, taking the woman by surprise. "You look after him for me."

"I will, dear."

They waved Harry and Mabel off under the attentive care of Lucy.

Katherine slipped her hand into Anna's. "You appear to have warmed to Mabel."

"If Dad's happy, I'm happy."

"That's what I like to hear." Katherine tucked a stray

curl behind Anna's ear and pushed her lips against Anna's.

It was a fleeting kiss, for which Anna was grateful. Anything more and she would have been tempted to drag Katherine away from the party and straight back to Abbey House to devour her.

"Come on, let's dance some of the delicious cake off our hips." Katherine pulled her back into the barn and onto the dance floor.

An hour later, and with her body aching from exhaustion, Anna collapsed into the nearest chair to rest for a few minutes. She was grateful her feet weren't aching too. She grinned down at her Doc Martens. Comfort in life was all a matter of the correct footwear.

Tom bundled a sleepy Woolf into her arms. "Anna, can you take him? We *have* to dance to this one."

He and Abigail ran onto the dance floor where everyone, including Katherine and Rebecca, were dancing to 'Happy'. A smile stretched across her lips as she watched the two best friends, exactly where they should be: by each other's sides.

Abbey Barn's first wedding had gone off with a bang, luckily not of the Second World War variety. The room was loud and lively, as it should be, transformed from its rotting, dilapidated shell to a new space where important moments in the future would be celebrated. Even Tom and Gloria were dancing together, the young and the old of Nunswick finally finding peace together.

Anna stroked Woolf's soft, velvet nose as he slept. What adventures they were going to experience together. A heavy-lidded Moose traipsed over, sniffed at Woolf's blanket, and flopped sideways onto Anna's dress. She was too tired to tell him to get off, and truthfully, it only added to her contentment.

Her eye caught Katherine's, and she stopped dancing momentarily to blow her a kiss. Anna caught it with her hand and blew one back. This was a moment she wanted to remember forever.

WHAT THE CAT WITNESSED

*V*irginia tucked her head into her body and flicked her tail around to cover her eyes. The sun was bright today, even penetrating through to her hiding place between two bushes in the flower bed. It brought a welcome warmth where it reached her dark patches.

Her ear turned towards a shuffling sound nearby. She'd already been disturbed several times during her mid-morning naps by people coming in and out of her bedroom, so she'd taken herself off to a quiet place on her extensive grounds to sleep, only for them to follow her and chatter inanely beside her.

The tedious voices lowered until they disappeared altogether. At last, silence returned. With everyone gone, she could finally catch up on some sleep.

Her heavy eyelids closed just as the drone of music emanated from the building beside her. Why did they torture themselves with such noises? Silence was seriously underrated.

Her ear twitched as the music stopped, only for it to be replaced by the drone of a voice.

Was she to have no peace today!

It was time to check out one of her other spots. She stood and stretched, her tail receiving a tickle from the foliage above. Movement through the glass window drew her attention. What were they doing in there? Humans had some strange rituals, not least their toilet habits. Why not bury it?

Her humans were holding hands, watched by others, one of whom was a smaller, familiar human. Virginia surveyed them and spotted another one she knew. It was the old man; she'd missed curling up on his lap. Where had he been? Why did people come and then go?

The one person she had tolerated most of all had suddenly disappeared. One night she was curled up on the bed asleep with her; then she suddenly left and never returned. It had left her with strange feelings. As time had gone on, she realised she would have to tolerate the remaining person if she was going to get fed, the one that other people referred to as 'cat' — peculiar since she was most definitely not a cat. She had been the one to bring her to this place. It was a suitable hunting ground, but the house lacked the smell of the previous one. The person that had later moved into the house was also on her list of those to be tolerated, near the top. She had brought the old man with her.

"Meow," Virginia cried at the window. "Meow."

Why was no one looking?

She needed to find a way to him.

Emerging from the flower bed, she made her way over

to where they had stood by the big wooden doors. The entrance was ajar enough for her to fit through, so she made her way inside.

The old man was in a different chair from the rest. His chair had wheels, like those awful things that flew around the village.

"Meow." It was only right to announce herself.

Her humans turned to her. Finally, some acknowledgement. Everyone in the room turned to look at her.

"Virginia!" her human said, in the voice she reserved for her when she was misbehaving.

The old man patted his legs and called out with a tone she much preferred.

"Virginia."

She jumped onto his lap, pleased he remembered her too. A quick twirl and she settled in a tight ball.

A little later she opened one eye to see the humans were kissing. Yuk! When they did this in her bed, it would often result in her being squashed and forced to leave. The one time she repositioned herself further down the bed, she'd watched them cleaning each other. It didn't quite have the same elegance of a cat cleaning itself!

THE END

If you enjoyed this book, please consider leaving me a review on Amazon, BookBub or Goodreads. Just a rating or a line is fine. Reviews are life-blood to authors, boosting visibility and connecting new readers with our books.

FORGIVE NOT FORGET

Amazon review link...

JOIN MY READERS CLUB

If you'd like to hear about my new releases, sign up to my newsletter and receive a FREE sapphic romance,
The Third Act…

At the suggestion of her daughter, Amy, widowed Fiona attends an art course at the local college where she meets the confident, inspirational teacher, Raye.
Raye awakens feelings long suppressed, but as Fiona rediscovers her sexuality, fear grows over how Amy will react.
Can Fiona find the courage to follow her heart, or will she be destined to spend her third act alone?

5* - Absolutely loved this book! Great story line, well developed characters and beautifully crafted. It is really refreshing to see the older lesbian represented for a change!

www.emilybanting.co.uk/freebook

EMILY BANTING

Sydney MacKenzie, personal assistant to the rich and famous, is looking forward to a well-earned break to go travelling in her beloved VW camper van, Gertie — that is, until Gertie cries off sick. When her boss calls in a favour, one that will pay Sydney handsomely and put Gertie back on the road, she can't refuse.

Internationally renowned actress Beatrice Russell — adored by her fans and despised by those that know her — is splashed across the tabloids, all thanks to her broken leg.

She limps back to her palatial English country estate to convalesce for the summer, where she finds herself in need of yet another new assistant.

Enter Sydney, who doesn't take kindly to the star's demands, attitude, or clicking fingers — much less her body's own attraction to the gorgeous diva. If not for that, and Gertie's worn-out engine, she would leave tomorrow. Or so she tells herself.

As the summer heats up, the ice queen begins to thaw, and Sydney glimpses the tormented woman beneath the celebrity bravado, drawing her ever closer to the enigmatic actress — sometimes too close.

Can Sydney reach the real Beatrice and help heal her wounds before the summer ends and she returns to filming in the States, or is the celebrity broken beyond repair?

Available on Amazon.

GOODREADS REVIEWS

"One of the best books I've ever read, period!"

"I have read over 200 books this year. This is the best written book of the year for me."

☆ ☆ ☆ ☆ ☆

"Oh. My. God. I couldn't put this book down."

☆ ☆ ☆ ☆ ☆

"One of the best books I've read in a long time."

☆ ☆ ☆ ☆ ☆

"This book spoke to me and I wish there were some way to make it required reading. The emotional and social insights are wonderful even when difficult."

☆ ☆ ☆ ☆ ☆

Syd and Beatrice are supported by a cast of some of the most beautifully developed side characters I've seen.

☆ ☆ ☆ ☆ ☆

Printed in Great Britain
by Amazon

47155610R10189